Spirit of a Highlander

Katy Baker

Published by Katy Baker, 2018.

While every precaution has been taken in the preparation of this book, the publisher assumes no responsibility for errors or omissions, or for damages resulting from the use of the information contained herein.

SPIRIT OF A HIGHLANDER

First edition. October 20, 2018.

Copyright © 2018 Katy Baker.

Written by Katy Baker.

Chapter 1

THEA THOMAS EDGED QUIETLY through the undergrowth. She crouched low, camera clasped in both hands, moving with as much stealth as she could muster. The ground underfoot squelched and she could feel cold water seeping into her boots. She barely noticed. She was so close to her goal. Just a little further...

In the clearing ahead her target lifted its head, ears flicking. Thea froze.

Don't see me. Don't see me, she thought.

She'd trekked for hours for this opportunity. She couldn't lose it now. After a few tense moments in which Thea was sure she could hear her heart hammering in her chest, her target dipped its head and carried on drinking from the pool in the clearing's center.

Thea crept forward, resisting the urge to hurry. Carefully she edged into the clearing, keeping low so the high grasses hid her, and went into a crouch, bringing her camera up to her eye.

"Easy, boy," she muttered to herself. "Just stay right there."

Her target sprang into focus on the viewfinder. It was the perfect shot. The moose lifted his head and looked right at her, his large, liquid eyes, fixing on her with mild curiosity. His magnificent antlers, grown to all their glory now the rut was so close, spread at least four feet to either side.

Thea pressed the button on her camera, sending it into automatic mode, the little motor whirring as she snapped shot after shot. Finally! She'd got what she came for! Her editor would be ecstatic and, if Thea was really lucky, this would kick start her new career and her new life.

She took a step forward and a branch snapped beneath her foot, sounding as loud as a gunshot in the still mountain air. The moose bounded away, disappearing into the trees in a heartbeat.

"Damn it!" Thea growled, cursing her clumsiness. What kind of wildlife photographer was she?

She drew in a deep breath and let it out slowly through her nose. Her stomach growled and she realized she'd not eaten all day. She was tired, hungry and really wanted to get these pictures to her editor. Yes, definitely time to get going.

Shouldering her pack, she turned on her heel and strode away through the woods. It was a long trek back to the motel. Her GPS device ensured she didn't get lost and as she walked, she kept her camera ready in case she spotted anything interesting. She didn't. It seemed the local wildlife had all cottoned on to the fact that she was prowling.

A couple of hours later she finally reached her motel, footsore and ready for a long soak and a big glass of wine. Thea hurried up to her room and was grateful to be able to kick off her boots, drop her backpack, and sink onto the soft bed. With a sigh, she lay back and closed her eyes, allowing herself to revel in the luxury of doing nothing for a moment.

SPIRIT OF A HIGHLANDER

Then, with a sigh, she sat up. She might just be able to catch her editor if she hurried. Crossing over to the desk, she got out her laptop, connected her camera and eagerly took a seat, hunched over as she scanned through the images she'd captured today.

As always, many of the pictures were no good. Some were blurred; others were overexposed or too dark. But then one flicked onto the screen that sent excitement racing through her. It was a picture of the moose with his head raised, looking directly at the camera, diamond droplets of water falling from his mouth. The setting sun had turned the background gold and orange and was reflected in the animal's eyes like tiny flames.

"Ha! Got you!"

She quickly logged into video calling and dialed her editor's number. It took a few seconds to connect before Amy, the picture editor of *World Wanderer* magazine, answered.

"Hi, Thea," Amy said. "You better make it quick. I'm just about to go into a meeting."

"Sure. I got it!" Thea said breathlessly. "The picture you wanted for the cover?" She quickly emailed it over.

Amy glanced to the bottom of her screen and nodded. "Sure. That's a great shot." She looked up at Thea. "But I'm afraid we've already commissioned the picture for the next edition's cover. Adrian, one of our regular freelancers, sent us a still of two eagles fighting in mid-air. It's amazing."

Thea stared at Amy, her mouth working like a landed fish. "But...but...we agreed!"

"No, honey," Amy said patiently. "That's not how it works. I said we'd consider it if you got the shot we needed.

You're a freelancer, remember? There are no guarantees. Our first responsibility is to our readership and what we think they'll like best. And that's Adrian's picture."

Thea's stomach fell. "But...but..." she said, her voice small. "What am I supposed to do now?"

Amy smiled sympathetically. "It's still a great shot. Look, I'll send it off to a few editors I know. Maybe one of them will take it."

Thea nodded, forcing a smile onto her face. "Sure. Great. Good night."

She ended the call and spent a moment staring at the blank screen.

Get over it, she told herself. *It's only a stupid picture.*

But it was much more than that. After a difficult year it was her chance to start over, to follow her dreams. Having her work taken by a prestigious publication like *World Wanderer* would lead to other gigs, perhaps even a staff job. As she'd nursed her grandmother through the last stages of her illness and then after, when she'd lost the house to the creditors, it was this thought that she'd clung to. One day she *would* be a wildlife photographer.

She'd never wanted to do anything else. Brought up by her grandparents after her mother left, it was her grandfather who'd instilled a love of photography in her. That's why, instead of doing something 'useful' at college as her grandmother wanted, she'd studied photography instead.

I should have done dentistry like Gran wanted, Thea thought. *Then I might actually have a future.* She sighed. *Right. Tomorrow I'll go home and start looking for waitressing jobs.*

But that was for tomorrow. She had one night left in the motel before her money ran out and right now she had the overwhelming urge to drown her sorrows. Without bothering to change, Thea grabbed her purse, put her boots back on, and made her way down to the bar.

It was busy, with most of the tables occupied, so she perched herself on a stool by the bar and ordered a large glass of red wine. She drank it quickly and ordered another.

"My, that is someone wanting to drown their sorrows if ever I've seen it," said a voice.

Thea looked up from her contemplation of her glass to find an old woman perched on the stool next to her. She hadn't noticed her arrival. The woman was easily old enough to be Thea's grandmother, or even great-grandmother, by the deep wrinkles that framed her face and the iron-gray bun pinned to the back of her head. She was so short that her legs dangled from the tall stool and she wore a large coat held shut with a deer-shaped brooch that made her look wholly out of place in the ultra-modern bar.

Thea smiled at her and lifted her glass. "Nothing better for it than red wine."

The old woman shook her head. "Nah, lass. Ye want whisky. A good single malt will sort ye out a treat."

The woman had a broad Scottish accent and a twinkle to her eye that made Thea smile despite herself.

"I think I'll stick to the wine. Whisky gives me a headache."

The woman smiled, her dark eyes twinkling. "Most wise." She stuck out her hand. "I'm Irene by the way. Irene MacAskill."

Thea took it and was surprised to find that, despite her advancing age and diminutive size, Irene had a grip like iron. "Thea. Thea Thomas. Pleased to meet you."

"Not half as pleased as I am to meet ye, my dear. Aye, now that I look at ye, I'm certain ye are the one. Ye will do just fine."

"I'm sorry?" Thea asked, puzzled.

Irene cocked her head, regarding her with an intense gaze. "What are ye doing up here, lass? What are ye looking for? And I dinna mean what ye are trying to find at the bottom of that glass."

Thea smiled wryly. "A shot. *The* shot. One that will make my career. That was the plan but you know what they say about the best laid plans."

"Ah, and here's me thinking ye were searching for something else entirely." Irene's dark gaze caught and held Thea's and she found herself unable to look away.

"What else would I be searching for?" Thea asked with a nervous laugh.

"Somewhere to belong?" Irene replied. "Yer place in the world?"

Thea opened her mouth and closed it again. "I...I don't know what you're talking about."

The smile Irene bestowed on her was kindly. "Aye, but ye will. A choice is coming, lass. There will soon be a fork in yer road, a choice of which path yer life will take. Which will ye choose? Yer current path: adrift and alone, searching for something ye can never find? Or will ye choose a new path: fraught with danger but one that may ultimately lead ye to where ye are supposed to be?"

A shiver walked down Thea's spine at the old woman's words. She felt suddenly cold. "Why are you saying these things to me?" she demanded. "Who are you?"

"Somebody who wishes ye well," Irene replied. "And to see events take their proper course." She hopped down from her stool and patted Thea on the arm. "Keep yer eyes open, lass. Ye never know when opportunity will come knocking."

Then without another word, she strode away, disappearing through the door and out into the night. Thea stared after her, feeling oddly unsettled. What the hell was that all about?

She turned back to her wine glass but found her heart wasn't in it anymore. Pushing the glass across the bar she climbed down from her seat and made her way back up to her room. She'd have a shower then go to bed. The sooner this day was over, the better.

But when she arrived at her room, she saw that Amy was trying to call her on her laptop. She sprinted across the room and quickly accepted the call.

"Hi, Amy."

"There you are!" Amy said. "I've got some great news. I've shown your photo to our European office, and the editor loves it!"

"She does?" Thea said a little breathlessly. "So they want to buy it?"

"Better than that! She's just had one of her photographers quit and needs an urgent replacement. She wants you to fly over to Scotland for an assignment! They'll pay your air fare and everything!"

Thea stared at the screen, trying to make sense of what she was hearing. It sounded like she was being offered a job! But that couldn't be right, could it? Things like that just didn't happen to her.

"Um...I beg your pardon? Could you just say that last bit again?"

Amy rolled her eyes. "I told you it was a good picture, didn't I? Look, I'm emailing over the details now. She says you've got until 9am tomorrow to accept or they'll need to find somebody else. Okay?"

"I...um...yes. Thanks," Thea stammered.

Amy ended the call and Thea sat staring at the screen for a long time. Irene MacAskill's words came back to her. *Ye never know when opportunity will come knocking. There will soon be a fork in yer road, a choice of which path yer life will take.*

Had the strange old woman had a hand in this? If she had Thea would give her a bear-hug and plant a big sloppy kiss on her cheek if she ever saw her again! Elation washed through her. All the months of anguish—losing her grandparents one by one, then being thrown out of the house she'd grown up in were suddenly bathed in the warm glow of something she'd not felt in a long time. Hope.

She was going to Scotland!

Chapter 2

LOGAN MACAULEY RAN his hands across the horse's shoulders. "Easy boy," he said soothingly. "This willnae hurt a bit."

The piebald plow horse rolled his eyes but stood placidly as Logan took the horse's hoof between his knees and began trimming it, ready for the new shoes he'd made. He worked diligently, cleaning each foot then attaching the shoes with short, sharp taps of his hammer.

Despite the cool wind blowing in off the sea, by the time he'd finished a sheen of sweat covered his brow and stuck his hair to the back of his neck. He smiled wryly to himself. What would his father think if he could see him now? The mighty Laird MacAuley reduced to working as a blacksmith and farrier?

Better this than the alternative, he thought. *At least my people are safe. And there's honor in good honest toil.*

"Logan! Ye should've called me!" a voice yelled. "I would have come to help. Dale is a grumpy old beast at the best of times. Ye are lucky he didnae take a bite of ye!"

Logan looked up to see the blond figure of Rhodry MacAuley crossing the barnyard towards him. "Grumpy?"

Logan replied with a grin. "Nah, he's been a grand old lad, havenae ye, Dale?"

The horse flicked an ear idly at Logan and then began sniffing at his plaid, looking for treats.

"Well isnae the world full of surprises?" Rhodry replied. "Ye have my thanks. How much do I owe ye for yer time?"

Logan waved a hand. "Naught, man. Like I've said before, I'm happy to help."

Rhodry frowned. "Aye, but that willnae put food in yer belly. Ye must allow me to give ye something."

They'd had this discussion many times. Logan was reluctant to take money from his friend, especially as he knew how he and Ailsa struggled to make ends meet and raise enough crops to feed their family on this poor soil.

He considered for a moment. "I'll call in the favor some time."

Rhodry nodded. "I'll hold ye to that. Now, at the very least, ye will join us for some food and ale."

"Aye," Logan replied with a smile. "That would be welcome. My stomach is growling so loudly I'm sure they can hear it up at the castle."

Rhodry barked a laugh and the two men made their way into the small cottage Rhodry shared with his wife, mother-in-law, and three children. Inside Ailsa was bustling around the hearth, whilst Mary, Ailsa's elderly mother, sat by the hearth sewing a tunic, with the children at the table practicing their letters. The children all looked up as the door opened.

"Uncle Logan! Uncle Logan!"

They jumped down and clustered around him, chattering excitedly and asking a hundred different questions all at once.

Logan laughed. "Lord above! Ye do sound like a gaggle of squabbling geese!"

He picked up Maisie, a toddler of two, who proceeded to yank his hair with one chubby hand.

"Will ye tell us a story, Uncle Logan?" David, a boy of six, asked.

"Aye and then come see our new pups?" Anna, the eldest, added.

"Hush!" Rhodry scolded them. "Let Logan take a breath afore ye begin badgering him! Mayhap he'll tell ye a story later—if ye behave yerselves. Off with ye now, back to yer letters, whilst I speak to yer ma."

Logan put Maisie down and the two eldest reluctantly returned to the table and their lesson whilst Maisie toddled off to where a black hunting hound was curled up on the hearth. Rhodry crossed to Ailsa and scooped his wife up in a hug, planting a kiss on her lips.

"Och! Get off me, ye big oaf!" Ailsa cried. "Ye are all sweaty!"

"I thought ye liked me that way," Rhodry replied, giving her another kiss, despite her protests.

Logan looked away, uncomfortable with such shows of affection. Such a life was not for him. He'd known that when he'd entered into his bargain all those years ago.

Ailsa extricated herself from her husband. "Be seated, both of ye. I'll fetch ye some ale and the stew will be ready anon."

Logan settled gratefully into a chair by the fire. His muscles ached and he'd built up a mighty thirst. He nodded his thanks as Ailsa handed him a mug of ale and took several long pulls before sighing appreciatively.

"Ha!" Rhodry laughed, taking a seat. "Drink yer fill. There willnae be much more unless we can find a way to bring in some coin."

"Still nay luck with the northern fields?"

Rhodry shook his head. "I canna stop it flooding. Every time it rains the field becomes a bog."

"Have ye spoken to the laird?" Logan asked. "Mayhap he could send ye some lads down from the castle to help irrigate it. If ye dig a ditch along the eastern edge, it will drain into the river."

Rhodry snorted. "Ye really think our laird would lend such aid to the likes of me?"

Logan was surprised by the bitterness in Rhodry's tone. When he'd been the laird, he wouldn't have thought twice about such a thing. Every seventh day, together with his brothers, Camdan and Finlay, he'd held an audience where any of his tenants could bring their difficulties before him. After all, wasn't it the duty of a laird to do all he could to help his people? Logan was sure his cousin Eoin, the new laird of the MacAuley, would be just the same.

Before he could say as much, Mary, Ailsa's mother, looked up from her needlework and tutted. "Our new laird is far too busy to worry about the likes of us, what with trying to find a wife and all."

Logan looked up sharply at that. "Eoin—I mean Laird MacAuley—plans to wed?"

"Aye," Mary replied. "It's the talk of the valley. Although he hasnae arranged a match yet." She fixed him with a penetrating gaze. "And ye might have heard it yerself if ye spent a bit more time around people instead of alone on that croft of yers. Mayhap ye should follow our laird's example and find a wife of yer own."

"Mother!" Ailsa said from where she was stirring the pot by the fire. "Logan didnae come here to be lectured by ye!"

Mary was undeterred by her daughter's rebuke. She set her needlework down and narrowed her eyes at Logan. "I only speak the truth. It isnae right a strapping young man like ye living all alone out here. Ye should have a woman by yer side and bairns sitting by yer feet. Ye would make a fine husband and I know many a young lass who would agree."

Not if they knew the truth, Logan thought. *If they knew the truth they would run as far and as fast as they could. And they would be right to do so.*

He shifted awkwardly under Mary's stern gaze. This was the last topic he wanted to talk about—it came too close to secrets he needed to keep hidden.

"Leave the poor man be, Mother," Ailsa said, coming to Logan's rescue.

She handed out bowls of stew and Logan tucked in eagerly, grateful for the diversion.

THE GPS ON THEA'S PHONE beeped. Thea pulled up, turned off the engine, and got out of the hire car. It was a fine, bright day with a stiff breeze that tugged at Thea's hair and clothes, sending it streaming out behind her as she surveyed the landscape.

She was literally in the middle of nowhere. Inland, the Scottish Highlands rose in a series of hills towards snow-capped mountains and in the other direction scrubby fields gave way to rocky inlets being lashed by the Atlantic. Thea squinted at her cell. According to the display she was about half a mile from where she needed to be.

Moving to the trunk of the car, she got out her backpack. This was a recce trip, so she was only carrying the basics: her hand-held camera, the map emailed to her by her contact at *World Wanderer Europe* and a flask of coffee. If she found some good photo opportunities, she'd return with her full gear later. Hefting the backpack she set out, holding her cell out in front of her so she could follow the GPS signal. The trail led her over the scrubby fields towards the coast and she soon found herself walking between two sand-dunes and stepping out onto a rocky shore stretching down to the roiling gray ocean.

Thea stopped and looked around. Sea birds were circling in the sky and she picked out cormorants, kittiwakes and gannets. She snapped a few shots and then carried on walking. She wasn't exactly sure what she was looking for. Her instructions were a little vague.

We're after something unique, the email had said. *Something that evokes the essence of the Highlands. There's a place on the coast that's rumored to have just that.*

There'd been the GPS coordinates and nothing else. No mention of exactly what *kind* of wildlife she was supposed to snap. Thea wondered whether there might be golden eagles here, or even better, the elusive Scottish wildcat. So far she'd seen evidence of neither.

She continued walking and suddenly something up ahead caught her eye—something sticking up from the water line. Intrigued, Thea hurried closer and found to her surprise a ring of standing stones rising out of the waves like jagged teeth. She counted five in all, but one had fallen against its fellows to form a triangular archway through which Thea could see the waves stretching out to the horizon.

Thea walked down to the water's edge and peered at the stones. She took out her camera, kicked off her boots, rolled up the legs of her jeans, and waded into the water. It was cold enough to make her gasp but didn't reach much past her ankles. Carefully she edged closer to the stones, feeling slimy sea weed squelch between her toes.

As she reached the circle, she realized the stones were each made from solid granite and must be incredibly heavy. What ancient people had gone to the trouble of erecting them here? she wondered. And what did they use them for?

Perhaps the coastline used to be further out, she thought. *And the stones used to be on dry land.*

Squinting through the viewfinder, she snapped photos of each of the stones in turn, carefully documenting them just as she'd been taught. Then, on impulse, she reached out and pressed a hand against one of them. For a moment she felt nothing but its warm, coarse surface under her palm but then something like electricity shot right up her arm and she yanked her hand back with a cry.

What the hell was that? Thea stared in surprise as a design began to spill across the surface of the stone like spilt ink—a design she was damned sure hadn't been there a moment ago. The pattern was a series of interlocking coils, reminding Thea of the Celtic knot work decorating all the tourist junk she'd seen since she'd arrived in Scotland.

She blinked. Was she imagining things? Reaching out, she ran her fingers softly over the design, feeling the bumps and indentations of the ancient carving. A tingle walked up her fingers and something stirred within her. It was a feeling she couldn't quite describe, like a memory floating just out of reach. Lifting her camera, she snapped photos of the pattern.

"I knew ye were the right one," said a voice behind her. "It doesnae reveal itself to just anyone."

Thea spun, her heart leaping into her mouth. Irene MacAskill stood behind her, hands clasped, a smile on her wrinkled face.

Thea pressed her hand to her chest. "Jeez! You scared me half to death!"

"My apologies, lass. I did call yer name but ye were so engrossed with yer work ye didnae hear me." She didn't sound apologetic at all.

"What are you doing here?" Thea asked, a little rattled by the woman's sudden appearance. "You didn't tell me you'd be here. I assumed you were staying in the US."

"Didnae I?" Irene replied, her eyebrows rising. "Silly me, must have slipped my mind. I had urgent business calling me home, and it seemed the right time to come find ye—seeing as ye've begun yer quest and all. And look, ye have already found yer first clue."

Thea frowned. Irene was making about as much sense as the last time they'd spoken. "What is this place? I've not seen it marked on any map."

"Ye willnae find it on any map," the old woman replied. "They're called the stones of Druach and are old beyond memory. They've stood here, guarding the Highlands, since the hills themselves were young. It's said they're a place of power. A place of endings." Her eyes met Thea's and they were as dark as pools of ink. "And of new beginnings."

Thea shivered suddenly. She pulled her coat closer and looked around. She couldn't see a car or any indication of how Irene had got here. Surely the old woman hadn't hiked all this way?

"I...um...I guess I should thank you," she said. "For getting me this job. It was you, wasn't it?"

Irene smiled. "I said ye had a choice coming. It is here, lass. What will ye do?"

"Do? What do you mean? I'll do what you paid me to do: take some pictures."

Irene nodded. "Aye that is one of yer choices. Complete yer assignment. A permanent job offer will follow and ye'll soon have everything ye ever wanted: a career, an apartment, money." Her gaze sharpened as she watched Thea. "But what then? When ye have everything ye want and yet still find yerself adrift and unsure of yer place in the world, what will ye do?"

Irene took a step towards her and Thea found herself involuntarily taking a step back.

"There is a second choice, a different fork in yer road," the old woman said with a smile. "It isnae an easy choice. Ye could risk everything, throw yerself into unspeakable danger to help me avert a disaster and break a curse that is throwing the future out of balance. And in so doing, mayhap ye will find the thing ye've been searching for all yer life. All ye have to do is step through the arch."

Irene pointed and Thea turned to see movement through the arch formed by the fallen stone. At first she thought it was just the waves but as she looked more closely, she saw images: a tall man carrying a laughing child on his shoulders, a gray castle with pennants snapping in the wind, two armies facing each other at the mouth of a pass.

"What is this?" she whispered.

"Yer destiny," Irene replied. "And the chance to restore balance to the world. If ye so choose it."

A strange feeling formed in the pit of Thea's stomach. *What are you looking for?* the waves seemed to whisper. *Your destiny awaits*, the wind seemed to call. The archway seemed to pull her closer. Before she knew it she'd taken a step forward and another.

Stop! a voice screamed a warning in the back of her head. *This is crazy. Irene MacAskill is crazy! Turn around!*

But she didn't. Her fingers brushed the swirling pattern on the stones, feeling the little tingle that ran up her arm.

Thea stepped through the arch.

"THAT WAS GRAND," LOGAN said, handing his empty bowl to Ailsa. "I do declare ye are the best cook in all the Highlands."

Ailsa accepted the bowl with a smile. "And I do declare ye are the biggest flatterer in all the Highlands, Logan MacAuley."

Logan glanced through the window. It was dusk and night would soon be upon them. He shifted uneasily. He'd tarried too long.

Standing abruptly, he said, "I will bid ye all good night."

Rhodry glanced out the window. "It looks to me as though a storm is coming on. Will ye not stay? We could make up a bed in the barn for ye."

"Aye! Stay, Uncle Logan!" Anna cried.

But Logan shook his head. He dare not. He had already stayed too long, any longer and they would be in danger. He couldn't stay near anyone for long without his doom falling upon them. "I canna. I must be getting back to my smithy."

The children let out a chorus of disappointed noises and Rhodry climbed to his feet. "Aye. Well, I'll see ye out then."

Logan bid good night to Ailsa, Mary and the children, and then followed Rhodry out into the yard. The wind had picked up and there was the smell of a storm on the air. If Logan guessed rightly, it would be a wild night. He hoped he could get home before it struck.

Rhodry fetched Logan's horse, Stepper, from the stable. She was a handsome beast of fine stock and if anyone wondered why a humble blacksmith rode a horse fit for a nobleman, nobody commented. Stepper was one of the few reminders Logan kept of his old life. She pranced as Rhodry brought her out, eager for a run. Logan took hold of the bridle and clasped Rhodry's arm.

"Send word if ye have any difficulties with the plow horse."

"I will," Rhodry nodded. "Take care on the road, my friend. It looks as though it's going to be a bad one."

Logan nodded and swung up easily into Stepper's saddle. He bid Rhodry good night and then set his heels to his mount's flank, sending her trotting down the lane. Out over the sea, a black bank of storm clouds swallowed the last of the sunlight. The wind howled into his face, plucking tears from his eyes and swirling his copper colored hair around his head. He gritted his teeth, a wild smile pulling at the corners of his mouth. He welcomed the storm. The cold bite of the wind, the crash of the waves, the smell of brine in the air.

It reminded him he was still alive.

"Yah!"

He gave Stepper her head and she sprang into motion, galloping along the trail with fierce joy, reveling in the sudden freedom. They moved north, away from Rhodry's croft, and towards the humble cottage Logan now called home. It lay many miles distant and as he rode the wind howled around him lashing the waves into a frenzy and sending leaves and small branches raining down.

The storm suited his mood perfectly. His mind went blank, no thoughts, no worries, only this moment: the wind on his skin and the taste of sea-salt on his tongue. It was a blessed relief. Too often his thoughts ran in circles, chasing themselves through the myriad of possibilities that might have unfolded if he'd done things differently.

If he and his brothers hadn't made the bargain that damned them forever.

He kicked Stepper to greater speed, mud flying from beneath her hooves and her mane flailing like a whipcord in the ever-increasing gale.

He didn't see the figure ahead until it was almost too late. It was the lantern that gave it away, glowing through the gloom like a firefly, almost swallowed by the stormy night. Its meager light lit a small figure struggling along the path in front of him. It was an old woman.

"Ware!" he bellowed, certain Stepper would trample her.

He yanked savagely on the reins, and the woman stepped deftly aside with an agility that belied her advancing years. Logan guided Stepper to a halt and then sprang from the saddle.

"Lord, woman!" he shouted, advancing on her. "I could have trampled ye! What, by all that's holy, are ye doing out in this?"

The old woman seemed not in the least daunted by his outburst. She barely reached his chest and wrinkles creased her face. Nevertheless, the dark eyes that peered at him sparkled with either annoyance or amusement. Logan wasn't sure which.

"A fine question, Logan MacAuley," the woman said. "Have ye asked it of yerself?"

Logan started. "How do ye know who I am?"

The old woman raised an eyebrow. "And who else would ye be? Do ye know of another exiled laird who lives roundabout?"

Logan froze. "I dinna know what ye are talking about, woman. I'm no laird. I'm only a simple blacksmith."

The woman poked him in the chest with a bony finger. "Oh, my boy. Ye are far, far more than that, despite attempts to make ye otherwise."

Logan stepped back a pace, suddenly uneasy. How did this woman know who he was? "Who are ye?"

"My name is Irene MacAskill."

Her smile was kind but her eyes caught and held him so that Logan couldn't look away. He seemed to see eons spinning in her gaze, the slow swirl of the stars in the sky and the passing of ages. He was reminded suddenly of another night, a stormy night just like this one, when he'd stood with his brothers in a circle of standing stones and made a desperate bargain that would seal their fates forever.

"What do ye want with me?" Logan demanded, his voice harsh.

"Only what ye want for yerself," Irene replied. "A life. The life ye were meant to lead, not the one ye live now. Alone and forgotten."

Sudden anger flared inside Logan. Who was this woman? Why was she saying such things to him? "I dinna ken who ye think I am, woman, but ye are mistaken. I am a blacksmith. I have a life. It's the only one I need."

He made to walk away but her hand snapped out and grabbed his wrist. Despite her advancing years, she had a grip like iron pincers.

"Nay, lad," she said, her voice soft, yet cutting easily through the storm. "It isnae. I know the bargain ye made and why ye did it. I know ye ache with loneliness and a nagging sense ye canna be rid of. A sense that this isnae the life ye were supposed to lead. A sense that ye have taken the wrong path." Her grip on his arm tightened. Her eyes glinted like polished obsidian. "But there is always a way back. If ye have the courage to retrace yer steps."

Logan snatched his hand away. "There isnae," he growled. "There is no way back for me. I made my choice. Now I live with it."

Irene smiled sadly. "We shall see. Yer choice is still to be made, lad, and it is coming. If ye have the courage to seize it, things may yet be different. There is always hope."

"Hope?" Logan snorted. "I abandoned that a long time ago. It is for fools."

Irene shook her head. "Nay, lad. Despair is for fools. Hope is sometimes the only thing we have."

Logan opened his mouth for a retort but a sudden crack of thunder sounded overhead and a flash of lightning lit the sky so brightly that for a moment Logan was blinded. He threw his arm in front of his face and when he lowered it, found only an empty road before him.

Irene MacAskill had disappeared.

Logan spun, eyes scanning the stormy landscape. Nothing. He dropped to one knee, searching for footprints in the mud, but found only his own and those of his horse. He shivered, and not from the cold wind.

Mounting Stepper, he pulled her in a circle, taking one last look around, and then nudged her into a gallop for home.

Chapter 3

THEA STEPPED THROUGH the archway and stumbled. To her surprise, her foot came down, not on the ankle-deep sea water as she'd expected, but on solid land. The unexpected jolt sent her stumbling and she grabbed one of the upright stones for support. How the hell had that happened? Had the tide gone out even further?

She turned to speak to Irene. She'd had enough of the old woman's nonsense and it was about time she got to the bottom of what exactly she was up to. But as she opened her mouth to speak, the words died in Thea's throat.

Where the old woman had been standing was only an empty piece of grass, without even footprints to show she'd ever been there.

Thea blinked rapidly and then shook her head to clear it. "Irene? Where are you?"

She walked carefully around the stones of Druach but found no trace of the old woman. The stones hadn't changed, they were still rising from the ground like teeth, still pitted and weathered by time. They hadn't changed. But everything else had.

She was no longer standing on the shoreline and her bare feet felt warm, dry grass under them rather than cold wet rocks. The sea lay over a hundred paces to her left, white waves pounding the shore and throwing up spray. The sky, which had been bright blue a moment ago had turned a dark purple, like a bruise, and filled with angry storm clouds. A last streak of sunlight along the horizon told her that the sun was setting behind those clouds.

What the hell? It had been morning a moment ago!

Thea pressed her hands to her temples. *Did I fall and hit my head? Or am I going crazy?*

"Irene?" she shouted, turning in a slow circle and looking around. "Where are you? What the hell is going on?"

There was no answer but the pounding of the waves. Maybe she was getting a fever. Maybe she'd hallucinated the whole episode with the stones and Irene MacAskill. That must be it. She'd be fine once she'd had a bit of rest. Time to get back to the hotel.

She took a step but halted as she noticed something lying in the grass. It was a small, leather-bound book. Puzzled, Thea stooped and picked it up. The pages crackled as she opened it. It seemed to be a book of folk stories although she could find neither a title nor an author's name. On the inside cover she found a note scrawled in spidery writing.

This may help you find what you're looking for. I.

Shit. So she hadn't dreamt it all. Irene really had been here. Oh hell, what was going on?

Just get back to the hotel. Everything will make more sense once you've had a bath and something to eat, she told herself.

Taking a deep breath, Thea tucked the book and her camera into her backpack and looked around for the boots she'd discarded before wading out to the stones. There was no sign of them. Thea cursed loud enough to send a startled seagull flapping into the air. Then, in bare feet, she started walking inland, climbing up the sand dunes in the direction of the car.

But when she reached the top of the dune, she found no sign of a road and certainly no sign of her car. There was only a narrow trail that wound its way along the coastline, climbing higher as the ground rose into a cliff.

Thea stopped. The wind was picking up, sending her hair whipping about her face and plucking at her clothes.

Don't panic, she told herself. *The car can't be far away. Before you know it, you'll be back at the hotel eating one of Mrs MacGregor's lovely lunches.*

She took out her cell phone and switched it on. Scrolling through the apps, she brought up her GPS. The screen flared to life, showing her location as a tiny dot on a map. With a sigh of relief Thea brought it closer to her face and peered at it in the gathering gloom. All she had to do was follow the map, and she'd be back at the hotel in no time.

Then an error message suddenly flashed onto the screen. *A GPS signal cannot be obtained at this time.*

"What? No! You have got to be kidding me!"

She threw up her hands in exasperation. Just her luck that the damned weather was interfering with the satellite signal! Forcing herself to take a deep, calming breath, Thea considered her options.

Follow the coastline, she told herself. *Glenmorrow is right on the coast so if I just follow the cliffs, I'm bound to reach it eventually or at least come across someone with a phone I can borrow.*

Bolstered by this logic, Thea began walking, keeping the sea to her right, following the winding trail as it hugged the contours of the coast. As she walked the wind picked up, soon becoming a gale that whipped the sea into a swirling maelstrom of white-capped waves. Thea tied her hair back into a loose ponytail to keep it out of her face and pulled her coat tighter about her. At least it wasn't raining. Yet. But from the look of the sky a downpour could erupt any minute. The sooner she found shelter, the better.

The trail began to climb. To her right the shore became a sheer cliff with raging white water below. The trail ran closer to the edge than Thea would have liked but she had no choice but to keep to it or fight her way through thick clumps of heather further inland.

The evening darkened suddenly and a crack of thunder split the sky. A moment later, a hissing torrent of rain came sheeting down, turning the world gray. With an irritated growl, Thea pulled her hood up and hunkered down in her coat, hurrying along the trail as fast as she dared. Her bare feet were filthy and freezing by now and she kept stumbling every few yards.

A sudden shrill whinny cut through the air and she looked up just in time to see a figure from a nightmare bearing down on her.

It was a horse, all stamping hooves, flashing eyes, and flying tail, a huge shadowy figure clinging to its back.

Suddenly lightning lit the sky, so brightly it momentarily blinded Thea. She screamed, threw her arm in front of her face and staggered back, desperately trying to avoid the horse's path. Her feet tangled and she staggered, slipping on the wet trail. Then suddenly there was nothing beneath her but empty air.

A strangled scream escaped her as she fell. It lasted only a moment as her stomach tried to rise into her chest before she smacked into the freezing water with enough force to drive all the air from her lungs. Bone-chilling darkness enveloped her and a shot of pure terror exploded through her veins.

Kick! Kick for the surface.

She tried, but her heavy coat, so helpful in the storm, now became a millstone around her neck, dragging her down. Little lights began to dance in front of her eyes. Her lungs burned. Her limbs felt as though they were filled with lead.

She found herself sinking down, down into darkness.

LOGAN YANKED STEPPER to a halt so fast that the horse skidded in the mud, almost losing her footing. Before she'd even come to a stop, he threw himself from the saddle and pelted to the cliff edge.

That had been a lass on the road! And she'd gone over the cliff!

He studied the churning water below but it revealed no sign of her. All he could see were churning white-caps and spray. He tore off his cloak and boots, tossed them onto the grass, then took a running leap over the cliff, tipping into an expert dive. It was his fault the lass had fallen. If he'd not been riding like a mad man, he'd not have startled her so. He had to save her.

As he hit, the water parted beneath him and he speared down into the cold depths. He clamped his lips shut and forced his eyes open. With powerful strokes he swam downwards, eyes scanning the darkness for any sign of her.

There! Something pale glimmered in the blackness below. Logan powered towards it, kicking against the current. The pale object revealed itself into a hand and then an arm, and finally the lass herself. Her eyes were closed and her hair floated around her head like shimmering fronds of seaweed.

Logan wrapped his arms around her waist and kicked upwards, fighting the swell of the water. The lass was a dead weight. She wore a heavy garment that tried to drag both of them down but Logan didn't have time to try to remove it. The lass had already been in the water too long. He didn't even know if she was still alive.

Gritting his teeth and summoning all his reserves of strength, Logan forced his screaming muscles to fire, to propel them upwards. At last, his head broke the surface and he sucked in a great, heaving breath. Flipping the lass onto her back and doing his best to keep her head above the roiling water, he made for shore. It was difficult to keep his sense of direction. Towering black cliffs kept bobbing in and out of his view.

Fighting the current, he trod water whilst he searched for somewhere safe they could go ashore, somewhere they wouldn't be dashed to pieces on jagged rocks. He spotted a narrow strip of sand and a small inlet between two soaring cliffs where the water was calmer, sheltered from the worst of the gale. Logan made for it, dragging the lass behind him.

It seemed to take an age but he finally felt solid ground beneath his feet and half-stumbled, half-crawled onto the beach, hauling the lass with him.

He shoved her onto her side on the wet sand and thumped his palm into the space between her shoulder blades. She flopped like a landed fish but didn't respond. He did it again, harder this time, and on the third attempt her eyes flew open, she sucked in a huge breath, and broke into a fit of coughing, water exploding from her mouth.

Logan knelt beside her as she doubled over, retching into the sand. "Easy, lass," he muttered. "Get it all out."

She hacked and gagged, coughing until her throat must be raw. Finally the coughing fit passed and she looked up at him. Her eyes were round and huge, her hair plastered to her face, her skin as pale as bone.

"I...I...I..." Then her eyes went to the cliff top. "My camera!" she gasped. "Where is it?"

She had a funny way of speaking and her clothing was strange too. Under the coat she appeared to be wearing trews like a man but her feet were bare. An outlander, then, unless Logan missed his guess.

"I dinna ken what ye mean by the word 'camera' but ye are safe now," he said. "Do ye think ye could stand?"

She stared at him, unblinking. "It was you!" she gasped suddenly. "You rode me down! You scared me half to death!"

"Aye," Logan nodded, shame running through him. "Ye have my apologies, lass. I didnae expect anyone to be on the path tonight. Not in this. Where are yer kin? I should get ye back to them so they can take ye home."

"My kin? A long way from here. But I'm staying in a hotel just down the coast. Could I borrow your phone? I could call a cab. Or, failing that, I reckon Mr MacGregor would come get me if he knew I was out here."

Her stream of words left Logan baffled. Hotel? Phone? Cab? What on Earth was she going on about? "Listen, lass, I will take ye back to the trail. From there we'll see if we can find yer folks. Let's start by getting to the top of the cliff. Can ye stand?"

She nodded, pushed herself into a kneeling position, then up to standing. Logan took hold of her forearm and she gripped his arm fiercely in return, her legs splayed like a newborn deer as she fought for balance.

"Thanks," she muttered. "For saving my life. Even if it *was* your fault in the first place." She looked up, met his gaze, and Logan was suddenly struck by her beauty. She had high cheekbones, a scattering of freckles across her nose and striking green eyes the color of spring leaves. Hair as dark as a raven's wing fell down her back.

"Ye are welcome," he said gravely.

She nodded but then stumbled. Logan caught her. Her eyes fluttered closed and her head lolled on her neck. Pressing his palm against her forehead, Logan realized her skin felt like ice. Ah, curse it all. The lass needed shelter and warmth— and quickly. He bent his knees and lifted her, clasping her to his chest as he hurried to a narrow trail that led up the cliff.

It was a difficult climb on the rocky trail and Logan had to stop and regain his balance several times for fear he might stumble and drop the lass, but he drove himself onward, fear for her adding urgency to his climb.

Finally he stepped over the brink and found Stepper waiting at the top, watching Logan with ears pricked. By Stepper's feet was a black bag with shoulder straps. Was this the 'camera' she'd asked about? He carried the lass over to Stepper's saddle then bent to pick up the bag, slinging it over his shoulder. He turned in a circle, eyes scanning the storm-lashed landscape, searching for any sign of her folks or for any clue of where she might have come from.

He saw not another soul but he could pass within ten feet of someone and not see them in this driving rain. He hesitated. He had to get her indoors and properly dry and warm but the only dwelling nearby was his own. Dare he take her there?

What choice do ye have? he asked himself. *Ye canna leave her here.*

With one last glance at the churning ocean, he swung up behind her and then levered her into a sitting position in the saddle. She slumped against him, semi-conscious, as Logan reached around her to take the reins. He only hoped he could keep her in the saddle and guide the horse at the same time. He nudged Stepper into motion, man and beast forging a path through the howling gale.

His cottage lay only a few miles distant but the journey seemed to take forever. Finally he spotted the croft in the distance, half-obscured by the gray curtains of rain. The tiny, a one-roomed stone cottage with a thatched roof and a low stone wall encircling the yard, was a welcome sight. His smithy and a stable completed the simple croft. It was a humble home, a blacksmith's home, so far removed from what he'd once known. Nevertheless, he was mighty grateful to be back.

He rode Stepper through the yard and right up to the door of the cottage where he dismounted and carefully lifted the lass down from the saddle. She didn't stir as he kicked the door open and carried her inside. He'd banked the fire before he left and the coals were still glowing, sending a delicious warmth through the room that felt wonderful after the freezing rain. He laid her down on the hearth rug and then threw in chunks of wood until the fire was blazing merrily.

He shook her gently. "Wake up, lass. Ye must get out of those wet clothes before ye catch a chill."

She stirred and her eyes flickered open. "Wassup?"

"Yer clothes, lass. Ye must take them off. Here, put this on instead." He handed her one of his old plaids.

She took it. "Yeah. Clothes. Gotcha."

He turned his back whilst she undressed. When she'd finished, he turned around to find her clothes in a pile, and the lass wrapped in his plaid, already asleep on the rug. He dragged the pillow and blanket from his bed, wedged the pillow under her head and laid the blanket carefully over her, tucking it in so that no cold air could get underneath.

Then he stood. The shutters on the windows rattled and wind howled down the chimney. He didn't relish the thought of going out into that maelstrom but he had to see to Stepper and besides, he'd tarried near the lass too long. Being this close to her put her in grave danger. His curse would see to that. He had to get away from her. For both their sakes.

Wrapping his cloak tight around him, he yanked open the rickety door of his cottage and stepped out into the storm. It was raging now. The rain was so thick he could barely see his hand in front of his face and the wind howled like a tormented spirit, full of rage and spite. There was no sign of Stepper and Logan knew she would have taken herself to the stable where it was safe and warm. Gritting his teeth, he pulled in a breath and dashed across the yard.

Sure enough, he found Stepper, still saddled and bridled, in the stable, munching hay from the manger. She turned to look at him as he entered, giving a snort of greeting.

"Ye are warmer and drier than me by the looks of ye," Logan muttered as he removed her saddle and hung it on a peg.

He brushed out her coat before adding some oats to a wooden bucket. The warrior in him would always see to his horse before himself just as his father had taught him all those years ago. When Stepper was settled, he ducked back out into the storm and crossed the yard to his smithy.

The lean-to building, open on all sides for ventilation and to reduce the risk of fire, was drafty and cold but at least the thick roof kept off the rain. The forge sat cold and dark in the center of the building but he quickly stoked it to life. When he had a spark going he went to work with the bellows until the coals began to glow white-hot, sending out a blessed blanket of heat that slowly began to thaw out his freezing muscles.

Gingerly he stripped off his sodden clothing and dropped it in a heap in the corner then pulled on the rough smock he used when working the forge. The material was thin and patched in a dozen places but at least it was dry.

He banked the forge so that its coals would hold their heat through the night then hunkered down next to it, his back to the warm stones. Outside the storm raged, the wind sounding like cruel laughter. It had been a most unsettling day. First meeting Irene MacAskill on the road then saving a strange lass from the sea. Who was she? Where had she come from? And were the two connected somehow?

Yer choice is still to be made, lad, and it is coming. If ye have the courage to seize it, things may yet be different. There is always hope. The old woman's words echoed in his head.

Dinna be stupid, he told himself. *Just meaningless ramblings. The lass is just a lost traveler, naught more. Go to sleep.*

He screwed his eyes closed and tried to shut out the scream of the wind. Soon he fell into a fitful sleep where he saw dark waters, a standing stone, and a beautiful woman with green eyes watching him.

Chapter 4

THEA OPENED HER EYES slowly. They were gummy with sleep and as she reached up to wipe them she realized she was tangled in a thick blanket. She fought her arm free, wiped her eyes, and then propped herself up on her elbows. It took a moment for her sleep-addled brain to take in her surroundings. She was lying by a hearth with a fire died down to embers. There was nobody else in the room.

Looking around slowly, she spotted her coat hanging on a peg on the back of the door. She frowned, trying to figure out the significance of that. How the hell had she ended up undressed?

She threw back the blanket in a panic then paused as she saw she was actually wearing some kind of long tartan wrap and had leather moccasins on her feet.

What the hell?

She frowned, trying to piece together her fractured memories. She'd been walking, hadn't she? Walking along a cliff because she'd gotten lost and couldn't find the car. Then a storm had swept in, a horse had been bearing down on her and...

"Oh, my god!" she gasped. "I fell over the cliff!"

A dark memory of freezing, grasping water filled her mind. She remembered sinking, her lungs burning, her limbs flailing, so certain she was going to die...

And then strong hands grabbing her, pulling her back towards the light. Someone's body heat warming her as she was carried gently. And then...waking up here by the fire.

Carefully, Thea climbed to her feet. A wave of dizziness washed through her and she staggered before catching herself on the mantelpiece. Reaching up, she placed a hand on the back of her head and felt a large lump there. So. She'd hit her head. No wonder, with the ground so slippery and all those rain-slick rocks lashed by the storm.

The storm. Yes, there had been a storm. A wild one.

She paused, listening. There was no howl of the wind, no patter of rain on the roof. All appeared still and by the light coming in through the shutters, she guessed it was early morning.

She slowly looked around. The room was tiny, its walls made from river-worn stones with a thatched roof over her head. There was a small cot in one corner which she guessed must be a bed, a rickety table with two chairs, and a pot by the fire. Nothing else. No TV. No phone. Nothing.

Who would live in such a place?

A man. There had been a man. He'd been the one who'd pulled her from the water, the one who'd carried her with such strength.

With staggering steps she crossed to her coat and fumbled in the pocket until she found her cell phone. Frantically she pushed the buttons, trying to get it to turn on but it didn't respond, no doubt ruined by its dunking in the ocean.

She closed her eyes and sucked in a breath, trying to calm her suddenly racing heart. Her benefactor would let her use his phone, she told herself. She would call a cab and go back to the hotel. If her headache didn't clear up, maybe she'd see a doctor later.

She made her way over to the door, using the wall to support herself, and pulled it open. The light was so bright she had to squint. Holding up a hand to shade her eyes, she looked out on a fresh landscape. A small yard stretched out in front of her, covered in sparkling puddles. The sky was bright blue, with high clouds scudding along above.

"What a difference a day makes," she muttered wryly.

A small wooden building sat in the corner of the yard and a horse had its head stuck over the half-door, watching Thea with interest.

Thea took two tottering steps and breathed in the cool, still air. To her right the sea sparkled all the way to the horizon and to her left the undulating uplands of the Scottish Highlands spread out like a map. There was not another soul in sight.

Then Thea heard splashing coming from the other side of the cottage. She stumbled in that direction and peered around the corner of the building. Another structure sat on this side of the house, one with a high roof supported by thick wooden pillars. A stout rain barrel sat in one corner, brimming from the recent storm.

A man was standing by it with his back to her, stripped to the waist. He dunked his head in the barrel and then flung his head back, spraying water droplets that sparkled in the sunlight. He was easily over six feet tall, his shoulders broad and his arms and back heavily muscled as though used to hard labor.

The man suddenly spun and looked at her, an angry glint in his dark eyes. A swirling black tattoo covered his pectoral and something about it tugged at Thea's memory.

"Sorry!" she blurted. "I...um...I...didn't mean to interrupt."

"Ye didnae," he muttered. "I was done anyway." He dried himself and then pulled a linen shirt over his head and tied a tartan plaid at the shoulder. Then he walked over to stand in front of her, his eyes narrowed as he looked her over. He was so tall that Thea had to crane her neck back to look up at him.

"I'm mighty surprised to see ye up and around this early," he said. "I think ye may have hit yer head."

Thea shrugged, trying to make light of it. "Nah, it's nothing a good cup of coffee and a few pills won't fix. Although my head feels like I've had a heavy night of drinking. It's not fair having the hangover without the fun."

He didn't smile at her attempt at humor. Instead a look of puzzlement crossed his face. "Pills? Coffee?"

She waved a hand. "Never mind. I'm Thea by the way. Thea Thomas. I've just realized you saved my life and I don't even know your name."

To her surprise he gave her an awkward bow. "Logan. Logan MacAuley."

"Pleased to meet you, Logan MacAuley."

She smiled at him but he didn't return the gesture. He watched her with a serious expression. Now that it was beginning to dry she noticed that his hair was the color of burnished copper and fell to his shoulders in lazy tangles, framing a strikingly handsome face. Awesome. Just her luck to meet a gorgeous guy when she looked and felt like hell.

"Why were ye walking the coastal road alone, lass?" he asked. "And in such a storm as that?"

Thea paused. Her memories were hazy. She remembered Irene MacAskill, the ring of standing stones, stepping through the archway and then...everything changed.

"I wasn't supposed to be," she answered slowly, thinking through the course of events. "I was out with my camera doing a recce. I walked under an archway and then everything went...strange."

His eyebrows pulled into a frown. "Ye were out alone? Have ye gone daft, lass? There are still wolves in these Highlands although they're rarely seen these days. But there are brigands aplenty who wouldnae hesitate to take advantage of a lass out alone."

Thea bridled at his tone. She wasn't a child to be lectured. Who the hell did he think he was? "I hardly think I need worry about being set on!" she retorted. "The Highlands aren't exactly known as tourist-mugging hotspots."

But his frown only deepened. "I dinna ken most of what ye just said, lass. Yer speech is most strange."

"*My* speech is strange?" she replied, a little annoyed by his tone. "You're the one with the crazy-ass accent! Don't tell me you've never met anyone from the US before? You must get bus-loads of tourists out here."

"The US?" he said the word carefully. "I know of nay such place."

Thea stared at him. Was he making fun of her? She opened her mouth to speak but before she could form a response, he turned away.

"Are ye hungry?" he called over his shoulder. "I'll fix us both some breakfast before I see ye safely back to yer kin."

Thea almost sagged with relief. "Starving," she replied. "I could eat a horse."

Thea followed him into the cottage where Logan bade her take a seat at the table. Thea found she was glad of the rest. Just the short walk out to the yard had tired her out and she still felt a little dizzy. Perhaps she'd hit her head harder than she realized.

As Logan busied himself breaking eggs into a pan and setting them to fry on the fire, Thea looked around the cottage. Rustic wasn't the word. She could see no evidence of running water nor any light switches or plug sockets. Instead, candles sat in holders on the mantelpiece and in the middle of the table. Why did Logan live out here alone in a place like this? Maybe he was some city boy who came out here at weekends to escape the rat-race. She'd heard of people like that.

Logan took a loaf from a shelf, sliced it, and then placed the slices in the pan with the eggs. He moved with a surety that spoke of having done this many times before. Thea wondered about that. Would a city boy be this comfortable cooking on an open fire?

Finally he turned the eggs and fried bread out onto a wooden plate which he placed on the table in front of her. Thea ate ravenously. When had she last had a bite to eat? It must have been breakfast at the hotel yesterday. Logan didn't eat. He stood by the mantelpiece and watched her in silence.

When she'd eaten her fill, he crossed his arms over his chest. "Right. Ye have said some mighty strange things since ye woke. I think ye better start from the beginning."

Standing there like that he was quite the imposing figure. He was so tall and broad, he seemed to fill the room. His expression suggested he was suspicious of Thea's story.

"I already told you everything," she snapped. "I'm here photographing wildlife. I was on a recce, trying to find some good subjects. I spotted some standing stones sitting in the water and went to investigate. Next thing I know I'm in a god-damned storm!"

She glared up at him, daring him to contradict her or call her a liar. His frown deepened.

"Standing stones, ye say? Why, by all that's holy, would ye approach such things? Dinna ye know they are the province of the Fae?"

"Sure. Just like you can find a crock of gold at the end of a rainbow or trolls guarding a bridge! Look, if you could just point me in the direction of the road I'll be out of your hair."

"Where were these standing stones?"

Thea waved a hand vaguely. "That hardly matters, does it? I'm sure there are hundreds of the things round here. Which way to the road? I'll walk back to the hotel." If she was really lucky, she'd pass a bus stop or be able to flag down a passing car.

He shook his head. "I promised to escort ye safely to yer kin and I will do just that. Where may they be found?"

Thea ground her teeth. He went from condescending to protective in the space of a heartbeat. "I'm staying at the *Loch View Guesthouse* in Glenmorrow."

"I've never heard of such a place."

"That's fine. If you could just get me to Glenmorrow, I'll give you directions from there."

"Nay, lass. What I mean is, I've never heard of this place called 'Glenmorrow'. There is nay such place in the Highlands."

She stared at him. What the hell was he talking about? She bit her lip, biting back an angry retort. "Okay. Whatever. I'm grateful for you pulling me from the water and putting me up for the night. I'll be on my way now. I'll have your plaid laundered and sent back to you and have someone pick up my clothes. Goodbye."

She crossed to the door but Logan stepped in front of it, blocking her path. "I canna let ye go wandering the wilds alone."

"Let me?" she asked, her eyebrows rising incredulously. "You're not 'letting me' do anything. I'm leaving! Get out of my way!"

Anger flashed in his eyes as he stared down at her. "Are all lasses in yer homeland so wilful?"

"Are all Highland men such overbearing jackasses? Now get out of my way!"

She glared at him, fists clenched and he glared right back. She felt something uncoil in her belly. Anger? Or something else?

Then, with a muttered curse, he stepped aside to let her pass. Thea pushed past him into the yard. There was a narrow path that led from the cottage through the heather and up to a line of gorse bushes in the distance. Good. That was probably the line of the road.

She marched off, not looking back, trying to ignore the dizziness that threatened to send her staggering. She'd be damned if she'd show any weakness in front of Logan bloody MacAuley! *Let* her go wandering the wilds? Who the hell did he think he was?

She marched along the trail and reached the line of gorse bushes. But on the other side she didn't find the road, only another narrow trail with deep ruts filled with puddles.

"Damn it," she growled. She turned slowly, scanning the terrain. Where was the road?

She heard a thumping noise and turned to see Logan trotting up astride the horse.

"If ye are going to persist in this foolishness, I will escort ye to where ye wish to go," he said. "Mount up and we'll be on our way."

"No thanks. I'm fine walking."

She set off down the narrow trail, reasoning that it must eventually come out onto a road or if not, then at least she'd hit a settlement sooner or later as long as she followed the coastline. After a moment she heard hoof beats and Logan came abreast, walking the horse.

"Lass," he said. "Thea."

Thea looked at him sharply. It was the first time he'd used her name. Hearing it from his lips sent a strange sensation through her body.

"Thea," he said again, gently. "Stepper can easily bear the weight of two of us. Ride with me. It will be much quicker than walking."

Did he think she would so easily forget his rudeness and condescension just because he was offering her a lift? She opened her mouth to reply but before she could utter a word, a wave of dizziness sent her stumbling.

THE LASS STAGGERED and then crashed to the ground with a strangled little yelp. Logan knelt by her side, cupping her head in his hands. Her skin had gone dangerously pale and her eyelids fluttered.

"Thea?" he asked anxiously. "Lass?"

She passed a shaky hand over her forehead and then struggled into a sitting position, pushing determinedly away from him. "I'm fine. Just a bit dizzy. It's passed now."

She didn't look fine to Logan but he knew better than to comment. Lord above, the lass was as fierce and proud as a hawk, and had a temper to match. He wasn't used to having people in his home and hadn't been entirely sure how to handle this woman who'd dropped into his life out of nowhere.

"Listen, lass," he said, deliberately keeping his voice steady and reasonable. He'd learned she didn't take too kindly to being ordered about. "I dinna ken this settlement ye spoke of, but if ye give me directions, I'll do my best to get ye there. Would that be agreeable?"

She looked up at him and the sight of those big green eyes of hers nearly unmanned him. Lord above, but she was beautiful. Heat rushed through his body and he forced himself to take a long, slow breath.

"Yes," she whispered at last. "That would be agreeable."

Logan rose to his feet and pulled Thea up after him. She leaned on him heavily as he led her over to the horse and helped her into the saddle.

He swung up behind her and gathered the reins. "Which way, lass?"

"South," she mumbled. "A little valley where a river empties into the sea. There's a long pebble beach and the cliffs on one side are so steep there are no houses built on them at all."

The description of the estuary and the beach sounded like Tragavnen Cove which lay a few miles distant but there was no settlement in that valley. However, he suspected she wouldn't believe that if he told her and would insist on seeing it with her own eyes.

Clicking at Stepper, he sent her into a walk down the trail, as fast a pace as he dared with Thea seated in front of him. She clung to the saddle with both hands, obviously unused to horses, but made no complaint as they rode. Whenever there was a slight bump she was jostled against him and Logan had to admit that it felt good to have the solid weight of her back pressed against his chest.

How long had it been since he'd last been this close to anyone? A year? More? Her hair tickled his neck and her scent filled his nostrils. She smelled of spring flowers.

This part of the coast was wild and sparsely populated. The protection of the laird up at Dun Ringill didn't stretch this far and so the only folks who walked these paths were smugglers or brigands hiding from justice. Logan scanned the terrain continually as they moved, alert for danger, but he spotted not another soul.

Thea suddenly sat up straighter. "What's that?"

Logan followed the line of her gaze. "What's what?"

"That rock! The one shaped like a sleeping cat! I recognize it! It's on the hillside just above Glenmorrow! We're nearly there!"

High on the hillside to their left a large outcropping of rock stuck through the heather. It didn't look much like a sleeping cat to Logan's eyes but he didn't tell her that.

They continued past the rocks and around half an hour later they found themselves looking down into Tragavnen Cove. The valley had a wide, lazy river meandering along it, emptying out into the sea through a delta that grew thick with marsh grass. The cry of sea birds and the whine of the wind filled the air but there was no sign of any settlement.

Thea stared, her eyes wide. Then she turned to look back at the sleeping cat rocks then back at the valley. Logan could see her thoughts turning.

"This doesn't make any sense," she muttered, shaking her head. "This is the place. Look, there's the steep cliff I told you about. There's the river mouth. There's the sleeping cat rocks. So where the hell is Glenmorrow?"

Her words rose in pitch, tinged with panic. When she'd first claimed to be from this 'US', he'd thought she was being untruthful and when she'd wanted to return to Glenmorrow, a place Logan had never heard of, he'd been doubly sure. But now, as he looked at her panic-stricken face, he realized she really believed what she'd been telling him.

"Let me down," Thea muttered. "I need to take a look around."

She began wriggling in the seat, trying to get her leg over Stepper's neck. Stepper shifted under the sudden change in weight.

"Easy," Logan warned Thea. "You'll have us both unhorsed if ye aren't careful. Here."

He swung his leg over the saddle and dropped to the ground before helping Thea to dismount. She walked unsteadily to the valley edge, and looked out. Logan crossed his arms over his chest and watched from a distance, giving her space. That blow to the head must have affected her memory. Logan could only hope she could piece together where her kin really were or they were both in deep trouble.

"I don't get it," Thea whispered, her eyes round and worried. "This doesn't make any sense. What the hell is going on? I should have found myself a waitressing job then I'd be safe at home right now! Why the hell did I listen to Irene MacAskill?"

Logan's head came up at that. He strode to Thea's side and grabbed her arm more roughly than he intended. "What was that name ye just said?"

She gave him a puzzled look. "Irene MacAskill. Why? Do you know her?"

Logan didn't answer her question. A sudden fear gripped him. Irene MacAskill? She'd spoken to the lass?

"How do ye know the woman?" he demanded. "And what did she say to ye? Tell me. Every word."

"I...I..." Thea stammered. "She brought me to Scotland. Offered me a job, paid for my flights. I was supposed to do some photography work for her magazine. She met me when I was doing my recce by the stones but then she just...disappeared."

Logan released Thea's arm and took a step back. He sucked in a deep breath and then scrubbed a hand through his hair. Irene MacAskill. The same woman who'd accosted Logan in the storm, right before he ran into Thea. The same woman who'd disappeared into thin air as if she'd never existed. The same woman who Logan suspected was far, far more than the benign old woman she seemed.

The tattoo on his chest suddenly ached, sending pain searing across his skin, just as it had the day it had been branded into him, the mark of his bargain, of his curse. He staggered a few steps, gritting his teeth against the pain. It passed after only a moment, so fleeting he could almost believe he'd imagined it. Almost.

Thea was watching him warily. "What is it?" she asked. "You look as though you've seen a ghost."

"Maybe I have," he muttered. "Maybe we both have."

Could it be coincidence? Unlikely. He'd learned from bitter experience that such things didn't happen by chance.

"You know something, don't you?" Thea said. "Tell me!"

Logan straightened and drew in a deep breath. Was the lass somehow in league with Irene? Or was she just another unsuspecting victim pulled into her plans? And how was he to know?

"Let me get this straight: Irene MacAskill brought ye across the ocean, met ye here, and then disappeared?"

Thea nodded.

"And ye have no kin here at all? Nobody who could take care of ye?"

She shook her head, her eyes round. "I don't know anybody here. Only Mr and Mrs MacGregor who run the hotel. Look, could you take me to a police station or something? I just want to go home." Her voice sounded frightened now.

He held out a hand and spoke gently. "I would if I could, lass, but ye use words I dinna understand. I dinna ken what ye mean by 'police station' or 'hotel'. All I know is that I suspect Irene MacAskill is at the root of this. If I guess correctly, she is of the Fae and they are known for their mischief. What she wants with ye, I canna say. But if she is the one that brought ye here, she is the one that can answer yer questions and arrange for ye to go home—wherever that might be. We must find her."

Thea was staring at him incredulously. "Fae? As in 'fairy'? You are kidding, right?"

He didn't reply, only met her gaze steadily. They stared at each other for a moment then Thea threw up her hands. "This is crazy! You really expect me to believe that I've been whisked here by some fairy? I'm surrounded by crazy people! Look, thanks for your help but I'll find my own way back to the hotel from here—"

Her tirade cut off as she staggered again, eyes rolling back in her head. Logan grabbed her arm before she could hit the ground.

"Gerroff," she muttered. "I'm fine."

"Ye most definitely are not fine," Logan growled, pulling one of her arms over his shoulder. He'd seen people with head injuries on the battlefield and knew how unpredictable they could be. The lass needed a healer.

Curse the Fae and their damned meddling! Hadn't they done enough to him? He'd dared to hope he would be free of them after he made his bargain but it seemed they weren't done with him yet. Curse them all!

"Come," he said. "There is naught to be gained by lingering here. We must return to my croft."

"No," Thea protested weakly. "We have to find the road. And the hotel. I need to go home."

"Aye, I know that," he said. "And we will. We'll find Irene—I give ye my word. But not this instant. Right now ye need rest and healing."

For a wonder, she didn't protest as he carried her to Stepper and lifted her into the saddle. She swayed and for one heart-stopping minute, Logan feared she would fall, but she gripped the horse's mane in both hands and managed to steady herself.

Logan mounted behind her. "Here, lass. Lean back against me. I willnae let ye fall."

It was a measure of how bad she was feeling that she did so without complaint. Her body felt warm where it pressed against his and his skin tingled where her hair brushed him.

An unexpected surge of protectiveness welled inside him. Aye, she'd burst into his life like a thunderclap, turning it upside down, but he'd protect her, make sure she was safe. From everything. Even himself.

Pulling in a deep breath, he turned towards home.

Chapter 5

THE POUNDING IN THEA's head was so hard she was sure it was going to crack her skull. She wanted nothing more than to close her eyes and go to sleep, let all this craziness disappear.

Concussion, a voice whispered in the back of her mind. *You have concussion.*

That was why she'd dreamed all this up, right? Maybe she'd hit her head so hard that she was in some sort of hallucination. Maybe that was why nothing made sense anymore.

But no. Who was she kidding? The feel of the wind, the motion of the horse, and most of all the solid presence of the man behind her was way too real to be any injury-induced hallucination. So, as they rode steadily back towards Logan's cottage, she fought off the dizziness and lassitude that kept threatening to pull her into unconsciousness and forced herself to think.

It had all begun when she had stepped under that archway. She'd emerged in a different place. Since then she'd been unable to find any trappings of her normal life. No car. No phone signal. No Glenmorrow.

And no damned Irene MacAskill.

A terrible thought sprang to life at the back of her mind but she pushed it away. No. She would not think that. It was too terrifying to contemplate.

There had to be a rational explanation—she just had to find it. So, what did she know about her situation? She was still in the Highlands of Scotland. Logan, the only person she'd met since passing through the arch, lived alone in a rustic cottage with none of the comforts of modern life. He wore traditional dress and rode a horse rather than drove a car. He'd never heard of half the things Thea mentioned and claimed to have no knowledge of the US. Which was utterly ridiculous. Unless...

She suddenly sat bolt upright in the saddle, clutching at the saddle horn with white knuckles. That terrifying thought reared up again and this time it wouldn't be silenced.

The saddle creaked as Logan shifted behind her. "What is it, lass?"

Thea worked her jaw but no words came out. Images flashed through her head. Irene MacAskill's smiling face. A stone archway with blue sky beyond. A storm raging around her. Sinking, down, down, and then emerging somewhere....else.

She licked her lips, working up enough saliva to speak. She took a deep breath and asked the question which had been building inside her. "Logan, what year is this?"

"It is the twenty-seventh year of the reign of our King James V. 1540 Why? What year did ye expect it to be?"

Thea reeled and clutched the saddle horn even tighter. Logan pulled the horse to a halt and wrapped one arm around her to steady her.

"Thea? What's wrong?"

Oh god. Oh god, oh god, oh god!

Panic tried to claw its way up Thea's throat and for a second she could hardly think, hardly breathe.

Calm, she told herself. *Breathe. Think.*

Taking deep breaths, she forced the panic down. "I'm fine," she lied. "Just another dizzy spell."

Logan nudged the horse into a walk again but his arm stayed wrapped around her waist. Thea found herself clinging to him. His presence was the only thing of solidity in a suddenly shaky world.

She was in the past! She had traveled back in time by hundreds of years! It was the only thing that made sense. It would explain why the shoreline by the stones of Druach had changed. It would explain why there was no cell signal and no sign of her car. It would explain why Logan dressed the way he did and looked at her as if she was a lunatic when she'd asked him about getting a cab.

This couldn't be happening. It couldn't. How had a simple job photographing wildlife led to this? It had all started with Irene MacAskill. She was the one who had arranged for her to come to Scotland. She was the one who'd encouraged her to step through the arch. Could Logan be right? Could she be one of these 'Fae' with the power to bring her back in time? And if so, could Thea find her here, in this time? Could she send Thea home?

Yes, she told herself. *That's it. Find Irene and your problem is solved.*

By the time they reached Logan's home, Thea was feeling a little calmer although the pounding in her head had not abated and she staggered and almost fell when she tried to dismount. She didn't have the energy to protest as Logan picked her up, carried her into the little house, and laid her down on the bed in the corner.

She sank gratefully onto the mattress, surprised to find it soft and comfortable. Sleep was trying to pull her under again and her thoughts were starting to turn fuzzy. Logan knelt by her side. Concern creased his features.

Thea found herself staring at him. Those eyes. They were so deep she could drown in them. On impulse she reached out and cupped his cheek in her hand. He startled as though he would pull away but he didn't. He tolerated the touch for a moment before reaching up and gently taking her hand away.

"I have to leave ye for a while."

"Leave me? Here? Alone?" she said, hating the fear that filled her voice. She couldn't help it. He was the only familiar thing in this world of strangeness.

"Only for a little while. I need to fetch a healer. Sleep. I will be back before ye know it."

He threw a blanket over her and Thea was suddenly warmer and snugger than she could remember in a long time. She tried to fight it but the lethargy was spreading. Sleep rose up and grabbed her.

SHE WOKE WITH A JERK some time later. She glanced at her watch, only to realize that it, like her cell phone, had been ruined by her dunking in the sea. She couldn't tell how much time had passed but from the quality of the light, she guessed not much. There was no sign of Logan.

She pushed back the blanket and sat up, wincing at the pounding in the back of her skull. What she wouldn't give for a couple of aspirin right now! What did people do for headaches in this time? Grin and bear it?

Rubbing her sore head with one hand, Thea looked around. Her eyes alighted on a bundle sitting on the end of the bed and her heart leapt. Her backpack! It was sitting atop her clothes which had been neatly folded into a pile. She scrambled over to it and quickly undid the flaps. Sure enough, all the belongings she'd brought on this trip were inside—including her beloved camera.

She lifted it out, examining it carefully for any signs of damage. There were none. It must have dropped from her shoulder before she went over the cliff and Logan had rescued it. It was the first bit of good news she'd had since arriving in this time.

She set the camera reverently down on the bed and pulled out the rest of the pack's contents. There wasn't much: a thermos flask full of cold coffee, a money pouch with a few pounds in it—useless in this time—and the book Irene MacAskill had left for her by the stones. She frowned, turning it over in her hands then scanned the contents page. The first title read *The Troll and the Princess,* the second read *Spirit of Culmaggin* and so it went. Thea frowned. Why would Irene MacAskill give her a book of folk tales? She flipped to the front and read again the scrawled message on the inside.

This will help ye find what ye are looking for. I.

How would a book of folk tales help her find anything? Were there clues to how she could get home hidden in this book? She shook her head. How the hell was she supposed to know?

Thea reached for the flask and poured herself a drink—cold coffee was better than no coffee—then scooted back on the bed until her back was against the wall and sat with the book propped open on her knees. Sipping her coffee and doing her best to ignore her headache, she began to read.

Once upon a time, she read. Thea rolled her eyes. Great. She really was sitting here reading fairy tales.

The sound of hoof beats startled Thea from her reading. Voices came from outside. She quickly downed her coffee then stuffed her flask, camera, and Irene's book into her backpack and shoved it all under the bed.

She mustn't let anyone see her belongings. How would she explain them? The last thing she wanted was anyone suspecting the truth about where she'd come from. They might burn her for being a witch or something!

She scooted to the edge of the bed just as the door opened and Logan strode in. At the sight of him Thea's stomach did an odd little flip.

"Thea," he said in his deep voice. "I'm glad to see ye awake."

She nodded then winced as a shot of pain went right down the back of her neck.

"Aye, and it looks like she shouldnae be," said another voice. A woman pushed past Logan and knelt by Thea's side.

She had honey-colored hair gathered in a braid and looked to be around the same age as Thea.

"My name is Ailsa MacAuley of Clan MacAuley," the woman said. "I'm mighty pleased to make yer acquaintance, my lady. Logan fetched me to see to ye. He said ye took a tumble into the water and may have hit yer head."

My lady? Where had that come from?

"I...um...yes," Thea muttered, a little flustered. Not knowing what else to do, she stuck out her hand. "Please call me Thea."

Ailsa shared a startled glance with Logan and then reached out to take Thea's hand. Her eyebrows rose.

"Ye are burning!" Ailsa pressed her hand to Thea's forehead and tutted. "Logan!" she commanded brusquely. "Bring my bag."

Logan picked up a small hessian satchel from where it sat by the door and brought it over to Ailsa. The blonde woman took it and began rummaging inside. It was filled with little packets, all carefully labeled. She pulled out several and placed them on the floor by her feet.

She looked up at Logan who was hovering by her shoulder. "I canna work with ye crowding me," she said. "Go outside. I'm sure Rhodry could do with yer help."

"I will leave when I know Thea will be all right," he replied. He had a stubborn set to his jaw.

It didn't have any effect on Ailsa. "She will be well as long as ye give me the space to work. Now out!"

Logan looked from Ailsa to Thea and back again. He held up his hands. "Fine! But call me if ye need anything."

With that he turned and strode out, pulling the door shut behind him. Thea was left alone with Ailsa. The blonde woman smiled and rolled her eyes at Thea as if to say 'men!'

"I need to feel yer head if ye dinna mind," she said. "I willnae hurt ye."

"I...um...okay," Thea replied.

She bent her neck and Ailsa began gently probing the back of her head and neck with gentle fingers.

"Aye," she said. "Ye hit yer head all right. Ye have quite the lump on the back of yer bonce but the skin doesnae look broken so yer skull shoudnae be either. Ye will have a headache and some dizziness for a few days but once we take the edge off yer pain, ye should begin to recover."

She took two packets from the selection she'd placed on the floor and tipped some of their contents into a beaker of water. She stirred it then handed it to Thea. "Here, drink it all down. It will help with any dizziness or sickness. I will leave it here. Make sure ye take it three times a day."

Thea took the proffered beaker and sniffed it. A smell like pine needles assaulted her nostrils. "You're a doctor?" she asked.

Ailsa snorted. "Logan warned me that I may not know some of the words ye say. I dinna ken what ye mean by 'doctor' but if ye mean a healer then I suppose ye could call me that. I have some knowledge of herbs and their applications passed down from my mother and grandmother. Now drink it all down."

Thea set the beaker to her lips and downed the concoction in one long swallow. The taste was so bitter it made her grimace but she swallowed the lot. "Thanks. It's kind of you to come see me."

Ailsa waved her hand. "Think naught of it. When Logan arrived at our croft and told us yer story I knew it was the least I could do. It must be mighty frightening being lost so far from home, without illness and injury to add to it."

Thea met Ailsa's gaze and saw curiosity shining in her eyes. She wondered what Logan had told her. "Yes, it is."

Ailsa smiled and patted Thea's hand. "Come. Let me help ye wash and dress. I always find that a good soak and clean clothes make me feel better."

Before Thea could reply, Ailsa took down a large metal basin from the corner of the room and began filling it with water from the kettle. She added some cold from the water jug and then tipped in some powder from another of her packets. The smell of jasmine suddenly stole through the room.

"It isnae as grand as up at the castle of course. Up there they have tubs so big ye can lie in them and servants to bring hot water." There was a wistful tone to her voice. "Come, lift yer hair so I can unwind the plaid."

Thea gathered up her hair and Ailsa deftly untied the knot on Thea's shoulder, unraveling the plaid that Logan had lent her. Thea tried to hide her embarrassment as she was left sitting naked. Ailsa though, didn't bat an eyelid at Thea's state of undress. Maybe there were different ideas of privacy in this time.

Ailsa watched Thea patiently and Thea realized she was waiting for her to get into the tub. Heat flushed Thea's cheeks. Was the woman going to stay while she bathed? Was this how it was done in this time? She'd only just met the woman!

"Would you mind turning around?"

Ailsa laughed lightly then turned her back whilst Thea climbed into the tub, submerging herself until the soapy water covered her up to her chin. It felt wonderful. The warmth, coupled with the jasmine, coupled with whatever had been in the concoction Ailsa had given her, made her muscles relax for the first time in days.

"Oh my, that's good."

"Told ye," Ailsa said. "There is naught like a good soak for clearing the mind and body both. That's what my ma always says."

"Your mother sounds like a very wise woman," Thea replied. "I'd like to meet her."

"Then ye shall!" Ailsa said with obvious delight. "Ye must visit us as soon as ye are able. I know my mother would be delighted to meet ye, as would the rest of my unruly family."

Thea met Ailsa's gaze and smiled. She felt as though she'd made a friend. "I'd love to."

"That's settled then. Now lean forward and I will scrub yer back."

Thea did as she was bid although it felt strange. She'd not been this pampered since…well, she couldn't remember when. As Ailsa scrubbed her back and then her hair, Thea drew Ailsa into conversation. She needed to find out as much as she could about this strange place she found herself in.

"You said something about a castle?"

"Dun Ringill," Ailsa replied. "It's the seat of Laird MacAuley. We live on his lands although we're right on the edge. The castle lies many miles to the north. In better days I might have sent up to the castle for a healer for ye. The previous laird would have sent one, that's for sure." She sighed dramatically. "But I doubt the new one would." Then she smiled. "There! Yer hair is done. The water is growing tepid too. If ye've had enough, I'll help ye to dress."

Whilst Ailsa obligingly turned her back—with a small smile for Thea's prudishness—Thea dried herself with the blanket Ailsa offered her and then donned the clean undergarments Ailsa had provided.

It was amazing, she thought, as she dried herself, how a bath and clean clothes could make a person feel better. This, along with the remedy Ailsa had given her, had chased her headache to a background annoyance and the dizziness had abated.

Ailsa bade her sit by the fireplace whilst she dried and combed out her hair.

"You're very good at this you know," Thea observed.

"Do ye think so?" Ailsa replied, obviously pleased at the compliment. "To be honest, tis good to use my old skills again and to have another female around to use them on. I used to be a maid in Dun Ringill before I married Rhodry and gave it all up to be a farmer's wife."

"So you used to live in the castle?"

"Aye," Ailsa sighed wistfully. "It was a grand place back then. Of an evening we would gather in the Great Hall to play games, swap gossip and listen to stories. Every feast day there would be dancing on the green in front of the castle."

She tutted suddenly. "Listen to me, carping on about what used to be. It may be a hard life scraping a living out here on the land but I wouldnae have it any other way."

Ailsa's words sent a pang of longing through Thea. What she wouldn't give to be as content as her new friend. Now, it seemed, she was farther from that than ever. She was alone in a time and a place she didn't belong. A wave of homesickness washed through her.

Ailsa finished Thea's hair and then crossed to the bundle she'd left by the door. Untying it, she shook out several long dresses in varying colors. All were expertly embroidered with flowers and birds along the hems.

"I took the liberty of bringing ye some of my old dresses and some shoes," she explained. "They aren't much but I thought they may help ye feel more at home."

"They're beautiful," Thea breathed. She ran her hands down the soft fabric, enjoying the sensation of it under her finger tips. At home she wasn't really a dress kind of girl. They weren't really conducive to wildlife photography so she normally went around in jeans, boots and t-shirt. But if she was to fit in here, she had to look the part. Besides, the dresses really were lovely.

Not for the first time that afternoon, Thea was glad to have Ailsa's help. Dresses in this time, it turned out, had hooks up the back that were difficult to do up without help. Finally though, she managed to get one on and then she did a little twirl in front of Ailsa.

"Well? Do I look utterly ridiculous?"

Ailsa grinned. "Ridiculous isnae the word I'd use. My, but if ye were up at the castle ye would be turning heads."

Thea snorted. "I'll take your word for it." There were no mirrors in the room and Thea doubted that Logan even owned one.

"How is yer head now?" Ailsa asked. "Are ye feeling up to a little stroll?"

"I feel much better, thanks to you," Thea replied, smiling. "I don't know what you put in that concoction but it's certainly done the trick. My headache's gone completely."

Ailsa nodded. "That's good. Now, some fresh air is next. What did ye call me? Doctor? All right then. Outside with ye. Doctor's orders!"

Thea laughed. "Yes, sir!"

She took Ailsa's arm and the two women made their way out into the yard. The day had turned blustery again and the wind tugged at the hem of Thea's dress and brought the smell of the sea to her nostrils. There was no sign of Logan but Thea could hear voices coming from the other side of the house.

As she looked around, she realized that what yesterday had seemed like a rustic shack surrounded by wilderness now looked more like a neat-and-tidy holding, surrounded by wild but beautiful countryside. The cottage was well made, the stones of its walls fitting neatly against one another. The thatch on the roof was fresh and clean. The barnyard was well swept with a dry-stone wall around it.

The two women rounded the corner of the cottage to see Logan and another man, who Thea guessed must be Ailsa's husband, in the distance. They were busy carrying rocks over to a part of the wall that had collapsed.

"Ah! That's what I like to see!" Ailsa said. "Good honest work to earn yer bread! Keeping yerself out of trouble, husband?"

The two men turned. Ailsa's husband grinned at his wife but Logan's eyes leapt to Thea. They widened at the sight of her and something flashed in them. Thea couldn't have said what it was but it sent heat rushing through her body right down to her toes.

"Thea. I would like ye to meet my husband, Rhodry," Ailsa said.

Rhodry stepped forward. He was blond-haired like his wife, with an easy smile. "An honor to meet ye, my lady. Logan has told me of yer predicament. Being lost in a strange land is bad enough but to be rescued by Logan MacAuley? Well, it doesnae get much worse than that. Ye have my sympathies."

His eyes danced with amusement and Thea couldn't help but smile as Logan frowned at his friend's teasing.

"Thanks, Rhodry. To both of you. Ailsa has been most kind. I don't know what I would have done without her."

Ailsa waved away the compliment, embarrassed.

Logan stepped towards Thea. He looked her over, his expression unreadable. "Ye are well, lass?" he asked.

She nodded. "Better. Much better."

"I'm pleased to hear it. Rhodry owes me a favor so at first light tomorrow the two of us will ride out and see if we canna discover the whereabouts of Irene MacAskill. One old woman couldnae have gotten far. Trust me, lass. Ye'll soon be on yer way home."

"And until then I'm sure ye can put up with spending one night under the same roof as our Logan, canna ye?" Ailsa said. "Dinna worry, he's a gentleman. Well, most of the time."

Thea nodded. One night. That's all. Tomorrow they'd find Irene and she'd go home. She could put up with one night here couldn't she? She glanced at Logan and felt a little thrill go through her. Yes, one night wouldn't be too bad at all.

Chapter 6

LOGAN DID HIS BEST to stifle the storm of emotions that swirled inside him, but it was hard. Lord! It was hard! When Thea had first stepped outside wearing that dress and with her hair spilling over her shoulders in midnight waves, it had taken all of his self-control not to gawk like an idiot. Her beauty had hit him like a physical blow.

And now Ailsa was suggesting that Thea stay here at the cottage with him until they found Irene, and whilst the very thought of having her so close sent a hot spear of desire right through him, it evoked a stronger, more primal emotion.

Fear.

It wasn't safe for her. He could not let it happen.

"I'll just fetch my bag and then we'll be on our way," Ailsa said. "My mother has had the children long enough."

Logan followed her and when they were out of sight of Rhodry and Thea said, "She canna stay here."

Ailsa's eyebrows rose. "Why ever not?"

Logan groped to explain himself. He couldn't tell her the truth—that he was terrified of his curse falling upon her. It affected anyone who stayed near him too long and he'd already risked too much by allowing her to stay at his croft for one night. He dare not risk another.

"It isnae proper," he blurted. "What would folk say if they knew she was staying here with me? I willnae have her reputation besmirched. She must stay with ye and Rhodry."

That way she'll be safe.

"There aren't any folk round here to notice whether she's staying with ye or not, much less gossip about her," Ailsa replied firmly. "Ye know there isnae room at our cottage. Not now my ma is living with us as well. I'm sure ye can keep yer hands to yerself for one night."

Ailsa meant the words lightly but they cut through Logan like a knife. Keep his hands to himself? He couldn't even risk going near the lass! Before he could frame a reply Ailsa retrieved her bag from the house, then she and Rhodry were striding away down the track, leaving Logan alone with Thea.

She stood a little ways off, watching the couple leave. She had her arms wrapped around herself as if cold, her eyes holding a faraway cast. What was she thinking? About her homeland? About how much she wanted to return to it?

He scrubbed a hand through his hair. Lord above! How had he ended up in this situation? When he found Irene MacAskill he would wring her neck!

Logan ground his teeth, trying to think of something, anything, to say, but no words came. He watched Thea a moment longer then turned on his heel and strode across the yard to his forge.

A sack of half-finished horse shoes sat in the corner where he'd left them the night before he met Thea. He'd lost a full day's work already and that was something he could ill afford. His reputation as the best blacksmith in the area meant that the people of Dun Ringill were willing to ride the extra distance to his croft in order to purchase his work. But that would soon change if he started being late with his orders.

As he gathered his tools and began stoking the fire, his thoughts whirled. Normally working at his forge brought him peace. It chased the thoughts from his head and he was able to lose himself in the hard physical labor. Not today. Today thoughts and memories plagued him. Thoughts of Thea. Of Irene MacAskill. Of his curse.

These in turn led to memories. Of his old master, Albus, an enormous bear of a man, standing with his hands on his hips as he watched a young Logan shape his first sword. Of his father, Laird David MacAuley, and the smile of pride on his face as Logan had presented that first sword to him as a gift.

So long ago. Just memories now. Less than a whisper on the breeze.

Logan shook his head. What would his father think if he could see Logan now? Would he understand why he'd done what he did? Or would he denounce him for the fate he'd chosen? For the fate he'd condemned his brothers to?

For the first time in many long months, Logan thought of them. Old pain twisted his guts like a half-healed battle wound. Where were his brothers now? Were they well? Were they even still alive? He'd not seen either of them since that fateful night when they'd made their pact. Had they managed to carve a life for themselves away from the clan? He had no way of knowing. All he could do was live the half-life he'd made for himself and hope that his brothers had found some measure of peace.

Grunting, he heaved the sack of horseshoes onto a bench and opened it, counting them. They were fine work, some of his best, and he suspected they were headed for the laird's own stable up at the castle. He paused. The castle. A sudden wave of hopelessness washed through him. It was *his* castle. *His* stable. *His* horses that these shoes were destined for. And yet, were he to deliver these in person, nobody would even recognize him.

For a moment he railed at his fate. How things would be different if he was still the laird. Thea would be sleeping in a soft bed and a warm room rather than in a drafty cottage. Logan would have the whole garrison out looking for Irene MacAskill, not just himself and Rhodry. Thea would know the delights of clan life instead of being stranded out here alone with him.

Would ye change it? A voice whispered in the back of his head. *Would ye do things differently if ye had yer time over? Would ye have refused to make yer bargain?*

Nay, he answered himself, with a sigh. *I wouldnae.*

The sun was getting low in the sky and dusk would soon be falling. With it would come the chill of a Highland night. He thought of Thea, warm in his bed. With a growl of frustration, he pumped the bellows on his forge and set to work.

THEA WATCHED AS LOGAN walked away from her. He'd said not a word since Ailsa and Rhodry left. With a sigh, she made her way back inside the cottage. The fire had died low and the Highland evening already had a chill to it. Crouching by the hearth, she carefully fed sticks into it until there was a merry fire blazing, chasing away the cold.

Thea knelt by the bed and pulled out her pack from underneath. Clutching it to her chest, she sat down on a chair. It creaked under her weight and she noticed that one of the legs was loose. She frowned. She would have to fix that.

For now though, she opened her pack and carefully took out her camera. At the sight of it, a sense of dislocation went through her. It looked so out of place in this time. Just like her. She turned it on and was relieved when the red light on the top flashed and the screen on the back lit up. Once the battery ran out that would be it. She had no way to recharge it. But for now at least, she had this tenuous link to home.

She selected the gallery function and began scrolling through the photographs. There they were; the pictures she'd taken since she'd arrived in Scotland. The hotel. The rental car. The bustling streets of Glenmorrow. Right now they felt so far away as to be on a different planet. She continued scrolling. A Highland cow peering at her over a fence. A pair of horse-riders waving at her as they trotted by. A kestrel riding the thermals above. On and on the pictures went and with each new one, Thea felt the despondency spreading. How had she ended up here? How would she get back to the places in these photos?

The next image flashed onto the screen and she gasped.

It was the archway.

The stones reared up out of the water like dark sentinels, their straight lines seeming harsh against the waves of the sea. Even in a photograph there was something about them that seemed to draw Thea in. She ran the tip of her finger down the tiny screen, tracing their outline. How on earth could a stone archway transport her through time? None of this made any sense. It was crazy. Crazy!

She used the zoom function to look more closely, searching for any kind of clue as to what had happened. The pattern carved into the stones' surface sprang into focus, a pattern of interlocking coils. Thea frowned. She'd seen this pattern somewhere else recently. But where? The concussion had made her memory hazy and she couldn't quite piece it together. With a 'humph' of annoyance she turned the camera off so as not to waste the battery, returned it to her pack, and pushed the whole thing under the bed. She felt a huge wash of homesickness.

One night, she told herself. *You only need to last one night.*

With this thought running through her head, she seated herself on the rug and stared into the fire. Her eyes drifted closed.

The next morning Thea woke slowly. Her back ached and there was a cramp in one leg. It took her a moment to realize that she'd fallen asleep on the rug in front of the fire and that the bed hadn't been slept in. She looked around bleary-eyed. Where was Logan? Hadn't he returned to the cottage last night? Where had he slept?

With a groan she sat up and rubbed her eyes. She had a headache again and she knew Ailsa would not be happy with her for sleeping on the hard ground. She climbed to her feet, shuffled over to the water jug in the corner, and poured herself a drink of the cold, clear water. Then she mixed up her medicine and downed it in one, gritting her teeth at the acrid taste.

Weak gray light was seeping under the door and Thea guessed it was early morning, perhaps not yet dawn. She took a deep breath.

Today, she thought. *Today Logan will find Irene MacAskill and I'll go home. Tonight I'll be sleeping in a comfortable hotel bed binge-watching my favorite shows, drinking wine and gorging on ice cream.*

She had a quick wash from the water jug, gasping as the icy water chased away the last of her sleepiness, and took her time stretching her arms over her head and trying to work the kinks out of her neck. There was still no sign of Logan but she could hear a clinking noise coming from behind the house.

She pulled the door open and stepped into the yard. Stepper stuck her head over the stable door and snorted. Dawn was just beginning to turn the sky orange and the rim of the sun was yet to appear above the hills. A soft breeze stirred Thea's hair and sent goose bumps riding up her arms.

She drew in a great, deep breath, allowing it to fill her lungs. As it did so, an unexpected sense of peace settled inside her. This place was wild and untamed, so different to what she was used to. And yet it was beautiful. It was so...so...Thea groped for a word. So now. So present. Without the distractions of TV, internet, the constant notifications on her cell phone, Thea felt...liberated. In this place there was only the now. This moment. And then the next. It felt strange but comforting.

She crossed the yard to the stable and scratched Stepper behind the ears. The mare leaned into the touch and then sniffed at the front of Thea's dress, hoping for a treat.

Thea laughed. "I don't have anything. But I promise I'll find you a carrot or an apple or something. How would you like that? Now where's your master, eh?"

She left the stable and made her way around the back of the cottage to the low-roofed building that sat a little apart from the rest. Sure enough, the clinking she'd heard was coming from inside.

"Logan?" she called but there was no answer.

She ducked under the low eaves and into the building. A wall of heat hit her. It was like stepping into an oven. The space around the edge of the room was taken up with racks holding tools of all kinds. Several huge water vats stood in one corner and in the center of the room was a stone built kiln-type thing holding coals that burned white-hot. Next to this stood a huge anvil where Logan was busy hammering at a piece of metal.

He had his back to her and was so intent on his work that he'd heard neither her approach nor her call. He was stripped to the waist, with only a leather apron covering his chest and thick gloves on his hands. His shoulder-length hair clung to his neck in damp tangles and a thin sheen of sweat covered his skin, highlighting the contours of his muscled back and arms as he raised a hammer high over his head and brought it pounding down onto the strip of metal over and over again. Sparks flew from the white-hot bar but Logan paid them no heed and they dropped harmlessly to the hard-packed earthen floor.

A smithy, Thea realized. *Logan is a blacksmith.*

His movements were strong and sure as if he'd done this countless times before. The hammer he wielded had a huge iron head that Thea knew she'd struggle to lift but Logan swung it as though it weighed nothing at all. She watched him for a moment and she noticed that his back bore many scars. Several were puckered burn marks but others look like stab wounds. How had he gotten them?

He dropped the hammer onto the anvil and then, picking up the bar of metal with both gloved hands, plunged it into one of the water vats. It hissed and steamed, sending up a great cloud of water vapor. Then he returned the bar to the anvil, straightened, and wiped his brow.

Thea cleared her throat loudly.

Logan spun. He snatched up the hammer, holding it like a weapon. Then, realizing it was Thea, relaxed, placing the hammer down on the anvil.

"My apologies," he muttered. "Ye startled me."

"I shouldn't have snuck up on you like that. I did call you but I'm not surprised you didn't hear me over this racket."

He didn't reply. He was breathing heavily from his exertion, his broad chest heaving under the leather apron. Her eyes locked with his and a tingle went down her spine.

A coal popped in the forge and Logan turned away, poking at it with an iron poker.

"I...wondered where you were," Thea stammered. "You didn't come into the cottage last night."

"Nay," he agreed. He nodded at a pile of rumpled blankets in the corner of the smithy. "This place makes as good a bed as any."

"Now you're just trying to make me feel guilty," Thea replied, trying and failing to make her voice sound light. "I can't turn you out of your own cottage, not after all you've done for me. You should have slept inside."

An expression flashed across his face so quickly Thea could almost have convinced herself she'd missed it. It looked like fear.

"Nay, lass," he said. "That wouldnae have been proper. I willnae have yer reputation besmirched. We aren't married. It isnae right for us to share lodgings."

Thea frowned. Damn it. She had to remember that attitudes were different in this time. Was that why Logan had slept out here? Over concern for her honor?

Logan shifted his feet, looking uncomfortable. "Did ye sleep well?" he asked at last.

"Yes," she replied. He didn't need to know that she'd fallen asleep on the hearth rug. "And Ailsa's concoction worked a treat. My headache is all but gone."

"I'm relieved to hear ye say that. Ye had me worried for a while."

I did? Thea thought. He was watching her again. Her cheeks flushed and she took a step back. She cast around for something to say and suddenly remembered the broken chair leg.

"Do you have a hammer I can borrow? And some nails?"

He looked at her quizzically. "Whatever for?"

She crossed her arms. "You'll see. You aren't the only one who can use tools you know."

He raised an eyebrow but then crossed to a rack and took down a hammer with a good leather grip and a handful of nails. He held them out to her. "Should I be worried?" he asked with a faint smile. "I've seen yer temper first hand, remember."

Thea snorted. "Me? Temper? I've no idea what you're talking about."

He held out the tool and Thea took it. For a moment her finger brushed his. She glanced up and her eyes locked with his. They were dark, unblinking, his lips parted.

Thea stepped back, clutching the hammer to her chest. "I...um...thanks."

He blinked then cleared his throat. "Aye. Well. I'll just finish up here then I'll make us some breakfast."

Flustered, Thea could hardly choke out the words. "Breakfast. Yes. Great."

She turned away and hurried back into the house.

LOGAN BANKED THE COALS in the forge then stripped off his gloves and leather apron and hung them on a hook. Stepping outside he crossed to the water barrel and dunked his head into the icy water, allowing it to wash away the grime and sweat of his morning's work.

He grabbed his shirt from a hook and pulled it on, tying the sash of his plaid over one shoulder. Then, taking a deep breath, he strode across the yard to the house. They would have a quick breakfast and then ride over to Rhodry and Ailsa's croft. He and Rhodry would find Irene MacAskill and get some answers.

Simple. By the end of the day Thea would be gone, the short disruption she'd caused in his life would be over and he could go back to normal. He ought to be pleased about that. So why did he have an ache in his gut as though someone had punched him?

Gritting his teeth, he yanked the door open and stepped inside. Thea was kneeling on the floor, the broken chair upturned in front of her. She glanced over her shoulder as he walked in. She had two nails clamped between her teeth.

"Pass me the hammer would you?" she mumbled at him around her mouthful.

Logan stared at her, bemused. Then, when she gave him a flat stare, he picked up the hammer and handed it over. She took it without a word and turned to her work. Logan crossed his arms, watching.

"Ye are wasting yer time lass," he told her. "The wood is knotted. It willnae take anyone's weight, regardless of repairs."

Thea took one of the nails from her mouth, held it against a piece of wood she'd braced cross-ways between two of the legs, then deftly nailed it in with three precise taps. Satisfied, she spun the chair around and hammered the other end of the wood to the leg on the other side. She righted the chair and carefully sat down on it. Her repair creaked but it held.

She grinned. "Ta da!"

She looked mighty pleased with herself and Logan couldn't help the smile that pulled the corners of his mouth.

"It just needed a bit of TLC. These cross-struts will distribute the weight more evenly. It should hold now." She looked him up and down and then frowned. "Although you might be better off using the other one and leaving this for guests."

To Logan's surprise, he felt a laugh bubbling up inside him. "As ye say, oh wise one. Where did ye learn such skills? Woodwork isnae the kind of thing noble ladies would normally be versed in."

"My granddad," she replied, her eyes turning wistful as though she was thinking of fond memories. "He was into DIY big time. When I was a kid, he taught me all sorts. I think he was happy to have a willing helper. We lived in a big old house that was slowly falling apart around us so when he got too old I took over trying to keep the place standing."

Logan frowned. There she went again. DIY? What was that word? "So ye live with yer grandparents?"

Her smile faltered. "No. Not anymore. I went off to college. Then they died and I had to sell the house. It's just as well as it was too big for me anyway. I was renting an apartment before I came here."

There was an old pain shining in her eyes and it twisted Logan's heart to see it.

"Would ye like some breakfast?"

"I would. Fixing chair-legs is hungry work."

"Aye, nay doubt. I hope ye like porridge. It's all I have."

"Ah! Porridge! My favorite!" she said with a smile.

Logan fell into the routine he went through every morning. Only this time he was preparing breakfast for two. Thea said not a word as Logan busied himself by the fire but he could feel her watching him. He was acutely aware of her presence. The sound of her breathing. The tiny rustle of her dress as she moved. Did she realize the effect she had on him? He guessed not, which made it all the more potent.

Ye have been too long alone, he thought.

But it was more than that. There was something about Thea Thomas. She was unlike any woman he'd ever met. She was wild and reckless and brave. She held secrets about her like a cloak.

Ye are losing yer wits, he thought as he stirred the pot. *The sooner ye send the lass on her way the better.*

He served breakfast and Thea ate greedily. She had none of the dainty manners that he would expect from a noble-born lady. She scooped up her porridge in great dollops and ate like she was starving, nodding appreciatively at the taste.

He sat down opposite her and pulled his own bowl over. How strange it felt to be eating breakfast with someone else! He was reminded suddenly of breakfasts in the castle. He would sit at the high table with his brothers and they would banter and make plans for the day whilst the Great Hall hummed to the conversation of his clan.

Lord, it seemed a lifetime ago.

He'd been a different man then. Laird Logan MacAuley had died that day by the stones as surely as if he'd had a knife rammed through his heart. Another man had emerged to take his place. Blacksmith MacAuley, a loner, living apart from society and avoiding all bonds of fellowship. As it must be.

Thea finished her bowl and pushed it back, rubbing her stomach appreciatively. "That," she announced, "was possibly the most delicious breakfast I've ever eaten!"

He raised an eyebrow. "It was only porridge, lass."

"Porridge tastes like the gods' own ambrosia when you're as hungry as I was."

"If ye think that was good, ye should try Old Magda's cooking up at the castle. If there is a better cook in all the Highlands, I've never heard of her." He clamped his mouth shut as soon as the words were out of his mouth. Curse it! He had to be more careful.

"The castle?" she asked. "You mean Dun Ringill? Ailsa told me about it. You've been there?"

"Aye," he answered quickly. "I sell my wares there sometimes."

"Like that sword you were making this morning?"

He glanced at her. "Aye, like the sword. Although normally it's less grand things. Horse-shoes. Bridles. Tools. That sort of thing."

"And yet you live out here alone, miles from the castle. That doesn't make much sense to me. Surely you'd do better living closer to where your customers are?"

Logan shifted in his seat. *Aye,* he thought. *It would. But that's not possible. Not for me.* He shrugged. "I'm the best blacksmith in the district. People will travel the extra miles for my services."

He said it without bravado. It was a simple statement of fact. His master, Albus, had been renowned all over the Highlands, and Logan had been his best apprentice. There had been raised eyebrows when Logan's father had apprenticed him to a simple blacksmith. What need had the heir for such a trade? But his father had believed in ensuring each of his sons was trained in more than just leadership. So for him had come blacksmith's training, for Camdan soldiering, for

Finlay, music. Their father's foresight had become more important than any of them could have imagined.

"What about ye?" Logan asked, trying to turn the conversation away from himself. "Ye keep insisting that ye are no lady and work as a—what did ye call it?—a 'photographer'? What is that?"

She frowned. "How to explain it? I make pictures. I came to Scotland to make pictures of your landscapes and wildlife. People are very interested in that sort of thing in my homeland."

Logan leaned back in his chair, trying to make sense of what she was telling him. "So, ye are a painter?"

"Something like that, I guess," she said, nodding. "Although I never expected my assignment to end like this."

She met his gaze and he saw a flash of fear in her eyes. She was a brave lass, trying to appear confident when inside she must be reeling. How would he feel if he was lost in a strange land, surrounded by people and ways he didn't know?

Logan pushed back his chair with a loud scrape and collected up the dishes. "Tis time we were on our way," he said. "The sooner Rhodry and I ride out, the sooner we will find our errant meddler."

Once breakfast was cleared away Logan saddled Stepper, swung Thea up into the saddle, and climbed up behind her. He nudged Stepper onto the trail that led to Rhodry and Ailsa's croft.

As they moved he tried not to think about the fact that by tonight Thea would be gone.

Chapter 7

THEA FELT BETTER THAN she had in days. The concussion seemed to have faded and she was filled with energy. As she and Logan rode along the gently rolling trail, the wild hills to the right, the sighing sea to the left, she found her head continually swiveling from side to side, taking it all in. It was a beautiful morning, so different to the night she'd arrived. A gentle breeze blew in from the sea, bringing with it the smell of sea-salt and the haunting cry of gulls.

The breeze brought goose bumps to her skin and filled her lungs with its freshness. Logan's hard chest pressed against her back and his arms formed a protective cage around her, promising he would not let her fall. Every time the horse jolted, their bodies came into contact and each time it sent a warm tingling right through her.

Alive, she thought suddenly. *I feel alive. More alive than I've felt in a long time. It must be because I'm going home today. That's the only explanation.*

Something caught her eye and she pointed. "Puffins!"

The little black and white birds with their rainbow beaks were popping up out of their burrows all along the hummocky ground to their left.

"Aye," Logan replied. "They nest all along here."

Thea watched, transfixed. If only she could get her camera out and snap them! And look! Cormorants and terns, kittiwakes and fulmars filled the cliffs ahead of them, calling so raucously they cut through even the sound of the waves. *Oh, my,* Thea thought. *This is a photographer's heaven!*

"It's beautiful," she breathed.

"Aye," Logan agreed. "When I was a lad, we used to scale these cliffs to try to get a look at the chicks. I soon learned my lesson when a fulmar spit all over me. Ye have never smelled anything like it!"

Thea laughed. The thought of a young Logan covered in fulmar spit was enough to make mirth bubble up in her belly. "Oh, I would pay good money to see that! I bet you were incorrigible as a child."

"I was naught of the sort," he said in a mock-haughty voice. "I'll have ye know I was a model child."

She turned her head to look at him and found he had a serious expression on his face but there was mirth dancing in his eyes. Logan didn't smile much but that didn't mean he was serious all the time. She was beginning to be able to read the slight quirk of his lips or the look in his eyes that betrayed his amusement.

They made good time and were soon riding up to Ailsa and Rhodry's croft. As Logan pulled the horse to a halt in the barnyard, the door to the cottage opened and a gaggle of children came pelting out, followed more sedately by their parents. The children swamped Logan, all clinging to his legs and crying, "Uncle Logan! Uncle Logan!"

He hefted the youngest on his hip and ruffled the hair of the others. "Here now! That's quite the welcome! I hope ye have been behaving for yer ma and da!"

Thea stared, astonished. The last thing she'd expected was for Logan to be good with children. It hardly fit with his dour, loner demeanor. But the way Ailsa and Rhodry's children clustered around him, it was obvious they adored him. Who the hell was this man?

Logan put down the child and turned to Thea. He held out a hand to help her down from the saddle. Thea swung her leg over and slid clumsily to the ground. The children fell silent, staring up at this stranger with wide eyes.

"Children," Logan said. "This is Lady Thea Thomas. She's going to be spending the day with ye today. She's a visitor from far away across the sea and I know ye'll take good care of her while yer da and I go out riding. Isnae that right?"

The children nodded silently, obviously wary. Ailsa stepped forward and swept Thea into an embrace.

"Ye are looking better already, my dear!" she said. "There is more color in yer cheeks."

"I feel much better," Thea confirmed. "Thanks to you." She winked at the children. "Your mother is a miracle worker. She fixed my broken head. I have much to thank her for."

The children's eyes widened further at her strange accent and stared up at her in fascination.

"Ye talk funny," a blonde girl said. "Where are ye from?"

"Hush, Anna!" Ailsa said. "It's rude to say such things!"

"That's okay," Thea laughed. She crouched down so she was on eye-level with Anna. "I'm from America. It's a place beyond the wide sea. There we have magical things called pizza and doughnuts. If ye like I will tell ye a story about it later."

Anna's face broke into a smile. "Aye! A story!"

Rhodry shook his head at Thea. "Ye've done it now. They'll be pestering ye for the rest of the day. Ye willnae get a moment's peace until they've pried every scrap out of ye."

"I don't mind that," Thea said, smiling. "It's the least I can do for all your help."

"The morning is wearing on," Logan said. "We had best be moving." He approached Thea and stood looking down at her. "We'll return as soon as we find Irene and some answers."

She watched dumbly as Logan and Rhodry mounted up and galloped away, the thunder of the horses' hooves soon disappearing into the distance.

THEA FOUND SHE HAD little time to worry about Logan and what he might find. As soon as the men had ridden off Ailsa introduced Thea to her children who soon got over their shyness and began chattering so fast Thea could barely keep up with them.

Mary, Ailsa's mother, was sequestered in a chair in the corner when they entered the cottage, the clack-clack of needles filling the air as she knitted.

"Ma, this is Thea. The one who's visiting Logan?"

Mary's creased face broke into a warm smile and she set aside her knitting and patted the chair next to her. Thea sat down and Mary took her hands in hers. Her skin was warm and dry, reminding Thea suddenly of Irene MacAskill.

"Ah! So ye are the one who has our Logan in such a spin, my dear! Come, let me take a look at ye!"

It was hard to pinpoint exactly how old Mary might be. Lines creased her face and the skin on the top of her hands was spotted with age but vitality still shone in her eyes, along with a fierce intelligence.

"It isnae every day that we welcome an outlander to the Highlands," Mary said. "Let alone one who's captured our Logan's heart so."

Thea flushed. "I...I don't know what you mean."

Mary grinned. "Nay? Mayhap I was imagining the way he was looking at ye just now."

"Ma!" Ailsa said. "Were ye spying through the window?"

"Spying?" Mary said, looking affronted. "I canna help what I see. Tell me, my dear, are ye married? Do ye have children?"

"Mother!" Ailsa exclaimed.

"No to both," Thea replied, fidgeting uncomfortably in her chair.

Anna suddenly burst through the door and skidded to a halt, all but flying into Thea's lap. "Will ye come to the beach with us, Lady Thea?" the girl cried. "Ma said we could go cockle picking. Will ye?"

"Cockle picking? That sounds great! Count me in!" Thea said with a grin.

Anna gave a little cry of delight, grabbed Thea's hand, and tugged her to her feet. Thea allowed the girl to guide her outside to where the rest of the children were waiting. She breathed a sigh of relief. At least she was away from Mary and her probing questions.

The day passed quickly and Thea soon lost track of time. She and Ailsa spent the day on the beach with the children. They picked through rock pools and waded into the shallows collecting cockles and mussels which they put into a large woven basket Ailsa had brought for the task. Although there was a serious side to it—they were collecting food for the family after all—the children made it into a game. They splashed and chased each other through the shallows, hollering and screaming in delight. Thea found herself pulled into numerous games and by the time the basket was full and the afternoon was wearing to a close, she found herself wet through, exhausted and thoroughly content.

She and Ailsa were walking back to the cottage, the basket strapped to Thea's back, when the sound of hoof beats caused them both to look up. Riders came galloping down the trail. Thea's heart leapt at the sight of Logan, his hair streaming out behind him in the wind. But a moment later her heart sank again as she realized Logan and Rhodry were alone.

There was no sign of Irene MacAskill.

"I JUST DINNA UNDERSTAND it," Rhodry said for about the fifth time. "How could she have disappeared? One old woman canna cover many miles in a day and we've been to every village in the vicinity. Nobody has seen her." He shook his blond head and then speared a big chunk of meat from his plate.

Logan glanced at Thea and he didn't need to speak for her to know what he was thinking. *Fae,* he'd called Irene

MacAskill. A being with powers beyond human knowledge who had decided to meddle in both their lives. It would be easy for such a being to disappear.

They were gathered around the table in Ailsa and Rhodry's house, tucking into the hearty meal that Mary had cooked. As they ate Logan had quickly related the tale of their journey. They'd ridden north as planned, along the road where Logan had last seen Irene, asking after her with everyone they met. But nobody fitting her description had been seen in the last few days.

Thea found herself staring listlessly at her plate. Logan suddenly laid a hand on her arm and she glanced up.

"Dinna worry, lass," he said. "We havenae given up yet. We'll ride out again tomorrow. And the day after that until we find her. Could be she has an isolated croft somewhere that we havenae found yet. We'll find her, be assured of that."

Thea gave him a smile but her heart wasn't in it. She'd been so sure she'd be going home today. Where was Irene? Why would she bring her here and then just abandon her?

She put food into her mouth but barely tasted it. She thought back through everything that had happened since the day she'd met Irene MacAskill. Every word. Every facial gesture. Every bit of body language. What, exactly, had Irene said to her?

Ye will help me avert a disaster and break a curse that will throw the future out of balance. And in so doing, mayhap ye will find yer own place in the world. The one ye've been searching for all yer life.

Avert a disaster. Break a curse.

Had Irene brought her here for a reason? Was she supposed to do something? Then why hadn't she at least given Thea a clue as to what that was?

Thea paused, spoon raised halfway to her mouth. Wait. Perhaps she *had* left clues. The book. The book of stories that Irene had left for her. At the time Thea had thought it a strange gift but what if it was more than just a gift? What if it held the clues to what she was supposed to do?

She was suddenly sure that Logan would not find Irene. Not until she wanted to be found, and, Thea suspected, that would not happen until Thea had done whatever she'd been sent here to do. But what was that? And how would she figure it out?

"Well, we mayn't have found Irene on our travels," Rhodry said. "But we found plenty of trouble. There are rumors flying so thick you could almost pluck them out of the air."

"Rumors?" Ailsa asked. "What rumors?"

"War," Rhodry replied. "War with the MacKinnons."

Ailsa tutted. "Ye shouldnae listen to such gossip, husband. Ye know as well as I that the MacKinnons have been allies of the MacAuleys for generations."

Rhodry shook his head. "*Were* allies. But not anymore. Seems the stories of the laird demanding an increased tithe from the MacKinnons is true. The word is he wants six of their ships."

"Their ships?" Ailsa asked. "But how will they feed themselves? The MacKinnon's are fisher folk above all else."

"Exactly," Rhodry replied. "Which is why Old Laird MacKinnon has had enough. The word is that if Laird

MacAuley doesnae drop his demands, the MacKinnons will dissolve the alliance. Then the MacKinnons will ride against us."

Mary shook her head. "This wouldnae have happened in the old laird's time. Eoin isnae half the man his predecessor was!"

"Hush, Mother!" Ailsa hissed. "He's still our laird and ye shouldnae say such things!"

"I willnae be hushed," Mary replied, fixing her daughter with a hard stare. "Do ye deny it? Taxes up, the roads more dangerous than ever, no help for the outlying crofts and what does our laird do? Spends his time war-mongering and chasing anyone in a dress! I pity the woman he finally weds!"

Logan shifted uncomfortably in his chair, making it creak. "I'm sure Laird Eoin has reasons for what he does," he said carefully. "The clan needs an heir and for that he needs a wife."

"And these rumors of war?" Mary demanded, turning her stern gaze on Logan. "Do ye think he has good reason for that? Ye would think war would be the last thing on his mind after the trouble with the Irish raiders. We've had peace for the first time in years and he wants to shatter it!"

Logan looked away but Thea noticed that his grip on his beaker was white-knuckled. He stood abruptly, his chair making a loud scraping noise on the hard wooden boards.

"We must be going. I have much work awaiting me in the smithy."

Without waiting for an answer, he strode out into the yard. Thea put down her spoon and pushed back her own chair.

"I guess that's my cue to leave," she muttered. "Thanks for dinner."

She waved a hasty goodbye and then followed Logan into the yard. She could see tension in the set of his shoulders as he held the horse for her to mount. She set her foot in the stirrup and Logan boosted her into the saddle before climbing up behind her.

He booted Stepper in the ribs and sent her off at a canter, soon leaving the croft behind. Logan was a silent, brooding presence at her back and Thea knew better than to break that silence.

Besides, she had plenty of things of her own to think about.

LOGAN RODE IN SILENCE. He tried to concentrate on the road but his thoughts kept skipping back to what they'd found earlier. No trace of Irene but plenty of traces of unrest and discontent. Could Eoin really be preparing for war? And against their old allies, the MacKinnons? What would drive him to do such a thing?

He was relieved when his croft came into view. He rode Stepper into the yard, pulled her to a halt and jumped down. Thea was getting better at dismounting and she stumbled only slightly as she hit the ground.

"Ye go on in," he said. "I'll see to Stepper."

She nodded and walked off and Logan led Stepper into the stable. Once inside he worked methodically, removing her saddle and bridle and then rubbing her down and filling her trough with fresh oats.

That done, he hesitated then walked to the back of the stable and pulled away one of the bales of straw that was stacked there. Behind it lay a large wooden chest, blackened and battered with age.

Logan stared down at it for a long time. Then he knelt, unclasped the locks, and pulled open the lid. Inside, folded as neatly as the day he'd put them there, lay an ermine-trimmed cloak in the colors of Clan MacAuley, an embossed shield that stood at least half his height, and Logan's sword, it's grip stained and weathered from use.

Logan stared at the items. The shield and sword had seen good use and saved his life on more than one occasion. The cloak was more ceremonial than useful and he used to wear it when greeting visitors or holding court. Trappings of his old life. Why had he kept them?

Fool, he thought. *Ye should have burned them. Why cling to a past that is dead and gone?*

Annoyed with himself, he snapped the lid shut and threw the hay bale back in place. What did it matter to him if Laird Eoin chose to take his clan to war? What did it matter to him if his people simmered with unrest? He'd already given them everything. Was his life and those of his brothers not enough?

It isnae my business, he told himself as he stomped to the door of the stable and across the yard to the smithy. *I'm just a blacksmith. A blacksmith with an order to fulfill.*

Chapter 8

THEA SAT CROSS-LEGGED in the yard, her back against the cottage wall. Irene MacAskill's book lay open on her lap and Thea was doing her best to read, despite the sea breeze that kept whipping her hair in front of her face or trying to turn the pages of the book for her. She'd been at it for hours, searching for clues that Irene might have left, but was getting precisely nowhere.

If Irene had meant for her to do something, then why the hell couldn't she just have told her? Trying to find clues in a book of fairy stories was worse than trying to find a needle in a haystack!

She squeezed her eyes shut and leaned her head back against the wall. Four days had passed since Logan and Rhodry had first ridden out to try and find Irene. Since then Thea's days had fallen into a routine. Whilst Logan rode out to look for the old woman in the mornings, Thea helped Ailsa around their croft. The afternoons were spent back at Logan's croft poring over Irene's book whilst Logan worked in the smithy.

Determined to prove herself useful, Thea had found a hundred different things to do around the croft. In fact, she wondered how Logan managed it all by himself. There were repairs needed on the cottage which Thea had tackled without asking permission and which Logan had watched with a kind of bemused look on his face, particularly when Thea had clambered up onto the roof to patch a hole in the chimney. There was Stepper to take care of, along with the chickens Logan had allowed to run wild on the holding, and food to be harvested, stored or cooked. Nothing came easy in this time and everything she took for granted back home took a supreme effort. Hell, even getting water meant hauling up buckets from a well.

Thea had thrown herself into it with determination and Logan made no protest. In fact, he barely spoke to her at all and her evenings were spent alone in the cottage poring over Irene's book whilst Logan slept in the smithy. Thea could tell he was uncomfortable around her. He never stayed near her for too long and always had an excuse to be off doing something else if she sought him out.

Thea couldn't figure it out. Sometimes she thought she'd offended him. At others, she was sure he just didn't like her. But then she'd catch him watching her with a look in his eyes that sent her pulse racing.

She sighed and snapped the book closed. From the smithy she heard the 'clink-clink' as Logan worked at his forge and could feel the heat coming from it even at this distance. Movement suddenly caught her eye. Three riders were cantering down the hill towards the croft.

"Logan!" she yelled, scrambling to her feet and running to the smithy. "We've got company."

He set down his hammer and followed her outside, wiping his hands on a rag. He squinted against the sunlight, shading his eyes with his hand. "Laird MacAuley's men. Come to collect his horseshoes."

He glanced at Thea and a flicker of unease washed across his face. "It would be best if they dinna see ye, lass. I'll give them their order and send them on their way."

"I'll wait in the stable."

She darted round to the stable. It was empty, Stepper having been turned out into the paddock for the day. Thea approached the plank wall and found a gap where she could peek out.

The three men rode into the yard and Logan stepped out to meet them.

"Greetings," he called. "A fine day to be out riding, nay?"

The men jumped down. They wore plaid in the MacAuley colors with thick leather gloves and boots that came up to their knees. Each was heavily armed with a sword strapped to his back and a dagger on his hip. They swaggered up to Logan with the confidence of men used to getting what they want.

"Well met, master blacksmith," one of them called, taking off his gloves and tucking them into his belt. "Although whether tis a fine day or not depends on what ye have for us. Ye are late with yer delivery."

Logan watched the man approach. "Aye, and I sent word to the laird explaining the reasons for that. The recent storm caused much damage to my croft and I had to make repairs."

The man waved away Logan's explanation. "Show us what ye've got."

A flicker of annoyance flashed across Logan's face at the man's abrupt tone but he turned without a word and led the three men into the smithy. Thea backed up a step. From here she couldn't see into the smithy, nor hear what was being said. She needed a better spyhole. She shuffled to the back of the stable where small rectangular hay bales had been stacked. She leaned against them, trying to see through a crack in the boards. She stubbed her toe against something hard and hopped, gritting her teeth to stop herself cursing aloud.

She looked down and spotted the corner of something poking out between the hay bales. Puzzled, she pulled away the bales to reveal a large battered chest.

Thea hesitated. Then curiosity got the better of caution and she yanked open the lid of the chest. Inside she found a shield, a huge sword almost as tall as she was and a fur-trimmed cloak elegantly embroidered with an insignia she didn't recognize. She knelt by the chest and gently ran her fingers along the fabric of the cloak. It was thick, finely made, and she knew enough of history to guess that this wasn't the sort of thing a simple blacksmith would wear. It spoke of high status and plenty of wealth. The shield and sword, although notched as though they'd seen much use, were also very fine work.

Why did Logan have them? And why was he hiding them in the stable?

She scrambled to her feet as she heard voices emerging from the smithy.

"Aye, the laird will be pleased."

She heard the sound of coins changing hands and leaned forward, trying to find a gap between the boards. The lid of the chest suddenly fell shut with a heavy thud and two of the stacked hay bales behind it went tumbling, thudding into the wall of the stable with enough force to make it shudder.

"What was that?"

"Naught," Logan replied. "Take what ye came for and be on yer way."

Thea heard footsteps approaching and the stable door was suddenly pulled open, revealing a man standing there. He startled as he saw Thea then barked a laugh.

"Ha! He has a lass in here!"

The man grabbed her elbow and yanked her roughly out into the yard. With a cry of protest, Thea snatched her arm from his grip and spun on him.

"Get your hands off me, asshole!"

The man's grin broadened. "And a feisty one at that!"

The other two men approached and stared at Thea in surprise. She didn't like the hungry expressions on their faces as they looked her over. She suddenly felt like a rabbit cornered by wolves.

"So this is why yer order was late?" the leader said to Logan. "Nay wonder. If I was tumbling a beauty such as her I wouldnae pay much attention to my work either. Where did ye find her? I know all the brothels round here and I've never seen her before."

Brothel? How dare he? Thea felt heat rushing to her cheeks. She opened her mouth for an angry retort but Logan stepped close. His hands were curled loosely at his side and he made not a sound as he moved. His dark eyes raked the three men.

"Ye will keep a civil tongue in yer head whilst ye are on my land," he said in a deathly quiet voice. "If ye insult my guest again, ye will regret it. This is Lady Thea Thomas, a visitor from across the sea."

The leader spread his arms wide. He shared a look of amusement with his men although the smile on his face did not reach his eyes. "Oh, come now," he drawled. "There's nay need for argument. I canna blame ye for finding yerself a ride. It must get mighty lonely living out here alone. But there's nay need to be so greedy either. We are willing to share. I'll wager I can offer the lass more coin than she's seen in a year. The laird pays well these days." His eyes fell on Thea. "How about it, my lovely?" He stepped forward and grabbed Thea's arm.

There was a blur of movement, a heavy crack, and the man was suddenly on the ground at Thea's feet, blood leaking from his nose. Logan stood over him, his fist clenched.

"Get off my land," he growled. "Now."

The man glared up at him and slowly wiped the blood from his nose. "Ye will pay for yer impudence, blacksmith," he hissed. "Men!"

The other two guards drew their swords and advanced across the yard. Logan pushed Thea behind him.

"Stay back!"

Thea's heart leapt into her mouth. What the hell was happening? How had this turned so ugly so quickly? She could feel her heart thundering in her chest, battering against her ribs. The man Logan had downed climbed to his feet and joined his fellows. The looks on their faces were dark and ugly. Thea read violence in their eyes.

Logan didn't move. He just watched as they approached, arms hanging loosely. What did he think he could do against three armed men?

One of them lunged, his sword stabbing. Logan stepped to the left, allowing the man's thrust to take him past, then he grabbed the man's wrist and twisted savagely. The man gasped, his grip loosened, and Logan yanked the sword from his grip. He reversed the blade, smashing the hilt into the man's temple. He collapsed without a sound.

Logan didn't pause. He dodged under a wild swing from the second guard, smashed his knee into the man's groin, then, as he doubled over in pain, punched him square on the chin so hard that the man's head snapped back and he smacked into the dirt, writhing and groaning.

That left only the leader.

"Ye'll not find me so easy," he snarled.

He came at Logan like lightning, sword swinging. A jolt of pure terror exploded in Thea's chest as she saw a red gash open up on Logan's bicep. He grunted in pain but danced out of the way of the next blow, stepping close to the man and head butting him square on the nose. The man's nose exploded in a shower of blood and he crashed to his knees, clutching at his ruined face. Logan grabbed him and hauled him up by his shirt, holding his face close to his own.

"I said," he growled. "Get off my land. Now!" Then he hurled the man bodily away from him. The man went flying through the air and landed with a crash by the horses, which shied and whinnied in alarm. Pure fury twisted Logan's features as he lifted the other two men and flung them after their leader.

"Get out!" Logan roared. "Get out and tell the laird if he wants further orders he can send someone with some manners! If I catch any of ye on my land again, I swear by Holy God I will kill all of ye!"

Thea had no doubt he meant his threat. The men seemed to have no doubt either. They climbed painfully to their feet and mounted the horses. Kicking them into motion, they fled across the yard, up the hill, and were soon out of sight in the distance.

Logan watched them go, his chest heaving. Then he turned to Thea. His eyes blazed with fury and for a moment Thea felt a thrill of fear.

"Are ye all right?" he asked. "They didnae hurt ye?"

Something inside Thea crumbled. She threw herself at Logan, wrapping her arms around his neck and pulling him close. "Oh my god!" she muttered into his neck. "I thought they were going to kill you! Don't ever do that to me again!"

Logan stiffened under her touch as though he would pull away but then the tension leaked out of him and his arms came around her, pressing her close against him.

"I couldnae let them hurt ye," he whispered. "I willnae let anyone hurt ye."

Thea buried her face in his neck. It felt so good to be this close to him, to feel his chest against hers and his arms around her. He was sweaty from the forge but Thea didn't care. Then her eyes alighted on the wound on his arm, not two inches from her face and she stepped back.

"Shit! You're hurt."

He released her and glanced down at the cut. His arm was sheeted in red as though he wore a glove. Blood dripped slowly into the dirt. "It's only a scratch."

Thea fixed him with a hard look. "A scratch? Inside. Now. That needs cleaning and stitching."

His lips pressed into a line as though he would argue but Thea raised one eyebrow and cocked her head. He nodded then made his way into the cottage.

Once inside, Thea crossed over to the kettle that was always warming on the fire and shakily poured some hot water into a bowl. Logan sat at the table, a gasp of pain escaping him as he jolted his injured arm. The sight of all that blood made her stomach churn.

"Hold still," she instructed as she dunked a cloth in the water and began wiping the blood from his bicep.

For a wonder, Logan did as he was told. He sat still and silent as she worked, watching her with those dark, dark eyes. The water was soon tinged with pink and the cut was clean but deep, cutting almost to the bone. It would need stitching and keeping clean. She should go fetch Ailsa. The healer would know what to do.

No time, she thought. *It needs stitching now.*

She could dress a wound, treat a burn or splint a twisted ankle. But stitching a sword-slice like this? Without anesthetic?

She pulled in a deep breath. "Okay," she said. "Do you have needle and thread?"

"In the pot on the mantelpiece. And there's a bottle of whisky there too."

She fetched both, handing him the whisky which he opened and took a long swig. Thea cut off a piece of thread and threaded it through the needle. Then she dumped both in the kettle and put it back to boil.

"Why are ye doing that?"

"Infection," she replied. "They both need to be clean or it will fester."

After a few minutes she fished out the needle and thread and moved to stand by Logan's side. With gentle fingers, she probed the wound. A fresh wave of blood sheeted down his bicep and he gritted his teeth, taking another swig from the whisky bottle.

"Do it quickly, lass," he grunted. "I trust ye."

You do? she thought. *Oh god. I'm not sure I do.*

Then, before she could change her mind, she pinched the skin together and dug the needle through, pulling the thread tight. Logan hissed in pain but moved not a muscle and she quickly stitched the length of the cut. Thea marveled at his self-control. If it was her, she'd likely be writhing and screaming right now. She left a tiny opening at one end of the wound to allow any infection to drain out, then took the honey pot from the table, smeared the wound, then dressed it with a bandage ripped from a bed sheet.

It was done. Thea wiped her forehead with a shaky hand and stepped back, blowing out a long breath. A thin sheen of sweat covered her brow and her limbs felt weak. She staggered and caught herself on the table. Logan's good arm reached out to steady her.

She looked at him. He was so close. Seated not an arm's span away from her, she could hear his breathing and see the way his chest rose and fell under his plaid. His hand, where it rested on her arm, felt warm.

"You must keep it clean," she said hoarsely. "It will need redressing every day and fresh honey applied."

Logan nodded. "Thank ye, lass."

"You're welcome."

She couldn't stand up anymore. Her shaking legs gave way and she slumped onto the chair opposite Logan and leaned her elbows on the table.

"Will they come back?" she asked. "Those men? I've met plenty of assholes like them and in my experience they won't take kindly to the beating you gave them."

Logan shook his head. "They willnae be back. The laird willnae allow it. He and I have an ...understanding. He'll know better than to send them anywhere near here again."

An understanding? Between the laird and a simple blacksmith? She remembered what she'd found in the stable. None of that gear fitted with the image of a simple blacksmith. Secrets swirled around Logan like shadows.

"Where did you learn to fight like that?" she asked.

He shrugged. "I had two brothers. We were always brawling when we were younger."

His quick answer didn't fool her. "And where are your brothers now?"

He glanced at her and then away. For a long moment he stared at the fire. Then he whispered, "Gone." Shaking his head as if to clear it, he drew in a deep breath and looked at Thea. "What is the book ye keep reading?"

It was a very unsubtle attempt to change the subject. They both had secrets. They yawned like a gulf between the two of them. Sometimes Thea longed to tell Logan the truth about where she'd come from and how she'd got here. At times she felt sure he would understand. At others she was terrified that he would think her crazy and turn her out of his home. And then what would she do?

"Irene gave it to me. It's just a book of stories but I was hoping I might find a clue in there as to how to find her. Why would Irene have given it to me otherwise?"

Logan snorted. "Why indeed?" He sighed and leaned back in his chair, wincing as his wounded arm was jolted, and then climbed to his feet. "I must return to the smithy."

Thea's eyebrows rose incredulously. "You've got to be kidding! You can't work with that injury!"

"I must. Neither of us will eat unless I do." He strode to the door and out into the yard.

Thea watched him go, a little knot forming in her stomach. There he went again. Just as she thought he might be willing to open up he shut her out and left, unwilling to remain in her presence.

Fine. Let him keep his secrets. What did it matter to her?

She took Irene's book from the pocket of her dress, opened it on the table and began reading. She was about halfway through the book and so far she'd not found anything that might be a clue to why she was here. The poems and stories it contained were an eclectic mix. Some were long, rambling sagas about heroes she'd never heard of. Others were short humorous rhymes, some rude enough to make her blush. Still others seemed to be proverbs or moral stories put to verse. The book was beautifully illustrated with swirling scrollwork around the edges of the pages and pictures of strange beasts, flowers and stylized patterns. Thea guessed the tome would be worth a tidy penny to a collector.

There has to be something here, she told herself. *I just have to find it.*

She flicked through to a random page and scanned the title. It read *Laird's Curse*. It was a poem about three brothers who made a pact with the Fae. As a result, they were cursed to be always alone and to wander the Highlands for all time. Her eyes were drawn to a particular verse.

The mark of the Fae burned into his skin, a brand for all to see, tis the sign of his fateful bargain, and the way to set him free.

Thea sat back. A tingle walked down her spine. Something stirred in her memory. Something she couldn't quite put her finger on. She bit her lip, thinking through all she'd heard, all she'd learned since she came here. But the connection danced out of her reach the more she tried to grab for it.

With an exasperated sigh, she pushed the book away. It was starting to get dark. She stretched her arms over her head and yawned. From the smithy she heard the sound of hammer on anvil and shook her head. Stupid man! Didn't he realize he'd taken a sword cut to the arm today? He would tear it open if he wasn't careful. Not that he'd listen to her, of course. Logan MacAuley was about as stubborn and pigheaded a man as she'd ever met.

Grumbling to herself she threw herself down on the bed, hands behind her head, and stared at the ceiling. The words in Irene's book swam around in her mind, chasing themselves into a knot that got ever more tangled.

Chapter 9

AN ALMIGHTY CRASH WOKE her. She bolted upright, heart hammering and looked around wildly. There was no sign of Logan and the candle had burned down to a stub, giving only the barest illumination to the small room. Then a blinding flash lit the room and another crack tore the air. The shutters rattled and over the howl of the wind Thea heard the hissing of rain outside. Another storm. And a big one.

Thea gulped. Holy crap, the weather in the Highlands could be wild. Memories of the storm the night she'd arrived crowded in on her and the little room suddenly felt oppressive. She remembered driving rain, howling wind trying to tear her from the path, freezing waves reaching up to yank her under. Then Logan pulling her to safety.

Logan!

Where was he? Surely not still in the smithy? He would be drenched and freezing if he slept out there in this.

"Idiot man!" she cursed aloud. What was he thinking?

She climbed off the bed, pulled the cloak Ailsa had leant her around her shoulders, and made her way to the door. As she opened it, the wind snatched it from her grasp and slammed it against the outside wall. Wind and rain pelted her so fiercely it drove her back a step. Leaning into the maelstrom, she grabbed the door and closed it firmly before fighting her way across the yard. She held the cloak tight against her body, pulling up the hood and trying to keep out the worst of the rain. Another crack of lightning revealed the yard awash with water. From the stable came the sound of Stepper's terrified whinnies.

Thea squinted ahead through the driving rain. She couldn't see any light shining in the smithy. She ducked inside and was glad to be out of the worst of the wind. The low eaves of the roof were dripping water but inside it was blessedly dry although it was as cold and drafty as a cliff top.

She looked around and spotted Logan lying on the pile of blankets he'd made for himself in one corner. She picked her way around the racks of tools and crouched by his side.

"Logan! Come inside. It's freezing out here. We can rig up a curtain across the room if you're still worried about my reputation. You'll catch your death sleeping out here in this!"

He didn't respond. Thea leaned closer. He was lying on his back, his eyes closed and his copper colored hair making a halo around his head. The muscles in his face twitched as if he was dreaming and his sun-burnished skin had gone pale. A shiver of unease went through Thea.

"Logan?"

She grabbed his shoulder but snatched her hand back. His skin was like ice. "Logan!" she cried urgently. "You have to wake up!"

There was no response. Thea sat back on her heels, biting her lip. Tentatively she pulled the blanket away and inspected his arm. The bandage was still in place and looked clean enough but Thea knew that could be deceptive. She pressed a hand to his forehead and her palm came back wet with sweat.

"Logan!" she tried again, shaking him as hard as she could.

His eyes flickered open. They were bleary and unfocussed. "I had to do it," he whispered, his words slurred. "I had to make the bargain or we were all doomed." Then his eyes slid closed once more.

Thea hesitated. When she'd been ill Logan had picked her up and carried her as easily as if she was a doll but there was no way she'd be able to carry him back to the house. All she could do was make sure he was warm and dry until morning when hopefully his fever might break. Damn it all! What should she do?

She pulled back his blanket and burrowed in next to him, pulling the blankets over them both. She pressed her body against his, wrapping her arms around his broad chest. The cold from his skin seeped into her but she clung on, determined to warm him with her body heat. It was the only thing she could think to do.

His breathing evened out and she hoped he'd slipped into a proper sleep. She rested her head on his chest, listening to the thump of his heartbeat by her ear. It sounded strong and healthy. She shifted slightly, resting her head on his shoulder so the top of her head lay just beneath his chin. Outside the smithy the storm raged and howled, cracks of thunder splitting the sky and then flashes of lightning picking out the world in stark brilliance.

She lay awake for a long time, listening to the storm and the beat of Logan's heart, but eventually exhaustion washed away even the sound of the storm and sleep took her.

LOGAN OPENED HIS EYES slowly. Above him he saw pale morning light seeping through the rafters of the smithy roof. He blinked, trying to clear his sluggish thoughts. His memories were hazy. He recalled thunder and lightning. Had there been another storm? Or had he dreamt it? He'd also dreamt Thea had come to him in the night and they'd spent the night side by side, wrapped in each other's arms. He'd been having a lot of dreams like that lately.

A heavy lassitude filled his limbs and he felt weak and washed out. A dull headache pounded behind his eyes and he was ravenously hungry. Had he been ill?

He shifted and then froze as he spotted Thea curled up beside him. Her eyes were closed. A jolt of pure terror went through him, so powerful it was like he'd been stabbed.

No! He roared inside. *No!*

He rolled towards her, pushing her onto her back. She flopped like a landed fish. He shook her hard, making her head wobble from side to side. There was no response. Pressing his hand to her forehead he realized her skin was cold. She wasn't breathing.

"Thea!" he bellowed. "Wake up, lass! Wake up!"

She did not respond.

He rocked back on his heels, his pulse thundering. Oh, Lord above! What had she done? He staggered to his feet and out into the yard. His limbs were so weak they could hardly support him and he staggered to his knees on the wet ground, barely noticing as water soaked through his plaid. The words of his curse echoed in his head like rocks tumbling in an avalanche.

Alone shall ye always be. Only death awaits those who share yer life.

Lord help him, why had he allowed her to stay? He'd reasoned that as long as he kept his distance, as long as he slept in the smithy at night and left her alone in the house, she would be all right. And so it had been for days, until she'd come to him in the night.

Fool! he growled at himself. *How could ye have been so careless?*

Twice before he'd thought to test the limits of the curse and twice before it had bitten hard and deep, reminding him that there was no cheating the Fae. When he and his brothers had first made their bargain he'd taken work as a farm hand on a remote croft in the north. The family had been kind and he'd soon become careless, accepting a place to sleep by their hearth when they offered. Soon after that their cattle had begun to die and when one of the children suddenly took ill, he knew it for his curse and fled, before any other misfortune could befall them.

A second time he'd been wandering alone as night was falling. An old shepherd had offered him shelter in his hut and Logan had accepted, sure that one night wouldn't do too much harm. He'd woken in the morning to find the shepherd still and cold on his bed, eyes closed and a small smile on his face.

After that Logan had never pushed the bounds of his curse and kept everyone at arm's length. Until Thea.

Why didn't I send her away? he thought bitterly. *Up to the castle. Or persuaded Ailsa to let her stay with them. Lord, anywhere would have been better than here with me! Look at what I've done! Lord curse me!*

"Logan?"

He spun at the sound of the voice. Thea stood outside the smithy, rubbing her eyes.

Logan stared. "Thea?"

"Were you expecting someone else?"

He moved his mouth to speak but no words came out.

"What's wrong? You look like you've seen a ghost."

Logan shook his head, trying to clear his thoughts. "Ye wouldnae wake, lass. I thought...I thought."

She yawned hugely and then stretched her arms over her head. "I guess I was pretty tired. I've always been a heavy sleeper." She cocked her head. "How are you feeling? You had quite the fever last night."

Him? She was worried about *him*? "I'm fine, lass. Was that why ye came into the smithy?"

She shrugged. "Another storm came and you were injured. How could I let you sleep in the smithy? I came to convince you to come into the house but you had a fever and I couldn't wake you. I didn't know how else to get you warm so I stayed with you."

"How?" he whispered. "How is this possible?" He strode over and grabbed her upper arms. Looking down into her face, he studied her intently. "How do ye feel, lass? Are ye well?"

She gazed up at him, a puzzled expression on her face. "Fine. Why are you asking me this? Logan, you're hurting me."

He let her go and stepped back. He felt a grin spread across his face.

"Ha!" he cried, throwing his head back and laughing. "Irene! Thank ye!"

Thea's puzzled expression deepened. "Are you sure you're feeling all right, Logan?"

"Aye. Better than I have in a long time."

He stepped close and gazed down at her. Those eyes of hers were as green as spring leaves as she stared up at him. He put one finger under her chin and lifted her face.

"Thank ye, lass," he breathed.

"For what? I didn't do anything really."

He just shook his head. "Are ye hungry? I reckon I could eat a horse."

"That will be the fever," she replied. "I need to check your wound. You might say you're feeling better but you're acting a little odd."

Logan just laughed at that.

AS OFTEN HAPPENED IN the Highlands, last night's storm had blown through, leaving a clear day as bright as polished glass. As Logan guided Stepper along the trail he breathed deeply, feeling it tingle in his lungs. Was he imagining it or did the grass look greener this morning? The waves a brighter shade of blue? The calls of the seabirds more melodious than usual? He didn't know and he didn't care. All he knew was that it felt like a great weight had been lifted from his shoulders. For the first time since he'd made his bargain, he felt free.

He glanced at Thea. She sat up straight in the saddle, clinging to it with both hands, her head swiveling from side to side as she took in the landscape. Part of him was still angry at her for being so reckless as to spend the night in the smithy with him. Things could have gone so badly wrong. If his curse had come to claim her...

He could hardly believe that she was alive and warm and riding in front of him, watching the landscape pass by with child-like delight.

Why? Why was she immune to his curse?

Because she is an outlander? he wondered. It was the only explanation.

"Look!" she cried suddenly, pointing out to sea. "Dolphins!"

"Aye. Hunting by the looks of them," Logan replied, shading his eyes. "They've probably chased a shoal in close to the shallows and will pick them off now."

Thea's hands twitched as though she wanted to hold something then she folded them on the saddle in front of her. She watched intently as the dolphins zoomed right into the shallows, almost beaching themselves, then snatched up the silver fish that jumped into the air to escape them.

"I've read about such behavior," she said. "But never seen it in the wild. Oh, what I wouldn't give for my camera right now!"

Her delight was infectious and Logan found himself smiling as he watched her. She had an uncanny ability to live in the moment, to take pleasure in the simple things in life. Her eyes sparkled and the wind had put a rosy glow to her cheeks. Lord above, she was possibly the most beautiful thing he'd ever seen. He was taken by an almost irresistible urge to touch her. To run his fingers through that thick midnight hair or cup that soft cheek in his hand.

"Come, lass," he said thickly. "Rhodry will be waiting for us."

Thea nodded and Logan nudged Stepper into a trot. There were smoke rising from the chimney of Rhodry and Ailsa's croft and their three goats gathered at the fence to watch Thea and Logan ride past.

"Good morning!" Rhodry cried, crossing the yard to meet them. "I trust ye weathered the storm last night without damage?"

Logan glanced at Thea then cleared his throat. "Aye. Nay harm done. And ye?"

Rhodry laughed as he took Stepper's bridle to hold her steady while they dismounted. "Naught but a few frightened bairns and a goat who insisted on coming inside with us."

Ailsa appeared at the doorway with little Maisie on her hip. She waved. "A fine Highland night is what it was!" she called. "And look at the morning it's given us!"

"Uncle Logan! Lady Thea!"

Anna came pelting over, skidding to a halt and looking up at them excitedly. "Are ye going to come fishing with us today?" She looked between Logan and Thea expectantly.

Thea laughed. "Fishing? My, that sounds like an excellent idea. As long as your ma will allow it of course."

Anna waved a hand, dismissing Thea's concern with all the flippancy of a nine-year-old. "Nah, Ma doesnae mind. Shall we go tell her?"

Thea gave Logan an amused look as Anna grabbed her hand and dragged her over to Ailsa. Logan watched them go. Rhodry laid a hand on his shoulder.

"She'll be here when we get back, my friend. Where to today? St. Berrick?"

Logan tore his eyes away from Thea. "Aye," he said gruffly. "St. Berrick. There were rumors of someone who looked like Irene MacAskill over that way. Although I dinna fancy our chances in such a large town."

Rhodry nodded then the two of them swung up onto their mounts. As they rode away, Logan resisted the urge to look back.

ST. BERRICK WAS A LARGE town which meant it boasted several streets lined with shops as well as an inn. It lay just over the border in MacKinnon lands and as Logan and Rhodry rode into town, Logan was struck by the number of armed men he saw prowling the streets. Their MacAuley plaids drew several hostile glances and more than one muttered curse.

They rode to an inn and paid the stable lad to take their horses and then spent a couple of hours perusing the market and the shops, asking after Irene MacAskill. Again, there were rumors. An old woman spotted walking the hills alone. An old woman turning up at a croft where a sick child was miraculously healed. An old woman giving a warning to a fishing family that saved them from venturing out in last night's storm. But nobody could give them more than hearsay.

Come mid-morning, Logan was seething with frustration. Another morning wasted and still no closer to finding a way to send Thea home.

Is that such a bad thing? a little voice whispered in his head. He smothered the voice ruthlessly.

"My stomach thinks my throat has been cut," Rhodry grumbled as they wove their way through the crowds in the market. "What say we retire to the inn for something to eat before we ride home? I reckon we've earned it."

"Aye," Logan replied. "I reckon we have."

He led the way into the inn's common room. It was busy, with almost every available table occupied. Logan and Rhodry managed to find one at the back and ordered ale and food from the serving lass. Logan leaned back in his chair and surveyed the room. Almost everyone in sight wore the MacKinnon plaid and carried a sword. Some had shields propped against the tables and quivers of arrows lying by their feet. A shiver of unease went down Logan's spine. He knew a muster when he saw one.

When the serving girl returned with their food and drink, he asked, "Why so many soldiers? There isnae trouble here about is there?"

The girl's eyes roved over Logan's MacAuley plaid and she suddenly looked uncomfortable. "Laird MacKinnon has put out word for a muster," she replied. "There's talk of war."

"War?" Logan replied. "With whom?"

The girl shifted awkwardly. She glanced at the patrons, many of whom were watching Logan, then stared at the floor by her feet. "With the MacAuleys."

She hurried away before Logan could say another word. Logan leaned back in his chair, suddenly uneasy. So the rumors were true. Eoin was going to war with his family's oldest allies. It made no sense. Why would Eoin break that alliance?

"I dinna like this," Rhodry muttered, looking around at the patrons. "There's trouble in the air."

"Aye," Logan agreed. He was suddenly very glad he'd brought a sword though he doubted it would do much good if this crowd decided to turn on him. "I reckon it's time we left."

Rhodry grunted his agreement. They quickly ate their food, downed the ale, and then made their way to the door. Logan felt hostile eyes on his back but nobody did more than glare. He was relieved to reach the stable. They climbed into the saddles and made their way out of town at a fast walk. Now that he knew what to look for, Logan saw the signs of a muster everywhere. Wagons carrying soldiers, rations and weapons. Gangs of young lads roaming the streets, hoping to find work by enlisting into the laird's reserves. Heavily armed mercenaries playing dice outside the taverns.

A growl escaped Logan's throat. "What does he think he's doing? This isnae what we agreed!"

"What's that?" Rhodry asked.

"Naught," Logan replied, shaking his head. "I was just wondering what has led our laird to such strife with the MacKinnons."

Concern creased Rhodry's brow. "Aye, I thought we were free of it when the old laird won peace from the Irish raiders."

Logan looked at him sharply but Rhodry's eyes were fixed on the road ahead.

"Aye," he breathed "So did I."

They rode in silence, each wrapped in their own thoughts. Now that war was brewing it was more important than ever that he find a way to get Thea home.

"Dinna worry, man," Rhodry said as if reading his thoughts. "We'll find this Irene." His friend grinned at him. "Eventually. And until then ye will have the pleasure of Thea's company."

"What is that supposed to mean?" Logan snapped. "I made a vow to take care of Lady Thea until she can safely return to her kin and that's what I'm doing. There's nay more to it than that."

"Aye, of course there isnae."

Amusement danced in Rhodry's eyes. Lord but the man could be infuriating when he wanted to be!

"Out with it!" Logan growled. "Ye are clearly dying to say something."

A laugh burst from Rhodry. "Why canna ye admit it? There isnae shame in it, man! Tis obvious how ye feel about the lass. I dinna think I've ever seen ye smile as much as when she's around. The way ye look at her. The way yer eyes follow her when she's in the room."

Logan glared at his friend for a moment and then his shoulders sagged. "Am I that obvious?"

"Aye, man. Ye are. To me at least. The question is, what are ye going to do about it?"

"What is there to do? She'll soon ride out of my life forever. It's best if I do naught."

Rhodry rolled his eyes. "That's it? That's yer plan?"

Logan frowned. "What would ye have me do? Tell her the truth? Tell her how the sight of her sets my blood pounding? How I canna concentrate on my tasks in the smithy or around the croft for thoughts of her? That even though I made a vow, I dread finding Irene MacAskill because it will mean I lose her? I canna tell her any of that. She would run a mile!"

"Would she?" Rhodry asked. "Are ye sure of that? Mayhap ye should try."

For a moment Logan wavered. Thea had come to the smithy in a storm out of worry for him. What did that mean? Did she care for him the way he cared for her? Or was that just her way of repaying him for his hospitality?

He shook his head. "Nay. I wouldnae know what to say."

"Lord above, man!" Rhodry cried. "Ye dinna have to spell it out! Do something special for her—something she will appreciate."

Logan turned his head and watched the trail. He absently patted Stepper's neck as his thoughts turned. Do something special for her? Aye, he liked the thought of that. An idea came to him.

He turned to grin at his friend. "I know just the thing."

"OKAY, SO WHAT'S THIS bit then?" Thea said, pointing at the diagram she'd scratched in the dirt.

"France!" Anna cried. "That's France!"

"Very good," Thea said. "And next to it?"

"Spain."

Thea smiled and ruffled the girl's hair. The children were gathered in a circle around her whilst she tried to teach them the geography of Europe. They were as bright as buttons and absorbed everything like sponges, always eager for more. When they concentrated that is. They were usually far more interested in games of tag or stories about dragons and monsters and great heroes. Thea was just about out of those.

Ailsa came round the corner carrying a bucket. "All done! Meg says thank ye for the snack. It was very nice."

Thea grinned sheepishly and glanced down at the torn arm of her dress. Meg, Rhodry and Ailsa's goat, had taken a chunk out of it when Thea had tried to milk her. Then she'd butted Thea in the stomach and ran off, bleating angrily. There must be a knack to dealing with livestock that Thea was sadly lacking.

Thea rubbed the bruise. "That animal hates me. Look, she's glaring at me right now!" She pointed a finger at the goat that was standing with her head over the paddock wall, watching proceedings in the yard.

Ailsa laughed. "Aye, she knows she's got the upper hand now. Ye'd best watch out or she'll be after ye every chance she gets."

Thea stuck her tongue out at the belligerent goat, sending the children into paroxysms of laughter.

"She'd better watch it," Thea said, puffing herself up and frowning. "Back home I've been goat-wrestling champion two years in a row."

That set them all off laughing even more.

Thea grinned. It had been a satisfying if tiring day. It seemed that the tasks around Ailsa and Rhodry's croft were endless. They had gone down to the beach and gathered sea food. They had fed the animals and collected the day's eggs. Whilst Ailsa and Mary had busied themselves baking bread and pies, Thea had taken some of Rhodry's tools and fixed the fence around the goat-pen, repaired a hole in the chicken run made by an eager fox, and hauled enough water from the well to make her shoulders scream and her back ache in protest.

She sighed. Ailsa, Rhodry, Mary and the children had accepted her without a second's thought. She'd known them only a short time but it felt like she'd known them for years. She felt more at home here in sixteenth century Scotland than she ever would have dreamed and she suspected the reason for that. A face flashed into her mind suddenly. Dark, serious eyes that seemed to see right into her soul, copper hair curling onto broad shoulders, smooth, full lips that so rarely smiled.

Ah hell, she thought. *I have to stop thinking about him. I have to stop feeling these things.*

Mary came to the door and called the children over to help her churn the milk Ailsa had just collected. The children sprang to their feet and hurried over to their grandmother, leaving Ailsa and Thea alone. Ailsa folded cross-legged onto the ground beside Thea. Her eyes wandered over the map she'd drawn in the sand.

"My, ye must have traveled far indeed to know so much about the world," she observed.

You don't know the half of it, Thea thought.

"Not really," she said with a shrug. "I've just seen some pretty good maps. Where I come from they're easier to come by."

Ailsa cocked her head. "And ye'll soon be returning there?"

"Yes. I suppose I will."

"Ye dinna look too pleased by that."

"I am," Thea protested. "I am. It's just..." she trailed off, unable to find the words.

Ailsa smiled kindly. "It's just that ye think ye might have found a reason to stay?"

Thea looked at her sharply. "What do you mean by that?"

"I've seen the way ye look at him," Ailsa replied. "And the way he looks at ye. Tis obvious what is growing between the two of ye."

"Is it?" Thea asked in a strangled voice. Holy crap, was she that obvious?

"Aye. Is that so bad?"

Yes! Thea wanted to shout. *Because I don't belong here! I'm from 500 years in the future! We may as well be from different planets!*

"Of course it's bad. I'll soon be leaving."

"Ye dinna have to."

"Don't have to what?"

"Leave. Go home. Ye could stay if ye chose. Is there something that is pulling ye back to yer homeland?"

Thea stared at her friend, rocked by the suggestion. Stay here? She'd never even entertained the thought. Since the moment she arrived all her energy had been bent on getting home. But as the days had passed and she'd found herself drawn more and more to Logan MacAuley, that determination had begun to waver. Ailsa's question struck her. What *was* pulling her home? What had she to go back to?

Nothing, a voice whispered in the back of her head.

Before she could frame a reply the door to the cottage opened and Mary stuck her head out.

"Riders!" she said in a low, urgent voice.

Thinking it was Rhodry and Logan returning, Thea and Ailsa scrambled to their feet and turned to look up at the trail at the top of the rise. But it wasn't Logan and Rhodry. A group of eight riders were cantering along the trail in front of the croft. They wore dark clothing without any plaid or insignia that Thea could make out and she caught the glint of weapons in the sunlight.

"Inside, now!" Ailsa hissed at the children who'd come out after Mary to see what the fuss was.

She ushered them back inside and then stood in front of the door, holding it shut. Mary, Thea noticed, had a poker clasped in one hand and her eyes followed the riders as they thundered by. Suddenly one of them spotted the women and pulled his horse to a halt. Mary's grip on the poker tightened and a shiver of fear slid down Thea's spine. The man stared at them for a moment before wheeling his mount and thundering after his fellows.

Ailsa let out an audible sigh and Mary sagged, sliding onto the wooden bench alongside the cottage wall. She passed a shaky hand over her face.

"Who were they?" Thea asked.

"Mercenaries by the looks of them," Mary replied. "Hired thugs. Riding to a muster unless I miss my guess."

"These rumors of war again?" Thea asked.

"More than rumors if that sight is anything to go by. They were heading north. Towards MacKinnon lands. I dinna ken what the laird is playing at. Is he trying to destroy the clan? Hasnae he got enough trouble on his plate already?"

"He's not popular?" Thea asked.

Mary waved a hand. "Does his best I suppose but he never had the training needed for leadership. He should never have inherited the lairdship, not with his cousins ahead of him. But after what happened to those three lads...well, ye never know what fate has in store."

Thea looked at Mary sharply. The old woman's words sounded unsettlingly like those Irene MacAskill had spoken right before she'd sent Thea hurtling back in time.

"What happened to the old laird?" she asked.

Mary smiled sadly. "Nobody knows for sure. A fleet of Irish raiders were on their way and the MacAuley army was gathering to meet them—although there couldnae be any hope of success against such a force. Then the laird and his brothers disappeared. Nobody really knows what happened but the story is that they rode out of camp that night, telling nobody where they were going. Next morning scouts rode in to report that the enemy had been attacked in the night. Decimated. The survivors had boarded their boats and were fleeing back to Ireland. Nothing was ever found of those three boys, save their swords driven into the mud in the center of the enemy camp and their MacAuley plaids laid out on the ground."

A feeling of unease uncurled in Thea's stomach. Something about the story made the back of her neck prickle. "What were their names?" she asked.

"Their names?"

"Yes. Laird MacAuley and his two brothers. What were they called?"

"I...um..." Mary stammered. She looked puzzled. "Do ye know I canna remember! Ailsa, what were those boys called?"

Ailsa shook her head. "I'm nay sure. Oh! How odd! I'm sure it will come back to us eventually."

What's going on? Thea thought. *Why does nobody remember the old laird? And why does that story make me so uneasy? I've heard it somewhere before, I'm sure of it.*

She stared into the distance, watching the riders disappear over the horizon. Another secret. Another mystery. This land was full of them. Thea got the uneasy feeling she wouldn't be going anywhere until she solved them.

Chapter 10

THEA STIRRED THE STEW, leaning over to look into the large pot. Was it ready? Was it edible? Tentatively, she fished out a piece of vegetable. Blowing to cool it, she popped it into her mouth and chewed. Hmm. Not bad. Trying to cook a stew with nothing but a hearth fire was definitely not on her list of skills. Hell, cooking with a modern gas cooker with lots of temperature settings and a timer wasn't even on her list of skills. Microwave meals in front of the TV was about the best she could muster.

So why did you offer to cook supper? she grumbled at herself. *Did you want to poison your host?*

In truth, she'd wanted to do something for Logan. He and Rhodry had returned empty-handed once again and with dire news of the muster of forces on MacKinnon lands. Logan had seemed distant and distracted all the way home so cooking dinner seemed the least she could do. Now though, she wondered if she'd bitten off more than she could chew. She'd surreptitiously asked Ailsa's advice and had followed her instructions to the letter but still wasn't at all confident that the meal would be edible.

It didn't help that she could feel Logan's eyes on her as she knelt by the hearth. He said not a word but she could feel his presence filling the room like a storm.

"Ready!" she announced. "At least, I hope so."

She grabbed the handle of the pot with both hands and struggled to lift it from its tripod. Logan moved to her side, lifting the pot easily one-handed, and placed it on the table.

Thea frowned at him. "You didn't have to do that. I could manage."

Was that a smile trying to curl the side of his mouth? "I know that," he said lightly. "But it's only fair I do my part after ye've worked so hard."

"Oh really?" Thea said, raising an eyebrow. "Does that mean you're volunteering to do the dishes?"

Logan rolled his eyes. "Why did nobody warn me I'd taken in such a harridan?"

Thea snorted then sat opposite Logan and ladled out the stew. She took a mouthful and chewed. Oh. The pieces of turnip and carrot were a little hard. And the flavor was a little ...burned.

She watched Logan. His face was carefully expressionless as he chewed and then swallowed. He slowly put down his spoon.

"That is...." he trailed off.

"Horrible?" Thea supplied.

Logan met her gaze. "Aye, lass. Horrible."

Thea held a look of indignation for a moment but when Logan suddenly burst into laughter, she found herself joining in. The sound of Logan's laughter, so rare a thing, sent a wave of joy right through her. His eyes sparkled with mirth and his shoulders shook.

"Ah, my Thea," he breathed. "I think we've finally found a skill ye lack."

My Thea, she thought. He'd said it so casually but it sent a delicious shiver right up her spine.

"Okay, I admit it. I'm a terrible cook. Is it really that bad?"

Instead of answering, Logan rose from the table and fetched a loaf of bread, a crock of butter and a slab of cheese which he placed on the table.

"Ah! Sandwiches!" Thea said. "Now even *I* can make those."

She and Logan ate in companionable silence, the only sound the crackle of the flames in the fireplace. When they were finished Logan pushed away his plate.

"I have bad news, lass," he announced. "I must postpone the search for Irene for a while. The rumors place her to the north—in MacKinnon lands. Now, with all this talk of war brewing, it would be foolish to travel that way."

"I know," Thea replied quietly. "I guessed as much after what you found today." She fell silent, not sure how she felt about what he'd just said. She wasn't as bothered by his news as she ought to be. In fact, she felt a little sliver of relief. Calling off the search for Irene meant she had a little more time here. A little more time to figure out what it was she was meant to do.

A little more time with Logan.

He seemed to take her silence as something else. He reached across the table and clasped her hand, fixing her with an earnest gaze. "I *will* find her, lass. I made a vow. Dinna worry. Ye will get the chance to go home."

Thea didn't answer. Instead, she curled her fingers around Logan's. Her hand felt tiny in his. His skin was warm and calloused from his work in the forge. Logan glanced down at their clasped hands then his eyes rose to meet hers and the look in them set her heart racing.

He blinked, pulled his hand away, then stood. "It's getting late," he muttered. "Ye must be tired. I'll leave ye to get some sleep." He strode to the door.

Thea rose. "You don't have to sleep in the smithy. There's no need."

Logan met her gaze. "There is every need, lass," he breathed, his voice low and husky. "For both our sakes." He pulled the door open and strode out into the night.

After he'd left, Thea ran a hand through her hair and let out a long sigh as she tried to gather her thoughts. It wasn't easy with the way her pulse was racing. Logan was right. She knew it was a bad idea for him to stay and he'd done the sensible thing by sleeping in the smithy but the room suddenly seemed smaller and colder without him in it.

Remembering Mary's words from earlier, Thea knelt on the floor and pulled her pack from underneath the bed before seating herself cross-legged by the hearth, arranging herself so the light from the candles lit Irene's book which she propped open on her knee.

Flicking through the pages, she scanned each title. The fate of the previous MacAuley laird had sparked something in Thea's memory. It had sounded uncannily like one of the stories in the book she'd read.

There! She reached a page that she'd marked for further investigation. It was the poem called *Laird's Curse* that she'd read previously. Quickly she read it again then sat back, thinking. The poem and Mary's tale were uncannily similar. It told the story of how three brothers had saved their clan from an invading army and that they'd disappeared without a trace afterwards. Some of the details were the same, such as the three swords stuck in the middle of the battlefield but others were different, such as the bargain with the Fae that the story mentioned. Her eyes alighted on the last verse once more.

The mark of the Fae burned into his skin, a brand for all to see, tis the sign of his fateful bargain, and the way to set him free.

What did it mean? Did it mean anything?

With a yawn, she snapped the book shut. All this thinking was giving her a headache. She lifted the curtain and gazed out across the yard. Logan was out there, alone. Was he asleep? She moved to the bed, lay down and closed her eyes, but sleep was a long time coming.

LOGAN LAY AWAKE MOST of the night. Thoughts of Thea Thomas kept going round and round in his head. Even now, as he lay staring up at the rafters of the smithy, he could feel how her hand had felt in his, so small and soft. Her absence was a like an ache deep inside him.

He sucked in a deep breath and let it out slowly. Lord, but the Fae were cruel creatures. Why, by all that's holy, had Irene MacAskill sent Thea to him? Was this yet another cruel trick they were playing on him? To have her so close and yet be so out of reach? Did they take delight in such things?

Giving up on sleep, he rose, stretched his arms over head and made his way out into the yard. The sun had not yet risen over the horizon and everything smelt fresh and clean. Logan loved this time of day. It was as though the world had taken a breath and was pausing for a moment before springing into action.

Skirting the house, he leapt over the low stone wall and made his way across the lumpy ground towards the cliffs. At the edge he stood looking out, eyes scanning the water. The sea was quiet, seeming like a sheet of glass gleaming in the pre-dawn. He grinned. Aye, today was a grand day for what he had planned.

He returned to the croft and gathered the morning's eggs from the chicken house—much to the annoyance of the hens—and then made his way into the larder and collected items for breakfast.

He placed it all in a basket and covered it with a piece of cloth. Only when he'd gathered everything he needed did he make his way to the cottage door and knock lightly.

"Thea? Lass? Are ye awake?"

"Yes, I'm awake," her muffled voice answered. "That rooster of yours made damn sure of that."

He pushed the door open and froze. Thea was standing with her back to him, shrugging into a shift. For a second he got a glimpse of the creamy skin of her bare back and shoulders. He cleared his throat awkwardly but Thea merely pulled the shift on then tugged a dress over it, deftly reached round the back to do up the buttons and then turned to face him. Her hair was still tousled from sleep, falling around her face in messy tangles but even so, the sight of her was enough to steal Logan's breath.

"Good morning," she said.

Logan realized he was staring. He coughed and then stepped inside, closing the door behind him. "Good morning. I trust ye slept well?"

Thea nodded. "Very well. You?"

Me? Nay, lass. I tossed and turned all night, plagued by thoughts of ye. He shrugged. "Well enough. If ye are ready to start the day, there's something I'd like to show ye."

She frowned, the skin wrinkling on the bridge of her nose in a way that Logan found mesmerizing. "Oh? And what's that?"

"It's a surprise. Ye will have to trust me." He held out a hand. "Do ye trust me?"

She grinned in turn and reached out to clasp his hand. "Aye, lad," she said in mock-imitation of his accent. "I trust ye."

He curled his fingers around hers. "Come on then."

He yanked her towards the door. She looked intrigued and didn't argue as he led her outside, picked up the basket he'd left by the door and quickly guided her across the fields to the cliff edge where they took a twisting path to the beach below. The sun had risen now and the waves sparkled silver in the morning light. Thea paused, her expression full of pleasure as she took in the scene.

"Well, this was worth getting up early for."

"Aye, but this isnae what I wanted to show ye."

Taking her hand, he led her along the beach to a large spur of rock that stuck out into the waves, forming a natural jetty. There was a rowing boat tied to an iron ring he'd hammered into the rock. Logan crossed to it and tossed in the basket.

"After ye."

Thea eyed the boat dubiously. "You want me to get in that thing?"

"Aye. It's perfectly seaworthy. I've spent many hours fishing in Martha."

"Martha?"

"Aye. Every boat needs a name."

Thea smiled, amusement dancing in her eyes. As Logan held the boat steady she climbed aboard and took a seat on one of the benches, clinging onto the sides as the boat rocked. Logan stepped aboard, settled himself on the other bench, and took up the oars. He began to row. The water was so smooth that the little boat glided over the surface. As they moved, Logan scanned the water, searching for the telltale signs he was looking for. After her initial hesitation, Thea relaxed, letting go of the sides, and watching the waves skimming past.

"Where are we going?"

"Ye'll see."

They rounded a promontory and entered a wide, horseshoe bay. Two bluffs stuck out from the mainland, sheltering the bay from both sides. Here, he hoped to find what he was looking for. He shipped the oars and sat back, scanning the water. Sure enough, after only a few moments, he saw a sleek shape break the surface. He turned to show Thea but she was already pointing.

"Look! Dolphins!" she cried in delight.

She swiveled in her seat as more of the creatures broke the surface around them.

"There's a whole pod here!" she said. "I reckon there's at least twenty. And look! A baby! I wonder if they're the same family we saw from the cliff?"

She leaned over, trailing her hand in the water, and laughed with pleasure as a dolphin broke the surface a few feet away and regarded her for a moment before diving under again.

Logan leaned back and watched her. *Live in the moment*, his brother Camdan would have told him. It was good advice.

"Is this the surprise you mentioned?" Thea asked.

He nodded. "Aye, lass. I wanted to do something for ye. Something ye would like. When I saw how delighted ye were with the dolphins we spotted yesterday, well, I thought ye might like to see them closer."

Her smile faltered and was replaced by an uncertain expression. "You did this especially for me?"

"Aye, lass," he replied. "Do ye like it?"

DO I LIKE IT? Thea thought. *Is he kidding?* It was quite possibly the nicest thing anyone had ever done for her.

"I love it," she whispered.

Dolphins surrounded them now. Ever curious, they kept breaking the surface, regarding the humans with their large, intelligent eyes, before rolling on their backs or slapping the water with their tails as they herded fish.

Logan smiled. When he smiled the corners of his eyes crinkled. Jesus, he was gorgeous.

"Well, let's see them closer shall we?"

He stripped off the sash of his plaid and then his undershirt and boots, leaving him in only the kilt then stood up in the boat. His smooth, muscled skin was lightly tanned, a shade lighter than his copper hair. Her eyes came to rest on the black, swirling design of interlocked coils that was tattooed on his pectoral. Where had she seen that design before?

"Coming?" he said. Then he dived into the water.

Thea leaned over the side of the boat. Logan broke the surface a few feet away, his laugh echoing off the walls of the lagoon.

"Come on in, the water's lovely. Well, it's freezing actually but ye get used to it."

Thea bit her lip. It looked very deep and very cold. *Oh, what the hell!* she thought.

Standing up carefully in the rocking boat, she undid her dress and let it fall to the floor before kicking off her shoes and standing in just her under-shift. She had none of Logan's easy grace as she clambered over to the side of the boat and instead of spearing into the water in an elegant dive, she ended up catching her foot and falling head-first into the water.

She let out a squawk of surprise as she went under. It was so cold it snatched her breath. She sank. She felt a moment of panic as memories assailed her of another night in a storm and dark waves pulling her under.

Then a silver shape materialized out of the gloom, flashing past her in a quicksilver dash. As the dolphin disappeared another swam near and then darted away, intrigued by this newcomer to its domain. Thea's terror was forgotten in pure delight. She kicked hard and broke the surface of the water, gasping.

"They're everywhere!" she called to Logan who was treading water several feet away. "Did you see?"

"Aye, lass," he replied. "They're very inquisitive. Look, the baby is coming to see ye."

Thea turned to see the fin of the tiny dolphin they'd spotted from the boat approaching through the water. She took a big breath and ducked her head under. Sure enough, the baby hung in the water a few feet away, regarding her curiously. For a moment they watched each other before the dolphin's mother came and herded it away. Something grabbed Thea around the waist and lifted her.

Thea surfaced to find Logan right in front of her. His hair was plastered to his face and water droplets had gathered in his eyelashes.

"I think ye've made a friend," he said. "Take a deep breath. I've something to show ye. Ready?"

She pulled in a breath and held it. He grabbed her wrist and together they dived. He pointed out the dolphins as they flashed through the water below and around them and then guided her closer to the shore where a knot of darkness blocked her view. The knot of darkness soon revealed itself to be a kelp forest, tall fronds of seaweed that moved with the current and were home to all kinds of creatures. Thea saw huge shoals of fish that flitted in and out of the shafts of sunlight reaching down from above. She spotted gray seals hanging motionless in the water, watching Thea and Logan with as much curiosity as the dolphins had.

Thea broke the surface only long enough to take another breath before she dived again, eager to explore more of this underwater world. She knew of photographers who specialized in marine habitats but Thea had never even got her diving certificate. Now she realized what she'd been missing. There was so much to see, from the crabs in the shallows that scuttled away from them, to the seals who hauled themselves out onto rocks, only to disappear back into the water without even a splash if Thea and Logan got too close.

Logan was never far away and more than once he caught her by the wrist or touched her shoulder to point out something she'd missed. Each time he did her skin tingled. Thea lost all track of time and had no idea what time it was when the dolphins finally finished their hunting and swam out to sea. Thea and Logan trod water, watching them go.

"I reckon that's our cue to have breakfast," Logan said. "Swim to shore whilst I fetch the boat."

Thea did as she was bid, making her way to the beach. It was not a cold morning but the ever-present sea breeze was enough to chill her wet skin. She did her best to wring out her hair and her shift before settling on a large flat rock to wait for Logan.

Out in the bay, he swam over to the boat and hoisted himself over the side before settling onto a bench, taking up the oars and rowing expertly into shore. As the prow of the little boat scraped the beach, Thea hurried to help him tug it up the tide line until it was high enough that the tide wouldn't float it out again. Reaching inside the boat, Logan handed Thea a large basket that was so heavy she had to stagger with it two-handed up the beach to a large flat rock.

"What have you got in here?" she asked. "Cannon balls?"

She set the basket down and was grateful when Logan handed her a blanket to wrap around her shoulders as she folded cross-legged onto the rock. The sea breeze would dry her quickly but she realized the thin shift she was wearing was clinging to her body in a way that was a little too revealing. Logan pretended not to notice and seated himself next to her, pulling a blanket around his own shoulders and hiding the swirling tattoo on his chest.

Thea busied herself with the basket. Opening the lid, she took out bread, cheese, butter, boiled eggs and some greens left over from last night's dinner. There was a stoppered bottle of ale to wash it down with. The breakfast was a million miles from the chai latte and almond croissant Thea normally preferred but at the moment it seemed like the best feast she'd ever laid eyes on—and it was all because of the man who watched her intently as she laid it all out.

They ate in silence. The only sound was the sighing of the waves and the raucous cries of seabirds. When she'd eaten her fill Thea stretched her legs out and leaned back on her hands, watching the waves as they gently lapped at the shore. She let out a long sigh.

"What is it, lass?" Logan asked. "Is something wrong?"

"No," she replied, turning to look at him. "It's just the opposite. I feel...I don't know what I feel. At ease, I guess, being here like this. With you." She hadn't meant to say that last bit but the words tumbled out before she could stop them.

He watched her for a moment, his eyes dark and unreadable. "I'm glad. I thought ye might be distraught that we havenae found a way for ye to travel home yet. That ye'd be stuck here for a while longer."

She couldn't bear the intensity of his gaze. If he kept looking at her like that she would lose herself completely and say something stupid. Something like *no, I'm not distraught at all. In fact, I'm glad you didn't find Irene because that means I can stay here with you for a bit longer. Because I'm not sure I want to leave at all anymore.*

Such words were dangerous, leading her towards possibilities she dare not contemplate, so instead of answering she jumped to her feet and strode down to the boat. Reaching inside, she grabbed her dress that was crumpled in a heap on the bottom and pulled it over her head. The shift underneath was still damp but she could put up with that.

Behind her Logan cleared away the breakfast things.

"If ye are ready, lass," he said, coming to stand by her side, "we'd best be heading back to the croft."

She glanced up at him. "Thank you. For this morning. I can't tell you how much I enjoyed it." On impulse she went up on her tiptoes and kissed him on the cheek.

He startled and then went very still, staring down at her. His lips parted slightly and for a second she wished he would kiss her. But then he cleared his throat and stepped back, tossing the basket into the boat.

"Ye are welcome, lass. Now let's get aboard before the tide comes in."

Thea clambered into the boat and they began their journey home.

Chapter 11

THE NEXT TIME HE SAW Rhodry, Logan thought as they cast off from the beach, he would be sure to thank the man. It had been a grand idea of his to do something special for Thea. This morning had been perfect, far better than he'd dared to hope. When was the last time he felt so alive? So free?

As he rowed he couldn't help looking at Thea. She was leaning against the side of the boat, her chin propped on one hand, her other hand trailing lazily in the water. Ah, Lord but she was beautiful.

"Who's that?" Thea asked, shading her eyes against the sunlight as she peered ahead.

Somebody was standing on the end of the jetty. A sliver of unease went through Logan. Had Eoin's thugs come back after all?

But he relaxed when they drew closer and he realized it was only Gregor, an old farmer whose land adjoined Logan's. He guided the boat alongside the jetty and tossed Gregor the rope so he could secure it to the iron ring. Once the boat was moored, he leaped out and then helped Thea to disembark.

Curiosity shone in Gregor's eyes as he looked Thea over but he didn't say anything.

"Ye go on up to the cottage, lass," Logan instructed her. "I just need a word with Gregor here. I'll be along shortly."

Thea nodded, grabbed the basket, and walked off along the jetty.

Gregor came to stand next to Logan as he watched her go. "So that's the lass?" he said in his deep voice. "The outlander?"

"Aye, that's her," Logan agreed. "What can I do for ye, my friend?"

Gregor scratched his beard then hooked his thumbs into his belt. "It's more what I can do for ye. That old woman ye were asking about? Irene MacAskill was it? There's been word of her."

A jolt went through Logan. "When? Where?"

"My youngest, Seamus, has just come back from Dun Ringill. There's a woman there works the market sometimes by the name ye gave me. Sells herbs and remedies and such like. Lanced a boil for the wee lad by all accounts."

"When was this?" Logan asked. "How recently?"

"Day afore yesterday I believe. I thought I'd best come over and tell ye, ye being so keen on finding her and all."

Logan's pulse quickened. Irene was in Dun Ringill? Could it really be her? He nodded and clapped Gregor on the shoulder. "Ye have my thanks, friend. Will ye come back to the house and share a bite to eat and some ale?"

The old man shook his head. "I've left old Daisy and the cart by the trail. I'd best be getting back before Morag starts wondering what I'm up to. I swear she thinks I'm a bairn who canna look after myself."

Logan laughed. "Then ye'd better not give her any excuse to scold ye. Thank ye for bringing me this news."

He walked with Gregor to the end of the jetty where the old farmer's pony and cart were waiting. He waved him off and then began walking along the trail towards his croft, deep in thought.

This was the news he'd been waiting for. If Irene had a stall at Dun Ringill it was likely she lived in the town, or at least nearby. He had to tell Thea the good news.

Good news? he thought suddenly. *Is it? Irene will send Thea home and she'll be gone from yer life. Is that what ye want?*

His mood soured. Damn it all! Why did this have to happen now? After the perfect morning they'd spent together? If they rode to Dun Ringill this afternoon, by evening Thea could be gone.

The thought clenched his stomach so tight he stumbled, almost losing his footing.

One more night, he told himself. *I'll tell Thea in the morning and we'll go to Dun Ringill tomorrow. One more night willnae hurt, will it?*

His mind made up, Logan strode for home.

THEA SEATED HERSELF at the table but found she couldn't settle. Logan had returned briefly after talking to the farmer to tell her he was going to work in the smithy and then had promptly ducked out again. He'd seemed distant and distracted.

No different to me, she thought. *I can't seem to get my thoughts straightened out at all.*

It had been a wonderful morning but now Thea felt more confused than ever. She couldn't stop thoughts of Logan running through her head. The small room suddenly felt claustrophobic. She had to get out. On impulse she pulled her pack from under the bed and took out her camera which she slung over her shoulder. Taking a deep breath she stood and made her way out into the yard. From the smithy she heard the clink of metal.

She spun on her heel and onto the trail that hugged the cliffs. Soon the sound of the smithy was lost in the distance, replaced by the whine of the wind and the cries of seabirds and Thea felt her tension unwinding. She sucked in a great, deep breath and let it out slowly, allowing her mind to settle on the moment.

She held her camera loosely, scanning the terrain for anything that would make a good shot. Seabirds wheeled in the air but most were moving too quickly for her to capture, and besides, it was the dolphins she really wanted to snap.

Up ahead, she spotted the fork in the trail that led down onto the beach and scrambled down it. The tide was out, leaving a line of sea-weed and shells high up on the sand. Thea picked her way down to the water's edge and found herself a rock to sit on. She scanned the waves, searching for that telltale glint of a fin or a sleek back breaking the surface.

As she waited, eyes scanning the water, she felt herself settle into the serene stillness that always overcame her when on an assignment like this. There was only her, the camera and her subject. Everything else—thoughts of Logan, her worries about getting home—receded into the distance, leaving her feeling calm and centered.

The dolphins didn't appear—they'd probably swam out to sea or moved further down the coast—so Thea contented herself with photographing the wading birds down at the water's edge and the seals who were basking on the rocks.

She lost track of time and the sun was climbing towards midday when she decided to take a break and examine her pictures. The red light on the top of her camera was starting to blink, indicating her battery was running low. When it ran out, she would have no way of recharging it.

With a sigh she activated the screen, taking this final opportunity to look at her pictures before the battery gave out all together. As she scrolled through what she'd captured, the images of the wading birds and seals were quickly replaced by the photographs she'd shot before she fell through time. Her stomach clenched as she saw once more the images of the hotel she'd been staying in and the sights of Glenmorrow. What would Logan think if he saw these photos? Would he be as shocked as she'd been when she'd first arrived here?

She moved on, knowing what was coming next. Sure enough, a picture of the standing stones popped onto the screen and Thea shuddered as she looked at the arch that brought her here.

She hadn't looked at the image since the day she arrived but now she understood things a little better the arch took on a most sinister aspect. Her eyes alighted on the swirling pattern running down the pillars—the pattern that had only appeared when she touched it.

Activating the zoom function, she took a closer look. The pattern consisted of a series of interlocking coils, three joined spirals that seemed to have no beginning and no end. Where had she seen it before?

And then everything suddenly came together. Of course she had seen this before! Just that morning. In the tattoo that curled across Logan's chest.

She thought suddenly of the last verse from *Laird's Curse*.

The mark of the Fae burned into his skin, a brand for all to see, tis the sign of his fateful bargain, and the way to set him free.

A shiver walked down her spine. Oh god. It couldn't be. Could it?

"Thea?"

She spun, scrambling to her feet with a cry of fright.

Logan was standing a few steps away. "What are ye doing here?" he asked gruffly. His eyes flicked to her camera and widened in surprise.

Thea glanced down and realized the display was still showing the photo of the stones. Involuntarily her eyes strayed to Logan's chest, where the plaid sash crossed his pectoral. The tattoo was under there, hidden, like so much about him.

"What is that unholy device?" he demanded. "I've never seen the like. What manner of devilry could capture an image like that?"

His voice was wary and his stance defensive. Damn it. She'd been so careless. Why had she taken the camera out of the house? Did she really think Logan wouldn't find out?

He held out his hand. "Give it to me."

Thea snatched the camera away. "No."

"Why not?" Logan growled. "Because it might reveal who ye really are? Because it might expose the secrets ye've been hiding?"

"*My* secrets?" Thea cried. "That's rich! You've been lying to me from the start! Why don't you tell me who *you* really are, Logan MacAuley!"

He crossed his arms over his chest. "I dinna know what ye are talking about."

Thea glared at him, brandishing the image on the camera screen. "Why don't you tell me why you have a tattoo that exactly matches the one on the archway that brought me here? Why don't you tell me why you live out here alone? Why don't you tell me why you never want to talk about your brothers? Or why nobody can remember the old Laird MacAuley? Or why you look so god-damned uncomfortable whenever he's mentioned?"

A tiny vein throbbed in his temple, betraying his tension. He didn't say anything for a long moment but when he did, it wasn't the response Thea had been expecting.

"What do ye mean 'the archway that brought ye here?'"

Thea blinked. "What? I never said that."

"Aye, ye did. Ye said an archway brought ye here but that isnae what ye told me. Ye said Irene MacAskill arranged for yer travel from yer homeland. Which is it?" Quick as a flash he snatched the camera from her and peered at the image of the archway. He paled. "What do ye know of this place?" he demanded. "Tell me!"

Thea swallowed. Oh, shit. What was she supposed to say? *Oh, that place brought me from the twenty-first century. Are you okay with that?*

Logan took another step towards her. His eyes flashed with anger. "Ye will tell me the truth!" he growled. "What connection do ye have to the stones of Druach? Why do ye have an image of them? Tell me, lass!"

A shiver of fear walked down Thea's spine. She'd never seen Logan so angry. "I...I...that's where I met Irene MacAskill when I first came here. Then a storm came. You know the rest." She didn't mention that Irene had brought her through those stones from the future.

Logan cursed and his hands curled into fists. "Damn her!" he growled. "Damn all of them and their meddling! Why canna they leave me be?"

"Logan you're scaring me. What's going on? What is your connection to these stones? Why do you have a tattoo with the same markings?"

The thought of the truth scared her. What might it reveal about Logan, about her and why she was here?

She met his gaze. "Tell me, Logan. Please."

LOGAN GLANCED DOWN at the picture of the stones of Druach and then out at the sea. What, by all that's holy, was this thing of Thea's? The way it captured images was unnatural. Why hadn't she told him about it? And about her connection with the stones of Druach?

Irene brought her ashore by the stones, he thought. Coincidence? Unlikely. He had to work out what was going on here, for both their sakes.

"I hoped never to see this place again," he breathed. "It is a dark place. A place of the Fae."

He handed the camera back to Thea then pulled off his shirt. The cool sea breeze sent goose bumps riding across his skin—and across the black tattoo that covered one half of his chest.

"It is the mark of the Fae," he said. "It proclaims the bargain I made and the curse I bear as a result."

"*The mark of the Fae burned into his skin,*" Thea muttered.

She reached a hand towards his tattoo. He caught her hand before she could touch it.

"Nay, lass. Ye mustnae. Did ye not hear what I said? I am cursed."

"*A brand for all to see, tis the sign of his fateful bargain, and the way to set him free,*" Thea breathed. "My god, it's not just a story. It's all true." Her eyes snapped up to meet his. "You're him aren't you? The MacAuley laird? The one nobody can remember?"

He stared at her for a moment before letting out a long breath. "Aye. I was once Laird MacAuley. Long ago. In another lifetime."

"And your curse?"

Logan passed a hand across his face. "In return for the strength to save my people I sold my soul. I thought the Fae would take my life in payment. They didnae. Instead they cursed me to be forever alone. Anyone who stays near me too long dies."

Something cold slid down Logan's spine. He didn't want to remember that night, the night he and his brothers stood by the stones of Druach and spoke the words that sealed their fate. He didn't want to remember the terrible exhilaration that came afterwards and the power that ran through his veins as he and his brothers had destroyed their enemies.

"It's all in the book," Thea breathed. "Irene's book. There was a story in there that reminded me of what Mary told me about the previous laird—of how he and his brothers saved their clan from destruction but disappeared afterwards. I thought it was just a story because it talked of them making a bargain with the Fae." Her gaze sharpened. "But it was true. It told *your* story, Logan."

He scrubbed a hand through his hair as he tried to make sense of what Thea was telling him.

"I dinna understand," he said at last. "Nobody but a handful know the truth. How can my story be written down in a book?"

She didn't answer for a moment. Then she drew in a deep breath as if steeling her courage. "Eventually, many years from now, the disappearance of the MacAuley laird and his brothers will become woven into the folk stories of your people. It will become a myth handed down through the generations. Hundreds of years from now someone will gather those stories into a book and I will bring it back with me." She met his gaze. "From the future."

THERE. SHE'D SAID IT. It was all out in the open now. Thea watched Logan carefully, gauging his response.

"The future?" he said incredulously. "What are ye talking about?"

"I'm from the twenty-first century." Her pulse quickened as she said the words. Nerves fluttered in her belly. She felt strangely vulnerable as if her armor had been stripped away.

He didn't say anything for a moment. Then his gaze strayed to Thea's camera. "Time-travel?" he breathed. "Surely such a thing isnae possible." He laughed bitterly. "What am I saying? I shouldnae be surprised by anything the Fae are capable of. Why did ye not tell me, lass?"

"How could I? I didn't know you. It's not the sort of thing you tell somebody on an introduction."

"So tell me now," he commanded in a soft voice. "Tell me everything."

"I didn't lie," she replied, shaking her head. "I told you as much of the truth as I dared. Irene MacAskill *did* arrange for me to come to Scotland and she did disappear as soon as I got here. She met me by the stones in my own time and talked to me about destiny and fate and loads of other stuff I thought was bullshit at the time. Then I stepped beneath the archway and came back in time hundreds of years. You know the rest."

His expression hardened, anger flashing in his eyes. "Irene MacAskill," he growled, his hands curling into fists. "The Fae. They will answer for what they have done. I swear it."

"You're not angry with me?"

"With ye? Why would I be? Are ye not as much a victim of their meddling as I?"

Relief flooded her and she closed her eyes for a moment. "You don't know how glad I am to hear you say that. And I'm sorry I didn't tell you sooner. I never expected it to be an issue as I thought I wouldn't be here very long." She looked up at him. "But I'm not sorry you didn't find Irene. I'm not sorry I've had to stay."

A wry smile twisted his lips. "Even now? Even after ye know about the curse that hangs over me?"

She took his hand and curled her fingers around his. "Even now. Especially now. I finally know the truth about you and it doesn't scare me at all."

He shook his head. "Ye shouldnae say such things, lass. Ye *should* be scared. I am dangerous to be around."

"I don't believe that. And I don't believe in curses. And you? Do you want to run a mile now you know where I'm really from?"

"Run?" Logan replied. "I could never run from ye, lass."

He stepped closer, cupped her face in his hands, and kissed her.

A shock wave went right through her body. For a heartbeat she went rigid, unable to respond. But then she kissed him back, her lips moving against his hungrily. His hands dropped to her waist, resting there gently as the kiss deepened, his tongue forcing her lips apart and dancing into her mouth. A low groan escaped her and she tangled her fingers in his hair as his arms went around her, yanking her roughly against his hard body.

An ache lit deep in Thea's belly and traveled down to the spot between her legs. Oh god. She wanted him. All the pent up emotion, the feelings she'd been denying, came rushing to the surface. She kissed him fiercely, desperately, all thoughts vanishing, swallowed by his presence.

But abruptly, Logan broke the kiss and stepped back. He rested his hands on her waist and pressed his forehead against hers.

"Lass," he whispered. "Thea. We must stop. I willnae dishonor ye."

Thea tried to gather her scattered thoughts. She placed her hands flat against his chest, her fingers touching the black swirl of his tattoo and forced herself to take a breath.

"Dammit. Why do you have to be so god-damned honorable?"

An answering smile curled his lips. He took one of her hands, kissed it, then turned to grab his shirt from the ground and pull it over his head.

The two of them began walking back along the trail. As they walked, she kept glancing at Logan. She couldn't help herself.

Holy crap, what was happening to her? She'd had boyfriends before but none of them had ever affected her the way Logan did. It was ridiculous. They were so different—from different countries, different cultures, different times. They had nothing in common. But Thea had never felt so alive as she did with him.

"May I see?" he asked suddenly.

"See?"

"Yer pictures." He nodded at her camera.

"Oh!" she said, surprised. She held the camera out to Logan who took it carefully. "Press this button here."

He followed her instructions and jumped slightly as a photograph of the stones sprang into view.

"Incredible," he muttered.

"You scroll through them like this." She showed him the button to press and then watched with a smile as Logan examined them, his eyes widening at the pictures of Glenmorrow with its busy streets and speeding cars. It felt a little strange to be showing him this after all the effort she'd made to keep it from him but it also felt oddly liberating. He knew the truth. She could finally be herself.

He let out a low whistle as he handed the camera back to her. "Yer time looks to be an age of wonders, lass."

She shrugged. "It's not that different from here, really. At first, when I realized where I was, it felt as though I'd landed on a different planet but then, as I got to know you and Ailsa and Rhodry I realized it wasn't so dissimilar. People are the same wherever you are. It's only really the technology that makes things different. We have a lot of that."

"Like this device?"

"Yes, like this device. And a million other things besides. Our lives are full of it."

He cocked his head at her. "Ye must miss it terribly, lass."

She glanced at him and then picked a piece of grass from the trail and began shredding it as she thought through her answer. "I do miss it. Some things, at least. Coffee. Chocolate. But it's not those things that make a place home. It's the people."

Logan glanced at her but said nothing.

The sun was setting as they finally reached the house. Once inside Thea sat at the table while Logan crossed to the cupboard and took out two pottery cups and a bottle of whisky. He poured them both a dram and passed one to Thea. She sniffed it suspiciously.

"This smells like paint stripper."

Logan raised an eyebrow. "That is Clan MacAuley's finest malt. Drink it lass, it will put hairs on yer chest."

Thea gave him a flat look then shrugged and downed the whisky in one gulp. She broke into a fit of coughing.

"And it tastes like paint stripper!" she gasped out.

Logan grinned at her. "Ye'll get used to it." He poured her another dram and then sipped his gently. "And it might help if ye dinna gulp it like ye are dying of thirst."

Thea eyed her cup. "I don't suppose you have any wine?"

"Nay, lass."

Thea waved a hand. "It's fine. It's coffee I really miss." She looked at him hopefully. "I don't suppose you've got coffee?"

"I've never heard of it."

Thea's eyes widened. "Never heard of it?" She pointed a finger at Logan. "You are an uncouth savage, Logan MacAuley."

"Aye, lass," Logan laughed. "Ye'll get no argument from me on that score."

Silence fell between them. All Thea could hear was the crackling of the fire and Logan's steady breathing. Memories of their kiss flared and she ached to feel his lips on hers again. He was watching her steadily, his eyes dark and unreadable.

Then suddenly he cleared his throat, pushed back his chair and stood. "I...um...I'd best retire to the smithy."

Thea grabbed his wrist. He glanced down at her, his lips parted slightly as a low breath escaped him.

"What are ye doing, lass?"

Thea's own breathing quickened. "You don't have to go to the smithy."

He said nothing, only glanced at her fingers where they gripped his wrist. "Dinna say such things, lass. Unless ye mean them."

"I mean them," Thea breathed. She stood, turning to face him and feeling her heart flutter in her chest. "You don't need to go."

His eyes searched her face, the candlelight casting shadows along the contours of his cheekbones. His hair gleamed like burnished metal and the shirt pulled tight across his chest. Did he even realize how god-damned handsome he was? The sight of him made Thea's stomach tighten and sent a hot wave of desire pulsing through her. She felt brazen but also a little afraid.

"Thea," he whispered and there was a world of implications in that word. "My self-control has limits. I should go. If I stay I fear I may dishonor us both." He was trembling slightly.

"There is no dishonor," she whispered.

He reached out and stroked his thumb down the side of her cheek. She leaned into the touch and gazed up at him. Logan leaned down and pressed his lips against hers.

Thea wrapped her arms around his neck and tangled her fingers in his hair. In response, Logan pulled her close and suddenly she was up against the wall, his body touching hers, the hard bulge of his desire pressing into her stomach.

She swept her hands underneath his shirt and up his back, feeling the hard muscles underneath his smooth, warm skin. His tongue darted inside her mouth and she welcomed it, their lips hot on each others, before his kisses traveled down her neck to her shoulders. She gasped and leaned her head back against the wall.

With a growl, Logan picked her up and carried her to the bed. As he laid her on her back he was already kissing her again, his weight pressing her into the mattress. One of his hands traveled lower, hiking up her dress and trailing his fingertips up her inner thigh. She arched under him as the ache between her legs deepened.

Then Logan looked up, his eyes going to the door, suddenly alert.

"What is it?" she gasped.

He held up a finger for silence and Thea fell still, listening hard. Then she heard it. Hoof beats in the distance.

A cold stab of fear went through her. Who would be riding here at this hour? Logan jumped to his feet and Thea scrambled up after him, quickly smoothing down her dress. Logan crossed to the shelf and picked up a long knife, clasping it in his fist.

"Stay there."

He padded silently to the door. Something suddenly pounded on it so loud that it almost made Thea jump right out of her skin. She let out a little shriek then jammed her hands over her mouth.

"Who is it?" Logan demanded. "Who's there?"

A muffled voice came from the other side. "Logan? It's Rhodry. I need yer help!"

Chapter 12

LOGAN UNLOCKED THE door and pulled it open. Rhodry stumbled inside. His hair was disheveled and he looked exhausted. Logan grabbed his arm and helped him stagger to a chair.

"What is it, man? Ye look terrible."

"Anna," he gasped out. "Anna is missing."

Thea's hands flew to her mouth. "My God! What happened?"

Rhodry drew in a deep, ragged breath. "She went to collect firewood from the beach earlier this afternoon as she does every day. She didnae return. I've searched everywhere. Is she here? Have ye seen her? There were prints on the beach that led this way. I thought she might be trying to come and visit ye."

Thea shared an anguished glance with Logan.

"Nay, Rhodry, we havenae seen her," Logan said gently. "But we'll help ye search and we willnae rest until we find her." He clasped his friend's shoulder. "I give ye my word."

Rhodry nodded. "My thanks."

Rhodry dragged himself to his feet and the three of them hurried out into the yard. Dusk was thick in the air, with a chill coming on. They would have to work quickly if they hoped to find Anna before full dark fell. Logan jogged into the stable and reappeared leading Stepper. They mounted and left the croft at a canter, taking the cliff-top trail that gave a view of the beach below.

They didn't speak and traveled at a steady pace but not one that meant they might miss Anna in the gathering dark. Thea scanned the landscape, her eyes searching for any sign of the girl. From what Rhodry had told them, she'd been missing for several hours now. What could have become of her?

After a few miles they reached a fork in the trail. Here a path veered off to the left and snaked down the cliff to the shore below. Logan pulled Stepper to a halt, gazing at the smaller trail. His expression was troubled.

"What is it?" Thea asked.

"Dinna ye recognize this place?" he replied. "It's the place where ye went over the cliff."

Thea shivered, suddenly cold. No, she didn't recognize the place and maybe that was a good thing. What little she could remember of that night was dark and terrifying.

"Let's get away from here."

But Logan didn't move.

"What is it?" Rhodry asked. "Why have ye stopped?"

"There's something here," Logan muttered under his breath, so low that Thea could hardly hear it. "I can feel it." He turned to look at Rhodry. "Wait here with Thea. I'm going to take a look."

He scrambled down from Stepper and strode to the cliff edge. Rhodry jumped from his own horse and followed.

"I'm coming with ye."

"And me," Thea said, jumping from the saddle. "You think I'm going to wait up here whilst Anna might be in trouble? No chance."

Logan glanced at them both and nodded. Together they scrambled down the steep trail, slipping and sliding on the loose stones that rolled out from under their feet. They finally reached the thin strip of shore at the bottom. Here waves were pounding the beach and it was littered with driftwood and other detritus.

"There!" Rhodry bellowed, pointing.

A figure lay crumpled on the sand by the tide line. It wasn't moving. Heart in her mouth, Thea pelted after the men as they ran down the beach and skidded to their knees by the figure.

It was Anna.

Her eyes were closed, her skin pale, and there was a trickle of blood flowing down her temple.

Rhodry gathered up his daughter, pressing his hand to her forehead and then listening to her chest. He closed his eyes, letting out a long sigh. "She lives."

Thea sagged and Logan wiped a shaky hand across his brow. Anna lay as still as death in her father's arms. Despite Rhodry's soft shaking, she didn't stir.

"Why willnae she wake?" he asked anxiously. "What's wrong with her?"

"We have to get her home," Thea said. "Ailsa can take a good look at her and give her some medicine."

Anna didn't stir as Rhodry lifted her into his arms, her head lolling and her limbs flopping. They made their way quickly up the trail to the horses. Rhodry cradled Anna in front of him as they mounted and pounded down the trail to Rhodry and Ailsa's croft.

As they came in sight of the small farm they saw Ailsa and Mary waiting anxiously outside. Ailsa gave a little cry as they came riding into the yard and raced over.

"Ye've found her? Oh, thank the Lord!"

She examined her daughter as Rhodry held her, her gaze roving over the young girl's face. Fear flashed in her eyes.

"Get her inside. I've made up her bed."

Rhodry carried the girl into the house and deposited her on the small bed. Ailsa crouched by her side.

"Fetch my bag," she instructed her husband. "And warm some blankets by the fire and bring them here. She's mighty cold."

Rhodry followed his wife's instructions, returning a moment later with her medicine bag and some warmed blankets.

Thea knelt by the side of Anna's bed. She took hold of the girl's hand. Her skin was like ice. Grabbing the warmed blankets Rhodry had brought, Thea spread them over Anna while Ailsa mixed up a concoction from her bag of herbs. She held it to Anna's mouth but before any of the liquid touched her daughter's lips, Anna suddenly began to convulse. Her limbs flopped and her eyelids fluttered.

"She's having a seizure!" Thea said. "Get her onto her side!"

Ailsa's face was white as they rolled Anna over and put her into the recovery position. After a few moments the seizure subsided and Anna went still once more, her eyes closed but her breathing even. Ailsa let out a sob.

Rhodry knelt by his wife's side and laid a hand on his daughter's head, gently stroking her brow.

"All will be well," he said soothingly. "Our Anna is a fighter. She'll come back to us."

Thea climbed to her feet and made her way into the living room. Mary was telling a story to the rest of the children to keep them occupied. She looked up anxiously as Thea entered.

Thea gave her a small smile. "Anna's sleeping." Then she looked around. "Where's Logan?"

Mary glanced at the window. It was completely dark outside now. "The lad seemed distraught. Kept muttering about it being his fault. Then he left. He went out there. Into the night."

LOGAN WALKED INTO THE darkness. The springy grass became sand that crunched under his boots. From up ahead came the sighing of the sea and a sickle moon illuminated the waves crashing against the shore. Logan reached the water line and kept going, walking right into the icy waves until they swirled around his thighs. The cold sent a shock-wave right through him but he welcomed it. It was nothing compared to the ice in his soul.

What had happened to Anna was his fault. His curse had come to claim her.

It was not a coincidence that Anna had been found on the exact same beach where Logan had brought Thea ashore. A beach miles from Anna's home where she had no right to be. There were no coincidences where the Fae were concerned.

"Curse ye!" he bellowed to the empty sea. "Why could ye not just take me?"

A sound like harsh laughter carried on the wind. *Did ye think ye could cheat me? Remember yer bargain,* the wind seemed to whisper. *Remember...*

And Logan did.

It was a dark, moonless night and Dun Ringill was far behind them. Logan strode purposefully, Camdan on one side, Finlay on the other. He glanced at his brothers. Camdan wore a fixed, determined expression but Finlay was pale, unable to hide his fear. The three of them wore full warrior garb and were heavily armed. His father's sword felt heavy where it was strapped across Logan's back.

Shapes suddenly appeared out of the darkness and they halted, looking around warily. The weathered stones of Druach reared out of the earth like jagged teeth, framed against the ocean beyond.

Camdan frowned. "There's nobody here. What now?"

"Patience, brother," Logan murmured.

He heard movement and spun, drawing his father's sword.

"There isnae need for such things," said a voice from the darkness. "I am not yer enemy."

A man stepped out of the shadows. He was short, barely reaching Logan's chest and seemed old beyond years. His face was a nest of wrinkles and his liver-spotted pate held only a few wisps of silver hair. But his eyes...they were as black as onyx and glowed with power.

Camdan stepped forward, his sword clasped in his fist. "Who are ye? Name yerself!"

The old man smiled. "Oh, I think ye know who I am. Put yer toys away." He waved a hand and suddenly the pommel of Logan's sword grew scolding hot. With a curse, the brothers dropped their weapons into the dirt.

"That's better," said the man. "I canna abide the touch of iron. Now, shall we begin?"

Logan frowned. "Ye know why we are here?"

"Of course. Humans only come to the stones of Druach for one reason: to bargain. I know what ye would ask of me. Ye wish for me to save yer people."

"Aye," Logan replied. "That is the boon we seek. We were told ye could grant such things—for a price."

The man smiled and the sight of it sent a shiver down Logan's spine. It was a predator's smile. "Aye, I can grant such things. But I canna save yer people." He held up a finger for silence as Logan began to protest. "But I can give *ye* three the power to save them." He fixed them with his black stare. "For one night I will give ye the strength of the Fae. With it, none will be able to stand against ye."

Logan looked at his brothers. Camdan was watching the old man as you would watch a snake. Finlay's pale gaze was fixed on Logan.

"We must, brother," he said. "We agreed, remember? It's our duty to protect the clan. Ye know what will happen when the raiders arrive. There can be no victory against such an enemy. They will slaughter the men and rape the women. Clan MacAuley will be no more. What are our lives against that?"

Logan bowed his head. Finlay had always been the most sensible of them all.

"Aye," Logan replied. "But it's not *yer* responsibility. It's mine. I'm the laird. The responsibility falls to me." He looked at the old man. "Take my life. I give it freely but spare my brothers. I beg of ye."

Finlay and Camdan yelled in protest but the old man was already shaking his head. "Such a payment isnae enough. For this boon the price is three lives. The lives of the greatest of the MacAuley clan. Do ye accept this bargain?"

Logan looked first at Camdan and then at Finlay.

"Aye," Logan breathed. "We accept yer bargain."

The old man's smile widened. "Then come forward and seal it."

Warily the three brothers stepped close to the stones. The old man hobbled into the center of the circle and spread his hands wide. The temperature dropped suddenly and goose bumps rode up Logan's skin, his breath misting in the air. The old man spoke in a language Logan didn't recognize.

The stones began to hum with power and small flames suddenly burst to life in a circle around them as though hundreds of tiny candles had been lit. In the sudden light Logan saw that the stones were carved with a swirling design of interlocked spirals and, as Logan watched, they began to move, writhing against each other like the coils of a snake.

Logan forced down his unease. The Fae looked at each of the brothers in turn, his eyes shining with a dark malice.

"The terms have been set," he said. "In exchange for the power to defeat yer enemies ye will give me yer lives. Do ye agree?"

"We agree," they chimed in unison.

"Then set yer hands on the stone and seal our bargain."

Logan steeled himself, swallowing down the awful foreboding that filled him, and pressed his palm against the swirling design on the stone. The man stepped forward and pressed something against his chest. At once, a blinding pain exploded inside him, forcing him to his knees. For a moment it rampaged through him so strongly he couldn't see or hear and he was sure he was going to die.

But after a moment the agony passed and when he looked he saw that the design from the stones was now tattooed across his chest, marking him like a brand.

He forced himself to his feet. He felt light, full of a strange energy. His brothers met his eye and he saw they were similarly branded, Camdan on his left arm, Finlay down his back.

"It is done!" the Fae cried, clapping his hands together in glee. "Ye carry within ye the power of the Fae but it will last for one night only. Ye must hurry to complete yer task before the sun rises."

Logan nodded. "Aye. Let's be on our way. We have much to do before we die."

The Fae's grin widened. "Die? What are ye talking about? Ye aren't going to die."

Logan frowned at the creature. "We traded our lives for this power."

"Aye, ye did. Yer lives belong to me. Mine to do with as I will. But did I ever mention dying? Nay, that isnae our bargain at all." The man stalked closer, seeming to flow over the ground like smoke. He looked up at Logan and his dark eyes flashed with malice. "I choose to let ye live. But ye will be cursed. Ye will become shadow-people, living a half-life on the edges of the world. Ye will never know love. Ye will never know peace. All who stay close to ye will die. This is the price ye have agreed to pay."

Fury filled Logan as the Fae's words sank in. The Fae were tricksters, not to be trusted. Hadn't he been told such things since he was a child?

"Why would ye do such a thing?" he growled.

The Fae's grin widened and suddenly there was nothing human about this creature at all. "Because it pleases me."

Logan jolted back to the present. He had no idea how long he'd been standing in the water but his legs had gone numb with cold. With a grunt, he waded clumsily onto the beach.

How could he have been so stupid? Did he really think he could escape his bargain with the Fae? No mortal could. What a fool he'd been. His curse had taken Anna. It was a warning. Thea would be next.

He knew what he had to do. He should have done it from the start.

Sick with guilt, Logan walked back to the house. There was a faint smudge of light along the eastern horizon and Logan realized he'd been gone most of the night. As he stumbled into the yard, he saw Thea pacing outside the cottage. She whirled at the sound of his footsteps.

"Where have you been?" she cried. "I was so worried!"

She threw her arms around him and pressed herself close, ignoring his wet clothes. Logan took her by the shoulders and gently pushed her away from him.

"My apologies, lass," he muttered, not meeting her gaze. "I needed to think. How is Anna?"

"No change. Rhodry and Ailsa haven't left her side all night."

Logan nodded. "We must go, lass. Come, I'll fetch Stepper."

"We can't leave now," Thea replied. "Not until we know Anna is going to be okay."

Logan gritted his teeth. She had that stubborn set to her jaw again. He wanted to shout at her that it wasn't safe to stay here. He wanted to take her by the shoulders and shake her until she understood how dangerous being near him was. Instead he searched for a convincing lie.

"Ye need sleep, lass," he said in as reasonable a voice as he could manage. "And something to eat. There is naught more we can do here. Leave Anna to Rhodry and Ailsa. We'll return later to check on her."

Thea hesitated, glancing back at the house and biting her lip. Then she nodded. "Okay, I'll let them know we'll be back later."

She hurried into the house as Logan fetched Stepper from the stable. His stomach churned with guilt. How easy it had been to lie to her. The lies rolled off his tongue like venom. Lord help him, what kind of man had he become?

Thea reappeared, they mounted Stepper, and he nudged the horse into motion, leaving Rhodry and Ailsa's croft behind.

Chapter 13

THEA WAS SO EXHAUSTED she soon found herself dozing in the saddle, leaning against Logan's hard chest. He hadn't spoken a word since they'd left Rhodry and Ailsa's croft and Thea didn't have the energy to make conversation. Instead, she found herself drifting in and out of sleep. The horse lurched and she jolted awake suddenly.

"Naught to worry about, lass," Logan said. "A grouse startled Stepper."

Thea blinked the last of the sleep from her eyes and looked around. She didn't recognize the landscape they were traveling through. They were walking down a wide, paved road into a shallow valley. A settlement filled most of the valley, a hotch-potch of small thatched houses and larger two-story ones. People were walking along the streets of the settlement, more people than Thea had seen since she arrived in this time. Her eyes widened, taking it all in, and then her eyes widened further as she spied the building that stood at the road's terminus.

It was a castle.

Dominating the settlement, the castle crouched at the valley mouth like some great gray beast: high walls, towers and crenelated battlements. Even from this distance she could see figures patrolling the walls.

"Where are we?" she demanded. "What is going on?"

"This is Dun Ringill," Logan murmured by her ear. "The seat of Clan MacAuley."

"But...but..." Thea shook her head, trying to gather her thoughts. The sun was high in the sky, indicating they'd been traveling for several hours. "Why are we here?"

She looked over her shoulder and saw dark shadows under his eyes. His gaze was troubled.

"Ye must trust me, Thea."

Before she could say another word, he kicked Stepper into a trot, forcing her to grab the saddle and concentrate on keeping her seat. They rode down the hill and soon entered the settlement.

It was large enough to be called a town and Thea gazed around in astonishment as they rode through the streets of hard-packed earth. Stalls lined the road selling all kinds of goods. Thea saw leather work, bolts of cloth, and woven baskets cheek by jowl with pens full of goats and chickens. The streets were so busy that Logan was forced to slow Stepper to a walk. The noise and busyness after the quiet of Logan's croft was a little overwhelming. Everywhere she looked people were busy bartering, arguing or gossiping on street corners and everyone was dressed in the same plaid design as Logan's.

These people were Clan MacAuley, she realized. Logan's people. Yet not one of them recognized him. Their eyes slid over him and away again, not seeming to see him at all.

Thea's stomach clenched. Why had Logan brought her here? *Trust me*, he'd said. Thea tried. But she couldn't shake the feeling of unease that settled on her like a dark cloak.

LOGAN GUIDED STEPPER along the street and then up the road that led to the castle. The gates stood open and a steady stream of people were passing through. Most of them, Logan noted, were warriors bearing weapons. There were more guards on the gate than usual and everyone was halted at the gates and questioned before they were allowed through into the bailey. Logan slowed Stepper and waited with ill grace until they reached the front of the line. Five guards, all heavily armed, blocked his way. He didn't recognize any of them.

"State yer name and purpose," one commanded.

"Logan MacAuley," he replied. "I have an audience with the laird and I doubt he'd appreciate being kept waiting. The password is Megan."

Megan had been the name of the laird's mother. Only a select few knew the password and it would ensure they were taken straight through into the castle without having to wait in line with everyone else.

"Aye, go on then. Archie will escort ye." The guard nodded and a runner, a boy of around thirteen years hurried over.

The guards moved aside and Logan heeled Stepper through into the bailey. A deluge of memories assailed him as he entered. It had been three years since he'd ridden out of this very bailey, but it felt like a lifetime ago. The stable block had been expanded and now filled the whole of the far wall and it was dirtier than when he'd been laird, the cobbles unswept and a pile of broken barrels stacked against a wall.

Logan swung out of the saddle and then held out a hand to help Thea down. She ignored his proffered hand and dismounted on the other side, away from him.

"Are you going to tell me what the hell we are doing here?" she demanded.

Logan glanced around. "Not here," he muttered. "I'll explain once we're inside."

A stable lad led Stepper away and the runner bobbed his head. "If ye follow me, I'll take ye to the waiting room."

Logan nodded. "Aye, lad. My thanks."

He indicated for Thea to precede him and she did so grumbling under her breath, following the runner up the wide steps and into the castle. They passed the door to the Great Hall and Logan glanced inside. When he'd been laird the place had often rung to the sound of music and merriment but now it echoed with the sound of snoring. Hundreds of warriors were billeted there, rolled in their cloaks on the flagstone floor.

Logan frowned. No doubt they were new recruits or mercenaries that his cousin had hired for his upcoming campaign against the MacKinnon but this didn't excuse their lack of discipline. What self-respecting warrior would be abed at this hour? The sun had long since risen so they ought to be up and training or patrolling the castle. Why was his cousin tolerating such tardiness?

He and Thea followed the runner up a set of winding steps to the floor above, which was traditionally set aside for clan business. Up here the surroundings were more sumptuous, with a thick carpet covering the floor and bright tapestries on the walls. The runner led them to a small room with an inner door.

"The laird is currently engaged. If ye wait here, he will see ye presently."

Logan inclined his head and the young lad left. Logan steeled himself for the tirade he knew was coming.

THE MOMENT THE DOOR closed Thea whirled on Logan. "Right," she said, jabbing a finger at him. "You have some explaining to do."

Logan glanced at her and away again. Instead of answering he moved to the window and leaned on the sill, looking down into the courtyard below. His shoulders were hunched, belying his tension. A sudden worm of unease slid down Thea's spine.

"Logan?"

He let out a long sigh, closed his eyes for a moment and then opened them again. He turned to face her.

"Ye canna stay with me anymore. I was a fool to think ye could. To my shame I've been lying to ye. I know where Irene MacAskill is, lass. She's here in Dun Ringill."

Thea stared at him. "I beg your pardon?"

"Ye remember Gregor coming to see me yesterday? He told me that Irene had been seen here in the town. She works here as a healer sometimes."

Thea shook her head. "I...I don't understand," she said. "Why didn't you tell me this?"

"I should have," he replied. "But I am a weak and selfish man. I thought to keep ye with me for one more night. And because of that my curse took Rhodry and Ailsa's child."

"Anna? What has she got to do with this?"

"Ye think it a coincidence that she was found injured on the very beach where I first met ye? There are nay such things as coincidences where the Fae are concerned. It was a warning, one I must heed."

Thea pressed her hand to her temple where a headache was forming. "Hang on a minute, you think what happened to Anna was your fault? Are you serious? She had an accident that's all!"

"Then how do ye account for her being found so far from home and unconscious?"

"I don't know!" Thea said, throwing up her hands. "But there are a thousand other explanations without talking about curses and other superstitious crap!" She was shouting now but couldn't help it. She was angry but also a little afraid. What would happen when they found Irene? She didn't want to think about it.

He held out a pleading hand. "Dinna make this harder than it needs to be, lass."

"Harder than it needs to be? Are you kidding?" she exploded. "You bring me here without my knowledge, tell me you're going to send me home—after everything that's happened between us—and you expect me to be *okay* with this? Are you out of your mind? Why, Logan?"

"What choice do I have?" he growled. "I willnae let Anna's fate befall ye."

"You cannot believe that was your fault!"

"Of course it is," he snapped. "Ye canna stay with me any longer, Thea. If ye do, it will cost yer life. I willnae allow that, do ye hear?" His eyes flashed with anger. "Ye will do as I say for once, woman."

Thea glared at him. Stupid, stubborn man! Who the hell did he think he was, deciding her fate for her? "And did you not think to discuss this with me before you brought me here?"

"Would ye have come with me if I had?"

Thea opened her mouth for an angry retort and then snapped it shut again. He was right. She wouldn't have agreed to come with him, not while Anna was so ill, but that didn't give him the right to...to....kidnap her!

"Your curse had nothing to do with what happened to Anna," she said, forcing her voice to sound calm, even though her insides roiled with emotion. "She is injured or ill, not cursed. Surely you can see that?"

"All I can see is that I've made a terrible mistake in thinking I could cheat my bargain. If Irene is here, we will find her and she will send ye home. If she isnae here, my cousin will give ye refuge."

"And if I refuse?"

"Ye have nay choice."

"Damn you, Logan!" she shouted, her hands balling into fists. "Take me back right now! I won't leave Anna and Ailsa and Rhodry like this!" *I won't leave you*, a voice whispered in her head. "And if you won't take me, I'll make my own way back!"

"How will ye do that, lass?" he asked softly. "We are a long way from my croft and ye dinna know the way."

"Then I'll find someone to give me a lift!"

"With no coin to pay yer way? And ye an outlander? Nobody will take ye. Hate me if ye wish, lass. Lord above, it's naught more than I deserve, but I will have my way in this."

His voice cracked with command, his jaw set with determination. Thea saw the laird in him suddenly, the man born to lead.

"If you think for one minute—" Thea began but cut off as the inner door suddenly burst open and a young woman came storming out.

The woman paused long enough to spin around and shout back into the inner room. "I'd rather die a maid than marry that...that...lecher!" Then she stomped off without giving Logan or Thea so much as a glance. A moment later an old man, who Thea took to be the woman's father, hurried after her.

"Women!" said a voice from the inner doorway. "I swear the good Lord only put them on this earth to make men's life a trial!"

A blond haired man came out of the inner room. He was of a height with Logan but where Logan was broad-shouldered, this man was wiry, with a build more like a runner. He shared the same golden skin with Logan though and Thea guessed who this must be.

Logan nodded. "Cousin."

The man grinned. "Is that all the greeting I get? After all this time? I couldnae believe it when a runner came to tell me yer password had been used at the gate! Come here, ye big ox!"

Logan grinned in response and the two men strode forward and embraced, slapping each other on the back.

"My, it's good to see ye," the blond man said. "How long has it been? Three years?"

"And then some," Logan agreed. "It is mighty strange being here again, I can tell ye."

"And mighty strange seeing ye here again," his cousin agreed. "I never thought to see ye inside these walls after....what happened. What brings ye here, cousin?"

Logan stepped aside. "This is Lady Thea Thomas, an outlander who fell foul of the Fae, just as we did. Thea, this is my cousin, Laird Eoin MacAuley."

Thea had no idea what was the proper form of address for a laird. Should she curtsey? She contented herself with inclining her head. "Hi."

Laird MacAuley stepped smoothly towards her, giving her a courtly bow. "Honored to meet ye, Lady Thomas. Run afoul of the Fae, eh? Then ye have my sympathy. Our clan has had quite our fill of dealings with those creatures." He took her hand and kissed it. "Ye are most welcome to my castle, Lady Thomas. How may I be of service?"

Logan cleared his throat. "She came through the stones of Druach," he said quietly. "And can only go back that way."

Something flared in Eoin's eyes. "The stones of Druach?" he whispered. "I wonder what the Fae want with her?"

"What they want doesnae matter," Logan replied. "What matters is getting Thea home. Will ye help? I would ask ye to offer her shelter and do all ye can to find a woman named Irene MacAskill. She's the one who brought her here and she has been spotted here in Dun Ringill."

"Irene MacAskill?" Eoin replied. "I canna say I have ever heard the name but if she is in Dun Ringill then we will find her. In the meantime ye both will enjoy the hospitality of the castle. Now! A drink is in order!"

He crossed to a side table on which sat a decanter of wine and several glasses. Thea stepped up beside Logan.

"How come he knows who you are?" she murmured. "Nobody else recognizes you."

"It was part of the agreement," Logan murmured. "He was party to our plans from the beginning. Without him we could never have defeated the raiders."

"There!" Eoin said, carrying over three goblets. "A fine vintage. Italian. Brought all the way from Venice, or so the traders tell me. For all I know it could come from twenty miles down the road but as long as it does the trick, eh?"

Thea and Logan took a glass of the dark red wine. Logan didn't drink but Thea tossed hers back. A little false courage was just about what she needed right now.

LOGAN SWIRLED HIS WINE in the glass but didn't drink. Instead, he watched his cousin. He still remembered the awkward corn-haired boy who had come to live with them at the age of twelve, shortly after the death of his father. Through the years he had become a trusted advisor. Logan knew his cousin had a weakness for women but when it came to matters of the clan, nothing was more important to him. That was why, when the time came, Logan and his brothers had left the clan in his hands. Logan was sure he would do right by Thea.

He let out a long sigh. "Ye have my thanks, cousin. I know this canna be easy on ye."

A smile quirked the edges of Eoin's lips. "Lord above, man! It's the least I can do. Here, will ye have another wine?"

Logan shook his head. Eoin shrugged and knocked back another glass. Logan noticed that the decanter was half empty all ready. How many had his cousin had? Three glasses? Four? At this time in the morning?

"Who was that lass who went running out of here?" he asked.

Eoin grimaced. "Isabella MacMurray and the old fart with her was her father. He thought to buy my favor by offering his daughter in marriage but I'll not marry a shrew. The girl is unhinged and as highly strung as a colt. I offered her a polite kiss in greeting and she went hysterical. Nay. I need a woman with some metal to her."

Logan said nothing. He remembered Mary telling him that Eoin was looking for a wife. It would be a rare lass indeed who could put up with Eoin's wandering ways.

"I see ye are expanding the garrison," he said. "The town is fairly bursting with fighting men."

Eoin poured himself another glass of wine and gestured at Logan with it. "Aye. What of it?"

"I heard rumors that war is brewing with the MacKinnon. I thought it idle gossip seeing as the MacKinnons have been our allies for generations. But now I see a garrison preparing for war and the MacKinnons mustering on their land. What is going on, cousin?"

Eoin's eyes narrowed. "The last time I looked, it was I, and not ye, cousin, who was laird of the MacAuley. I will do as I see fit." The icy tone of his voice took Logan aback.

"Aye, ye are," he growled in response. "And the last time I looked the Laird MacAuley was duty bound to do the best for his people."

"Dinna ye think that's what I'm doing?" Eoin said. "Laird MacKinnon refused to pay his tithes. I seized his ships in recompense. He didnae like that and came here threatening me. Me! Laird MacAuley! Laird of a clan ten times as powerful as his!"

Logan went very still. The MacKinnons had always paid a tithe to the MacAuleys and in return the MacAuleys had protected the smaller, weaker clan from the encroachments of their aggressive northern neighbors. The tithe had never been more than the MacKinnons could afford.

What had caused the MacKinnon to refuse payment? Was the clan in dire straits or had Eoin raised it to a price he couldn't afford? And to seize his ships? Even Logan's father, who had long argued that the MacKinnon ships should work in concert with the MacAuley ones, had been reluctant to do that. What was going on here? Why was Eoin war mongering?

He opened his mouth to speak and then shut it again. *Ye are no longer Laird MacAuley*, he told himself. And the business of the clan is no longer yers. *Ye are only a blacksmith. Never forget that.*

There was a knock on the door and a young woman entered. She wore a plain yellow dress with an apron over the top. She curtseyed to Eoin.

"Ah! Rian! This is Lady Thea Thomas and Blacksmith MacAuley. Escort them up to the guest chambers and see they have everything they need." He turned to Logan. "Go with Rian. Take some rest. We'll talk more later."

Logan nodded. "Until later, cousin."

Rian smiled at them both. Logan recognized her. The last time he'd seen her she'd been in her teen years, helping her mother in the kitchen. There was no recognition in the lass's eyes though.

"If ye would follow me, my lady, my lord?"

Thea put down her wine glass, gave an awkward curtsey to Eoin, and then they followed Rian from the room. The maid led them along the corridor and up a short flight of stairs to the guest quarters where they were given rooms next to each other. Logan thanked Rian then as soon as the maid had gone he knocked on Thea's door.

THEA'S ROOM WAS AS swanky as anything in a high-end hotel. The walls were covered in wooden paneling, thick rugs decorated the floor and a huge four-poster bed that looked big enough for ten people dominated the room. Thea barely noticed.

She crossed to the window and looked out. Below was a large courtyard where horses were being groomed. People bustled around and the hubbub of a busy day floated up from below. It was a million miles away from Logan's quiet, wild croft. Oh, how she longed to be back there!

There was a knock on the door and she wasn't surprised when Logan pushed it open. Thea grabbed onto the window sill to keep from running to him. She longed to throw her arms around him, pull him close, and it took all her self control to remain by the window.

He stepped into the room and stood by the door, dark eyes searching her face.

"I...I...um. Do ye like yer room?" he asked lamely.

"My room?" she replied. "Is that what you came to talk to me about?"

"Nay, lass. Ye know why I came."

"Do I?"

"I came to see that ye were all right. Ye aren't going to make this easy for me, are ye?"

She crossed her arms. "Why the hell should I?"

He sighed. "Aye, I probably deserved that. I must go out now and search for news of Irene. I need yer word that ye will remain here."

Thea raised her chin and glared at him defiantly.

Logan frowned at her. "Yer word, lass."

Thea sagged, letting out a sigh. "Okay. Fine. I give you my word I won't try to leave town. Happy?"

He huffed out a breath, his shoulders sagging with relief. "I shouldnae be too long, a few hours at most. Eat. Rest. I'll be back as soon as I can." Then he strode to the door and left.

Thea stared at the closed door for a moment. What was she supposed to do now?

Restless energy burned through her veins. She paced to the window and looked down. She saw Logan emerge and cross the courtyard to the gates. He moved purposefully as though he knew exactly where he was going. Thea bit her lip, trying to get a grip on her anger. How could Logan do this to her?

He's doing what he thinks is best for you, she thought. *Best for me?* She answered her own thought. *What's best for me is being allowed to decide my own damned fate! Stupid, arrogant man! If he thinks I'm going to sit here like some good little woman while he decides my future, he's got another think coming!*

She'd promised not to leave town but that didn't mean she had to sit in this room and wait for Logan, did it? She strode to the door, pulled it open, then made her way down the stairs to a landing with weapons hanging on the wall. A woman carrying an armload of sheets approached her and Thea was relieved when she recognized Rian.

"Oh!" Rian said when she spotted Thea. "I was just bringing ye fresh bedding, my lady. I thought ye'd want to rest after yer journey."

"No, I'm not tired."

"Would ye care for something to eat then?"

"That sounds great," Thea said with a smile. "I'm starving."

Rian put down her sheets. "This way, then. Margaret will be serving breakfast in the Great Hall by now."

Thea followed Rian down the stairs and into a cavernous room with a high ceiling, tall windows, and a huge fireplace at one end. Thea had spotted it when they first came to the castle when it had been full of sleeping soldiers. It seemed the soldiers had been turned out for the day and now the room was full of long trestle tables at which people of all ages sat eating.

"This way," Rian said cheerfully, taking Thea by the arm and guiding her to a table near the fireplace where an aging couple were talking quietly. Rian introduced her.

"Margaret, Malcolm, this is Lady Thea Thomas, Laird MacAuley's guest. Lady Thea, I'd like ye to meet Steward Malcolm and Housekeeper Margaret. I'll leave ye in their care." With a squeeze of Thea's arm the young maid turned and left.

"Sit, sit!" Malcolm said, waving Thea to a seat on the bench. "My wife and I are mighty pleased to meet ye."

"Thanks," Thea replied, taking a seat. "It's good to meet you too."

"Ah! Ye are an outlander by yer accent!" Margaret said, leaning close. "Where do ye hail from? I canna say I've ever heard such an accent."

Thea thought quickly. "I'm English. From Cornwall."

"Cornwall? My, ye are a long way from home. I havenae ever been that far south myself but Cornish metalwork is some of the finest I've ever seen."

"Um, yes," Thea said. "I guess it is."

The smell of food wafted through the room, setting Thea's stomach to growling. She realized that she'd had nothing to eat since she and Logan had shared supper last night. Her cheeks warmed as she remembered what had happened after that. Logan's hands on her body, his mouth hungrily devouring hers... How could things change so suddenly?

Margaret waved over a maid who placed a steaming bowl of porridge on the table in front of Thea. It smelled delicious.

"Get that down ye, lass," Margaret said kindly. "And there's plenty more where that came from."

The couple seemed friendly so, as she tucked into the porridge, Thea thought she would take a chance.

"I don't suppose you know of a woman called Irene MacAskill do you?"

Margaret pursed her lips in thought. "Hmm. Irene MacAskill? Nay, canna say as I do. Malcolm?"

The old man shook his head. "The MacAskill clan live many miles to the east. We dinna see many of them in these parts. Why do ye ask?"

"I was supposed to meet her here," Thea replied carefully. "But she didn't show. I was told she works in Dun Ringill sometimes as a healer."

"Well, the best place to look would be the market on the main square. Many healers ply their trade there."

"The market square?"

"Aye, right in the center of town. Ye canna miss it."

Thea's heart thumped. Finally, a lead on Irene! If she found the old woman before Logan did, she could get her to explain to Logan that his curse was a load of horseshit and then they could go back to the way things were.

What about getting her to send you home? She asked herself. *Isn't that why you need to find Irene?*

She pushed that thought away, unwilling to explore it. She finished her porridge and dropped the spoon into the bowl.

"That was delicious. You've both been most helpful. Thanks!" She climbed to her feet.

"Wait!" said Margaret. "Are ye going to look for her now? If ye wait a minute, I'll arrange for a guardsman to accompany ye. It isnae seemly for a noble lady to wander the streets alone."

"Oh, that's fine," Thea said quickly. "I'll be okay." The last thing she needed was a damned chaperone!

Before Margaret or Malcolm could say anything else, she hurried from the hall, across the bailey and mingled with the flow of traffic exiting through the main gates.

Dun Ringill's streets were even busier than when she and Logan had first ridden into town. The middle of the main thoroughfare had become a churned up mass of mud from the numerous carts making their ponderous way up to the castle and Thea was forced to pick her way along the edges along with everyone else.

As she walked a barrage of sights and sounds assailed her. Stallholders and hawkers cried their wares as she walked by and the smell of cooking food, spices, animals and sour ale all mingled together to assail her nostrils. It was a little overpowering and Thea forced herself to breathe evenly and walk with confidence as if she had the right to be there. Even so, she found herself wishing Logan was by her side. He would have led the way with unerring confidence and bellowed at people to get out of their way.

She smiled at the thought, wondering where he was. *Out arranging to get rid of me*, she thought. Her mood suddenly soured. *Not if I find Irene. Then there'll be no need to hand me over to his cousin and we can sort out this damned curse of his.*

The main street was longer than she realized and she found herself walking for a good distance before it opened out into a square. Here the mud was replaced by flagstones and there were many stalls dotted around the square. Thea halted and looked around.

A small ferrety man, who was busy sewing a pair of boots, noticed her standing there. "Ah! Good day to ye, mistress!" he said. "Are ye looking for some fine new footwear? If so, ye have come to the right place! Ye'll find nay better quality in the whole of the Highlands—and reasonably priced too!"

"No, sorry," Thea replied. "I don't need any shoes. I was looking for a healer who has a stall here. Her name is Irene MacAskill. Do you know her?"

"Canna say as I do."

Thea bit down her disappointment. She thanked the man and then made a circuit of the square, investigating the stalls and asking after Irene. Although one or two knew her, none had seen her for a long time. Eventually Thea found herself back where she'd started.

She perched on the lip of a stone water trough and sighed. Was Logan having more luck? Thea doubted it. Irene MacAskill, it seemed, did not want to be found. And if that was the case, it meant Logan would abandon her, leave her here amongst strangers, believing he had no other choice. The thought made her stomach churn with fear.

"Now that is one fed-up face if ever I saw one," said a voice.

Startled from her thoughts, Thea looked up to see that a woman had perched on the horse-trough next to her. She looked to be a few years older than Thea with long, shiny hair falling unbound down her back and sparkling, merry eyes.

"Sorry," Thea muttered. "It's been one of those days."

"Ah," the woman replied. "I know all about *those* kinds of days. Maybe I could help?"

Something about the way the woman spoke struck Thea as odd. She had a strange accent, part Scottish, part...something else.

"No. Thanks," she replied. "I was hoping to find someone here, that's all."

The woman nodded. "Yes, I know first hand how infuriating searching for Irene MacAskill can be."

Thea's head whipped round. "How do you know who I'm looking for?"

A smile curled the woman's lips and she lifted an eyebrow. "You asked after her at most of the stalls around the square. It wasn't hard to work out."

"No, I guess not. Sorry," Thea replied feeling a little foolish. Then the woman's words registered and she turned to look at her once more. "Wait a minute. You know Irene?"

The woman nodded. "Yes." She leaned forward, holding out her hand. "My name is Kara Harris. I'm a friend of Irene's. Well, she's my grandmother actually. Although half the time I think the woman causes me more trouble than she's worth."

Thea reached out and shook Kara's hand. "I'm Thea."

"Yes, I know who you are."

Thea suddenly realized why the woman's accent sounded so familiar. She spoke more like Thea than the locals. She said 'yes' instead of 'aye' and the way she pronounced her vowels was different. An outlander then, like herself.

"Do you know where I can find Irene?" she asked. "I really need to talk to her."

Kara sighed. "I don't know where she is and even if I did, I wouldn't be able to take you to her. There are rules that must be obeyed and even Irene must adhere to them. She cannot interfere—the choices you make must be done of your own free will. I am pushing the rules by talking to you now but I think I can get away with it." Kara's piercing eyes fixed on Thea. "After all, I'm not the one who brought you here."

The back of Thea's neck prickled. How did Kara know that Irene had brought her here? And what was this talk of rules and free will?

"Who are you?" she whispered.

"A friend," Kara replied. "I was once like you: snatched from my own time without an explanation and I know how difficult this is for you. I know you want answers and to find a way home. But Irene brought you here for a reason. To keep the balance. I, like Irene, am a keeper of that balance. I am intervening now only because we have almost reached the point where the balance will be tipped irrevocably. Clan MacAuley is about to go to war with Clan MacKinnon. If that happens the intricate network of alliances means the whole of the Highlands will ignite in bloodshed, the repercussions of which will echo through time like a rock thrown into a pond. Only one man can stop it. I think you know who that is."

Thea stared at the woman. Her words had sent Thea's heart pounding against her ribs. Brought here for a reason.

She had always thought as much. Why else would Irene have given her the book and the story of Logan's curse?

"Logan," she breathed. "He's the one who can stop it."

Kara nodded. "And you are the key to him doing just that."

"How? What can I do?"

"You will have to figure that out for yourself," Kara replied. "Free will, remember?"

A hundred different questions swirled in Thea's head. She opened her mouth to ask them but the sudden crash of a cart overturning across the square caused her head to whip around.

When Thea looked back, Kara was gone.

She sprang to her feet. She spun around, searching in all directions. There was no sign of Kara Harris—as though she'd disappeared in a puff of smoke. A shiver slid down Thea's spine.

"What the hell is going on?" she muttered to herself. Fae and curses and the fate of the whole Highlands. How did she get mixed up in this? She closed her eyes and counted to ten before opening them again. When she did, she felt a little calmer. A little.

She'd been right all along. Irene *had* brought her here for a reason, and that reason somehow involved Logan's curse and averting a catastrophic war in the Highlands. The wind picked up, plucking at Thea's clothes with icy fingers. With a shudder, she pulled her cape tight about her and strode from the square.

Chapter 14

LOGAN FELT AS THOUGH he was walking through a dream. This town was his home, where he'd grown up, and yet it felt utterly alien. He could have been a ghost for all the attention its citizens paid him. In another life, when he'd been the laird, people would call out greetings and go out of their way to have a word or two. The shopkeepers would offer him samples of their wares and the innkeepers would invite him in for ale and food. Sometimes, if he had the time, he would indulge them and spend a pleasant afternoon visiting with the townsfolk. Now though, it was as though he didn't exist at all.

There had been rain here recently and the hard-packed streets were beginning to turn into a mess of churned-up mud, made worse by the tramp of horses' hooves and booted feet. Logan had never seen so many fighting men in one place. If he'd thought the muster at St. Berrick worrying, this was doubly so. Everywhere he looked there were signs of war. The blacksmiths, instead of advertising tools, horseshoes and bridles for sale, sported large barrels full of swords and spears. The taverns, instead of being full of farm laborers, were crammed to the rafters with fighting men, most of them mercenaries by the look of them, hard, scarred men who would kill for the highest bidder.

Logan scowled. Didn't Eoin realize how unreliable mercenaries were? What had possessed him to fill the town with such men? And where were the garrison patrols to keep the peace?

He gritted his teeth and tried to ignore the growing sense of unease that filled his belly. It wasn't his concern anymore. Eoin would lead the clan how he saw fit and Logan must be content with that. He was here for Thea, nothing else.

Finally he spotted his destination up ahead, a large tavern that in his younger days Logan and his brothers had liked to frequent. Annie and Gareth were known to brew the best ale in the area and the whisky wasn't too far behind.

Logan walked up to the large oaken door but hesitated before placing his hand on the smooth wood. Steeling himself, he pushed the door open and walked into the large common room. It was exactly as he remembered it. Clean rushes covered the floor and the oaken tables were scrubbed to a high shine. His eyes flickered to the mantelpiece. Sure enough, a large gouge in the wood above the fireplace was still there from where Camdan had once gotten into a fight with a Moroccan trader and had narrowly avoided the curved knife that had been flung at him. Over in the corner was the table where he and his brothers had liked to sit but now it was taken by three mercenaries dressed in black who were hunched over, talking in low voices.

Logan drew in a deep breath and walked over to the bar. A large man with a bald head and his left arm missing looked up from the pewter tankard he'd been polishing.

"Good day to ye, sir," he said in his booming voice. "What will it be? Food? Ale?"

Logan resisted the urge to grin. Ah, it was good to see Gareth again, even if his eyes showed no recognition as they gazed expectantly at Logan. Lord above, how many times had Gareth helped Logan home after he'd had too much to drink? How many times had he spun a yarn to his father when he'd come down here demanding to know why his sons hadn't turned up to training on time? But now he looked at Logan with a slightly puzzled expression, as though something about Logan tickled his memory but he couldn't quite place it.

"Aye. Both," Logan replied.

"If ye take a seat, my wife will bring ye food and drink."

Logan inclined his head. "My thanks."

He took a seat close to the door so he could see whoever came in. Annie appeared at the bottom of the stairs, had a quick conversation with her husband, before dunking a big tankard in the ale barrel and bringing it over to Logan's table. Annie hadn't changed much in the years since Logan had last laid eyes on her. Her hair was maybe a little grayer but her broad smile and rosy cheeks were the same. She turned that smile on Logan as she placed the mug of ale on his table.

"Ye look hungry, my dear," she said. "Would ye like some mutton?"

Logan watched her, taking in her familiar face and mannerisms. An unexpected pang of homesickness washed over him and for an instant he was taken with the overwhelming urge to tell her exactly who he was.

"Aye," he said. "My thanks."

Logan curled his fingers around his ale cup then leaned back in his seat to listen to the conversations going on around him. His father had taught him that taverns—and especially those frequented by fighting men—were an excellent place to gauge the mood of the populace and to pick up any bits of gossip and other information that might be going round. He hoped to pick up news of both Irene MacAskill and also the trouble with the MacKinnons.

A group of men dressed in the MacAuley plaid took up several tables nearby. From the colored sashes across their chests Logan knew they were members of the castle garrison but he didn't recognize any of them. By their glassy-eyed expressions it seemed they'd been in the tavern for some time. Two were engaged in a boisterous arm wrestling contest while the others spurred them on with shouts of encouragement.

A big man with a beard falling halfway down his chest slammed the arm of his smaller companion down on the table with a thud and then grinned round at his fellows.

"Ha! What did I tell ye? Our young Angus is all piss and wind! Ye'll have to do better than that, lad, when we come up against the MacKinnons."

The smaller man massaged his shoulder and scowled at the big man. "Nah. When we come up against the MacKinnons I'll have my claymore to ram up their arses."

Some of the other men laughed at this but the big man's scowl deepened. "Ye reckon it will be that easy? The MacKinnons have the best horse archers in the Highlands."

Logan turned his ale cup in his hands then cleared his throat and leaned forward. "Forgive my interruption," he said to the men. "But I couldnae help overhearing yer conversation. I'm new to these parts and I wish to avoid any strife. I was mighty surprised to learn of the troubles when I arrived in town. I was always led to believe the MacAuley laird was a peaceful man."

The big man raised an eyebrow and snorted. "Were ye? Then ye were misled, friend. The only thing our laird loves more than trouble is chasing women. If ye wish to avoid getting tangled up in it ye'd be advised to leave MacAuley lands as quickly as possible."

"Ranulf, ye damned fool," growled the youngster, Angus. "Ye shouldnae say such things about the laird. Ye dinna ken who might be listening."

"I'll say what I damned well like, lad," Ranulf growled back. "Now pass me the whisky before I decide ye need teaching some respect for yer elders."

Sensing the tension amongst the men, Logan said nothing more and leaned back into his chair, sipping at his ale. Before long Annie returned with a steaming plate of mutton in gravy which Logan tucked into. He was ravenous. He'd eaten nothing since the previous night, since the evening he'd spent with Thea.

Nay, he thought. *Dinna think about that.*

But thoughts of her came unbidden to his mind. Her warm lips on his. Her soft body beneath him, her scent filling his nostrils.

Enough, he told himself. *She isnae for ye. She will be leaving soon, the moment ye find that meddling old woman!*

Annie returned to collect his plate and Logan looked up at her. "I dinna suppose ye've heard of anyone by the name of Irene MacAskill have ye?"

Annie frowned. "I canna say as I have." Then she tapped a chin. "Wait a minute. One of the serving lasses mentioned buying a potion from someone wearing a MacAskill plaid. I only remember because we dinna normally see many of the MacAskills round here, it being such a small clan and all. Could that be her?"

Logan forced a smile onto his face. "Aye, mayhap it could. Do ye know where she might be found?"

"The market would be my guess. If she sells fertility potions and the like, mayhap she'll have a booth there."

Logan thanked Annie then pushed back his chair and made his way outside. So. Old Gregor had been right – Irene was here after all. Logan wasn't sure how to feel about that. He ought to be pleased but he wasn't. Instead of relief, all he felt as he strode towards the market square was a growing sense of despair.

THEA HALTED AND LOOKED around. She was in a narrow street lined with timber buildings that leaned together, making the street almost like a tunnel. She frowned.

None of this looked familiar. How the hell had she managed to get lost?

All I had to do was walk back down the main street! she thought. *How difficult was that?* But as she'd left the square she'd been so lost in thought about what Kara Harris had said to her that she hadn't been paying attention and before she knew it, had found herself in a maze of narrow side streets and alleyways that all looked the same.

Could this day get any worse? When she got back to the castle she was going to have a stiff drink or five!

She hurried down the street, head swiveling from side to side, searching for a landmark that looked familiar. There weren't any. The buildings in this part of the settlement were some of the most dilapidated she'd seen. The thatched roofs were half-rotten, the windows dirty, the doors ill-fitting.

She reached an intersection and paused. Four streets met, each winding off in a different direction but with little to distinguish one from the others. She placed her hands on her hips. Would it be too much to ask for this place to have street signs?

"Why the stern face, my lovely?" said a voice. "Mayhap I could put a smile on it."

She turned to find three men standing behind her. They were dressed in dirty plaid and from the stink of them, had been drinking for some time. They eyed her up and down, a hungry look in their eyes.

"Excuse me," she said, fighting down a rising fear. "I must be going."

She began to move away but the man who'd spoken, a large man with a scraggly beard, darted in front of her.

"Where are ye going, my lovely? When we've hardly become acquainted?" He stepped closer and the stink of his stale breath almost made her gag. "I'd like to get to know ye better. I havenae seen ye round here before. Are ye one of Marie's new girls?"

They think I'm a prostitute! Thea thought in horror.

"No, I'm not," Thea said, fighting to keep her voice steady. "There's been a misunderstanding. Now kindly step aside so I may be on my way."

The man's eyes narrowed. "Ye speak strangely, lass. A foreigner are ye?" he grinned. "I like the exotic ones. Ah, the things they can do." His companions laughed.

The man laid a dirty hand on Thea's arm and she reacted instinctively. She rammed her knee into his groin with all her strength then, as the man doubled over, she ran. But her feet slipped in the mud and before she could right herself someone grabbed her arm and slammed her back against the wall of a building. The bearded man's face was mottled with anger.

"I was gonna be gentle with ye but seeing as ye like to play rough that's what ye'll get," he growled.

"Go to hell," she growled back. She swung her fist at his face but he caught it easily and pinned her arms above her head.

"My, my, but ye are a wildcat. It's just as well I like them fiery." His leering grin made Thea's blood run cold.

Then a fist connected with the side of the man's head so hard that the crack echoed off the walls like a gunshot. The man staggered away, releasing Thea and slumping to his knees. Logan suddenly stepped in front of Thea. Her heart soared at the sight of him. She didn't think she'd ever been so grateful to see anyone in her life.

"Bastard!" the man spat blood into the dirt. "Ye will pay for that." He looked at his companions. "Dinna just stand there, ye damned fools! Get him!"

The two ruffians advanced on Logan. They were both burly men who looked used to fighting. Logan watched them calmly, hands held loosely at his sides. One of them swung a left-hook in at Logan's mid-riff but he side-stepped, grabbed the man's arm, and used the man's momentum to send him crashing into the wall. He slumped to the floor, out cold.

The remaining man pulled a knife and darted forward, the blade flashing. Logan caught the man's wrist then head-butted him in the face. Blood exploded from the man's shattered nose and as he staggered back clutching at his face Logan punched him square on the chin. His eyes rolled back and he collapsed unconscious in the dirt.

The man who'd grabbed Thea staggered to his feet. He looked from Logan to his downed comrades and back again. Then he turned tail and ran, disappearing down the street.

Logan turned to Thea, chest heaving. "Are ye all right? Did they hurt ye?"

In answer, Thea threw her arms around his neck and buried her face in his shoulder. His arms circled her, holding her close for a moment before pushing her to arms length. "Come on. This isnae a part of town to linger in."

They stepped over the unconscious men and into the maze of streets. Logan seemed to know exactly where he was going and he walked slightly behind her, his hand a reassuring presence against the small of her back. It didn't take long before they reached the main street and from there made their way up to the castle where Logan quickly escorted her up to her room.

Logan shut the door behind them then stood leaning against it.

Thea tried to gather her scattered thoughts. She had so much to tell him about meeting Kara Harris and what she'd said. But the incident with those men had left her shaky and disorientated and she couldn't seem to think straight.

"Logan. I need to tell you something."

LOGAN LAID HIS HEAD against the hard wood of the closed door and forced himself to breathe steadily. He took in the scent of the wood and the more subtle smells around him: the mud on his boots, the lavender of the soap Thea had used for washing. He breathed it all in deeply, trying to regain control of himself.

He'd never felt such a deep, visceral fear as he had when that scoundrel had pinned Thea against the wall. Not in battle, not when he'd made his bargain with the Fae. At the sight, a rage had come upon him the like of which he'd never known. He didn't remember much of the fight. It was hazy, like a dream. All he could remember was the burning, all-consuming need to protect her.

Now she was safe and the adrenaline was beginning to fade, leaving him a little shaky. And angry.

"Logan," Thea said. "I need to tell you something."

Sucking a deep breath through his nostrils, he looked at her. "What did ye think ye were doing?" he couldn't keep the growl out of his voice.

"Doing? What do you mean? I just went out to see if I could find anything about Irene."

"Against my orders!" he bellowed. "Do ye have any idea of the danger ye were in? Lord above, woman, do ye not have the sense of a bairn?"

Anger flashed in her eyes. "How dare you? You were the one who brought me here—against my will—and now you just expect me to follow your orders like a trained monkey!"

"Nay, lass, I expect ye to show a bit of common sense! This town is crawling with mercenaries – dangerous men who will take what they want without a thought to the consequences. What I do, I do to protect ye!"

"Protect me?" she cried. "Is that what you call handing me over to your cousin like I'm some piece of baggage? Is that what you call kidnapping me and bringing me to a strange town without so much as a by-your-leave?"

"Ye gave me yer word that ye wouldnae try to leave. Or is yer word worth nothing now?"

"I promised not to try and leave town!" she yelled. "I said nothing about staying in this god-damned room. What are you really afraid of, Logan? That I'll discover something all on my own? That I might find a way out of this damned mess?"

Logan crossed the space between them in two strides. He grabbed her shoulders. "Nay, lass, I'm afraid of losing ye! Dinna ye understand that yet? I see a future where ye aren't a part of my life and that terrifies me!"

She went very still and made no effort to break his grip. Something inside Logan snapped.

He grabbed her, slammed her against the wall, and kissed her.

Chapter 15

THEA DESPERATELY TRIED to hold onto her anger but the words Logan had spoken doused it like water poured on a fire. *I'm afraid of losing ye.* Oh Lord, did he feel the same way after all? Could there be a future for them?

She got her answer when he kissed her.

As his lips touched hers, desire lit every nerve in her body. All thoughts of Kara, of Irene, of the coming war, flew right out of her head as goose bumps erupted across her skin and the hairs on the back of her neck prickled. A hot ache lit between her legs, a deeply burning core of warmth that grew stronger with every moment that Logan's lips moved against hers.

She yanked him roughly against her and she could feel the hard bulge between his legs that told how much he wanted her. She returned his kiss with a hot, hungry passion, wanting to taste every inch of him, *feel* every inch of him. He placed his hands under her buttocks and lifted her effortlessly, hiking her dress up around her hips. Thea wrapped her legs around his waist, tangling her fingers in his thick hair and breathing deeply of the scent of him. It was intoxicating. *He* was intoxicating.

"If ye want this to stop, ye must say so now," he breathed against her ear, his breath hot on her neck. "I willnae be able to help myself if this goes any further."

In answer she turned her head, met his mouth with hers, kissing him with an almost savage need, a need which he answered. His teeth nipped her lip and then traveled down her neck, tracing a line of fire across her skin. Thea threw her head back and moaned, her fingers digging into the hard muscle of his shoulders.

He shifted his weight and his manhood pressed against her, igniting the core of warmth between her legs to an almost unbearable ache. She reached down and gently stroked it. With a moan, Logan's eyes slid closed and he shuddered slightly. Then he pulled away from the wall and carried her to the large bed where he laid her down. She grabbed his shirt, pulling him down after her, finding his mouth and slipping her tongue inside.

His hands were suddenly on her body, sweeping across her belly and up to her breast which he squeezed until her nipple came painfully erect against the rough fabric. Thea plucked at his shirt and Logan obliged by rising onto his knees and yanking the shirt over his head and tossing it away. He was left in only the kilted part of his plaid and his bare chest gleamed a dull bronze in the sunlight flooding in through the window, the dark tattoo swirling across his chest. Thea drank him in, her eyes roving over the deep contours of his chest and arms.

Logan flipped her onto her belly, his fingers working deftly at the laces that held her dress closed. It took only seconds for him to get them undone and to slip the dress from her shoulders and down her back. She shivered as she felt his lips against the skin of her back, traveling gently down the length of her spine and up again.

He tugged the dress over her hips and Thea lifted herself slightly to allow the fabric to slip from under her. She was naked now and the cool air sent a chill across her skin. But only for a moment. The next moment Logan rolled her onto her back and took her nipple in his mouth, sucking and massaging until heat seared across her skin once more.

His hands moved lower, his fingers trailing ever so lightly up her inner thigh to the sweet spot between her legs. Thea gasped, her back arching as he began to expertly massage her there, sending pulses of pure electricity through her body. It was too much. She couldn't stand it. She needed him within her.

"Logan," she whispered. "Logan."

When he looked up at her, a question in his eyes, she began tugging at his plaid. She wanted nothing between them. She wanted to feel every inch of his hot skin against hers. Sensing her need, Logan ripped off his kilt and tossed it onto the pile on the floor. Thea's eyes traveled to where his manhood jutted out, every swollen inch of it testifying to his desire for her. She reached out and gently stroked it, running her fingers along its hard length and then back again. Logan groaned, his breathing heavy.

His eyes met hers and the raw lust in them almost knocked Thea flat. There was a primal, almost animal need in Logan's gaze as he pushed her down and positioned himself above her, nudging her knees apart with his own. Logan gazed down at her, his dark eyes locked with hers. Then he shifted, pushing his weight forward and driving himself into her with a hard, deep, thrust.

Thea cried out as he filled her, sending a shudder of ecstasy through her body. Logan growled deep in his throat as he began to move, making love to her in deep, steady strokes. Thea kept time with him, moving her body to meet his thrusts, her hands feeling the muscles of his back bunch and relax as he moved.

Thea had never felt anything like this. Her body was on fire. Every sense was heightened: from the tingling of her skin, to the scent of Logan filling her nostrils. She felt as though she was drowning in this man.

Logan's movements became faster. He thrust into her harder and deeper, his breathing ragged, his breath hot on her neck. Thea began to come apart. The sensations rocketing through her were too much. She felt it begin to consume her body. It was as though she was carried up on a wave of ecstasy. Up, up, up, she went—and then she toppled over the edge into blinding oblivion.

She arched her back and shuddered out her climax. He growled by her ear and then jerked as he reached his own peak. For a moment that could have lasted a lifetime, Thea lost all sense of time and place. Then slowly, as the pleasure began to ebb, she came back to herself. Logan's weight was on top of her, pinning her to the bed, his skin hot where it touched hers. Then he lifted his head and looked at her.

The lust was fading from his eyes and they shone with something like joy. He smiled at her, and it was so full of delight that it made her heart ache.

"Thea," he whispered.

He levered himself up onto his hands so he could look down at her. His hair brushed Thea's face. Leaning down, he kissed her gently before rolling onto his back and pulling her into the crook of his arm. Thea pressed herself against his side, resting her head on his shoulder whilst his arm came around her protectively. He kissed the top of her head.

A deep, heavy lassitude filled Thea's limbs. She felt more sated, more content than she could ever remember. She fought to clear her thoughts. There was something she had to do. Something she had to tell Logan. Ah, yes, her meeting with Kara Harris and what the woman had told her.

But it could wait. Everything could wait. The only thing that mattered right now was the fact that Logan was hers. Oh, how she had longed for this! And when it came it had been every bit as good as she'd dreamed. Every bit of fear and doubt that had assailed her since they'd come to Dun Ringill melted away. Logan wanted her every bit as much as she wanted him.

And she wanted him again already. Leaning over, she kissed him. Logan responded and arousal roared to life in her again.

It was going to be a long night.

LOGAN HAD NO IDEA WHAT time it was. He guessed it was almost dawn but he couldn't sleep. Lord above, he didn't *want* to sleep. He wanted to watch Thea. Her breathing. Her hair as it spilled across the pillow. He'd lost count of how many times they'd made love last night but he'd soon discovered that her passion matched his own and he could hardly contain his desire for her. Even now, watching her sleep, he felt his desire rise once more. Oh, how he longed to kiss her awake and make love to her again, to feel her body against his, the hot touch of her skin and her little cries of pleasure. Heaven help him, he would never stop wanting this woman. Not for as long as they lived.

He reached out and gently brushed his thumb across her cheek. She shifted slightly but didn't wake. Logan's breath suddenly caught in his throat. He'd never seen anything so beautiful and an uncouth lout like him had no right to possess something so delicate.

"I love ye," he whispered.

He'd known it for a long time, deep down, but he'd been denying it, even to himself. Now, finally able to admit it, he felt something inside he'd not felt in a long, long time. Hope.

Thea was not afraid of his curse. Twice now she'd slept by his side all through the night and not come to harm. Logan didn't know what that meant. All he knew was that if Thea was willing to take the risk, then so was he. He would find a way to protect her, no matter what it took.

Yesterday he'd had no luck in finding Irene. Today would be different. Today he would go to Eoin, enlist his aid in turning out the garrison, and they would scour every inch of Dun Ringill until they found the old woman. Then Logan would make a new bargain: he would do anything Irene asked in order for Thea to be safe. Then he would beg Thea to stay with him—forever.

Hope. It was a rare thing, so alien to Logan, and yet it filled his heart with joy. He might have a future. A future with the woman he loved.

Careful not to wake Thea, he climbed out of bed and gathered his clothes from where they lay scattered on the floor. Dressing quickly, he strode to the door and left, making his way through the familiar corridors of the castle until he came to his cousin's rooms—rooms that had once been his. He knew it was early but Eoin had always been an early riser, getting up well before dawn.

Logan knocked on the door and waited. There was no answer. He knocked again.

"Eoin? It's Logan. I need to speak to ye."

Still no answer. He turned the door handle and opened it a crack. "Eoin, I'm coming in so make sure ye are decent."

Poking his head around the door, Logan spied the large sitting room that had once been his. The curtains had been thrown open and dawn light filled the room. There was no sign of Eoin and the door to the large bedroom stood open, showing that was empty too. Logan strode inside and looked around. The suite of rooms were immaculately tidy, as was Eoin's wont, and the bed had clearly not been slept in.

Logan frowned. Where would Eoin be at this hour? Then he had it. When Logan had been laird Eoin had often spent all night in his study, poring over the old documents and maps he was so fond of. It was during one of these all night study sessions that Eoin had found the key to enacting their bargain with the Fae.

Striding from the room, Logan made his way through the castle, avoiding the servants who were already up and about, and reached a quieter, less used part of the castle close to the servants' quarters. He halted outside a plain wooden door. Sure enough, candlelight spilled from under it.

"Eoin!" he called, knocking gently. "Are ye in there?" He pushed the door open and walked into Eoin's study.

He took a few steps and then halted in shock. Instead of a room crammed to the rafters with shelves of books and documents as it had been in Logan's day, the room had been cleared entirely and the flagstone floor was taken up by a ring of four rounded stones about the size of Logan's head that marked the cardinal points on a chalk circle that had been drawn on the floor. The sight of it set Logan's hair on end.

"Eoin?" he called. "Are ye in here?"

He moved to the edge of the chalk circle and halted. Something warned him not to cross its threshold. Soft laughter echoed around him and suddenly the room changed, his surroundings melting away like candle wax.

Logan found himself sitting at a small square table. Someone was seated opposite him but a hood covered the face. Then a voice spoke.

"Do ye really think ye can cheat me?"

The figure lifted the hood and Logan's heart skipped a beat when he recognized the Fae with whom he'd made his bargain. The wizened old man was wearing the MacAuley plaid and had a copper torc around his neck.

Fear surged in Logan's veins. "What is going on here? Where am I?"

The old man waved a hand. "That doesnae matter. What matters is what ye will do next. I ask again: did ye really think ye could cheat me?"

"Cheat ye?" Logan replied. "I have done my best to abide by our bargain! It is yer kind who willnae stop meddling in my life!"

The old man shrugged. "It is in our nature. Just as we always call in our debts."

He vanished and Logan saw that there was a bed at the far end of the room. Pushing back his chair he approached the bed. Anna was lying in it, her skin deathly white, a thin sheen of sweat on her brow. Rhodry and Ailsa sat by their child's bed. Rhodry's face was ashen and Ailsa was gently sobbing into her hands.

Then the scene shifted and Logan found himself digging a hole in the ground. It was already waist-deep but Logan needed to make it deeper. He drove the shovel into the soft brown earth and dug until his shoulders burned. He didn't want to look at the shroud-wrapped figure lying by the graveside but his eyes were drawn to it nonetheless. The soft muslin that wrapped her wasn't thick enough to obscure her face and Logan stared in horror at Thea's closed eyelids and pallid skin. His punishment was only fitting: condemned to dig the grave of the woman he loved.

The soft laughter came again and Logan found himself seated back at the table with the old man.

Logan lunged across the table and grabbed him by the throat. "If ye hurt her I will kill ye!"

A force slammed into him, pinning him against the chair. Something dangerous flashed in the Fae's black eyes and a slow smile spread across his face. "How touching. And how naïve to think ye can harm me."

"What do ye want?" Logan growled. He strained to move but the invisible force held him pinned. "Why are ye here?"

"I have always been here," the old man replied. "In the background, weaving my webs. I am patient and it has taken many years for my plans to ripen. But now that ripening is here and ye willnae be allowed to disrupt them, Logan MacAuley. Irene and her protégé were foolish to think they could ever find a champion who could stop me. Ah, they had such hopes for ye. But ye stepped into my trap as blindly as a babe and gave me the means I needed to achieve my ends."

"What are ye talking about? What plans?"

He leaned forward, grinning malevolently. "Chaos, of course. Bloodshed. The destruction of the balance. Soon the MacAuleys will ride against the MacKinnons and the whole Highlands will be engulfed in a war that will drench the pages of history in blood. Ah! Glorious anarchy!"

Cold fear drenched Logan at the creature's words. "What has the conflict with the MacKinnons got to do with ye?"

His grin widened. "Everything. Ye can come out now!" he called behind him. "Yer cousin is suitably subdued."

Eoin stepped into the room. Another seat appeared at the table and he sat, smiling at Logan.

"My, my, ye look surprised, cousin."

"What, by all that's holy, is going on here, Eoin?" Logan growled. "Explain yerself!"

Eoin crossed his arms over his chest and leaned back in his chair. "There ye go again. Ordering me around. Ye canna help yerself, can ye? But ye aren't the laird here anymore, Logan. I am."

Logan stared at his cousin. There was a smirk on his face and a kind of malevolent glee Logan had never seen before.

"Aye, ye are," he agreed. "Because of the bargain I made with this creature." He looked into his cousin's eyes. "A bargain suggested by ye. Lord help me, Eoin, please tell me I'm wrong. Please tell me ye aren't in league with this creature."

Eoin smiled. Then he reached into a knapsack he had hanging from one shoulder and pulled out an object made from iron. Logan's skin prickled at the sight of it. He knew a branding iron when he saw one. Eoin laid it on the table between them.

"Do ye recognize this?" he asked softly.

The branding iron was shaped into an elegant swirling design of interlocking coils. When heated and pressed against skin it would leave a mark identical to one that Logan knew only too well.

The tattoo across his chest suddenly flared with pain causing him to gasp.

"Ah, ye do recognize it, I see," Eoin said. "I would be surprised if ye didnae, seeing as this was once pressed into yer flesh to seal yer bargain with the Fae. Look closer, Logan. What else do ye see?"

A lock of hair was wrapped around one of the coils. With cold certainty Logan knew it was one of his.

"Damn ye, Eoin," he breathed as everything suddenly became clear. "It was ye. Ye who suggested the bargain with the Fae, ye who arranged it. Ye were in league with the creature all along!"

Eoin clapped sardonically. "Finally! I thought ye were never going to figure it out!"

"Why?" Logan grated. "Why would ye do such a thing, Eoin? Why would ye betray me like this?"

"Why?" Eoin spat, his face suddenly contorting with anger. "Why, ye arrogant sack of horse-shit? For my rightful place, that's why! Ye think I was happy to play second fiddle to yer damn brothers all those years? Ye think I was content with the scraps ye left me? Me, Eoin MacAuley, who is far cleverer than any of ye! I would never get what was rightfully mine whilst ye and yer brothers were around."

"So ye sold yer soul," Logan said. "And betrayed yer clan."

"Betrayed my clan? Hardly! I *saved* the clan! Who else came up with a way to defeat the raiders? Ye? Camdan? Finlay? Nay, it was I who found the means to defeat them!"

"And promised to give this creature war and chaos in return for his help betraying yer kin. Ye are a liar and a coward, Eoin MacAuley, and ye will bring ruin to our people. I will kill ye for this."

Quick as a flash Eoin drew a long dagger from his belt. "Kill me, will ye? Nay, cousin, it will be the other way around." He lunged at Logan but a force suddenly slammed him back into his seat.

"How dare ye?" the Fae said softly. "Do ye not remember the terms of our bargain, Eoin MacAuley? Yer cousin's life is mine to do with as I wish. Ye willnae touch him."

"Ye will let him live?" Eoin spat. "Then ye are a fool! Ye should have killed him when ye first had the chance!"

"Killing is easy, human. I prefer despair. It is much more potent. When I am finished Logan MacAuley will be set free to wander the world alone, watching as everything he once loved turns to ashes. That is what it means to truly take a life."

"Aye," Eoin breathed, looking at Logan thoughtfully. "Mayhap ye are right. I will take great delight in watching that."

"But until then he canna be allowed to interfere with our plans," said the old man. "Good night, Logan MacAuley."

The force holding Logan to the chair suddenly intensified. Then a blow of power hit him in the side of the head with all the force of an upper-cut. Darkness descended and Logan knew no more.

Chapter 16

THEA WOKE SLOWLY, ROUSING bit by bit from a deep and dreamless sleep. She lay still, eyes closed, savoring the moment. After the small cot in Logan's cottage the huge bed felt luxurious in the extreme and the feather pillows finished it off perfectly.

But this wasn't why she'd slept so well. She and Logan had explored every inch of each other last night and she guessed it was almost dawn when they'd finally been sated and had fallen into exhausted slumber. Now her limbs felt a little achy but she'd take that any day as payment for the night she'd spent with Logan.

Thea stretched her arms over her head and opened her eyes. Sunlight was pouring in through the window and the sounds of a waking castle came from the courtyard below. She rolled towards Logan only to find his side of the bed empty. Sitting up, she looked around but he wasn't in the room. His clothes were gone from the floor.

Thea shrugged it off. He was probably off getting some breakfast or seeing to Stepper. She felt a little pang of disappointment that he wasn't here when she awoke but she knew Logan was an early riser and probably wouldn't have wanted to wake her.

She swung her legs over the edge of the bed and then yanked off a sheet to wrap around her naked body. Like this she crossed to the dresser where there was a bowl and a pitcher of water and began washing. The water was freezing but it helped to clear away the last vestiges of sleep. When she was done, she dried herself with the sheet and dressed. She found herself humming as she sat at the dressing table to brush her hair. Glancing in the mirror she saw that there was a healthy pink blush to her cheeks. She was looking forward to starting the day.

The door opened and Thea turned around. "I hope you've been to fetch some breakfast—"

She trailed off as she saw it wasn't Logan standing in the doorway. It was Eoin. His expression was one of sadness.

"What is it?" Thea asked, standing so suddenly her chair tipped over. "What's happened? Where's Logan?"

Eoin closed the door behind him and stepped into the room. He held something out to her. "He's gone, Thea. He left at first light this morning. He asked me to give ye this."

Thea stared at him in uncomprehending silence. She blinked. Gone? Left? What the hell was he talking about?

"Here, take it," Eoin said.

She glanced at the object in his hand. It was a letter, neatly folded and sealed with a blob of wax. Thea's arm trembled slightly as she took it.

Eoin smiled sadly. "He asked me to take care of ye and I will. A MacAuley always keeps his promises."

With that Eoin left the room. Thea stared at the closed door for a long moment then looked down at the letter in her hand. Her brain didn't seem to be working properly. Logan had left her? How ridiculous! Of course he hadn't!

She swallowed thickly and then broke the wax seal and unrolled the parchment.

We could never be together safely. I willnae put ye at risk. Eoin will take care of ye now. Forgive me. Logan.

It was Logan's writing—she'd seen it often enough in the ledgers he kept for the smithy. Thea stared at it, unable to believe what she was seeing. She read it a second time. And then again. By the fourth time her heart was hammering in her chest and she felt tears gathering in her eyes. She blinked them away mercilessly. Then she ran to the door, yanked it open, pelted along the corridor, down the steps and out the main doors of the castle. She didn't slow until she reached the stables.

One of the stable hands looked up in alarm as she skidded to a halt in front of him. "Can I help ye, my lady?"

"Yes, you have a horse in your care called Stepper. I'd like to see her please."

The stable hand looked puzzled. "I dinna know any horse by that name."

"A white mare, tall, fine-looking. Oh, never mind." She pushed past him into the stable, hurrying down the aisle until she reached Stepper's stall.

It was empty.

She looked around frantically, examining every horse whilst the stable hand watched her, nonplussed. She reached the end and doubled back, checking them all a second time. It did no good. Stepper was gone.

"If ye wish to go riding, I could have one of the laird's ponies saddled, my lady," the stable hand said.

She glanced at him. "What? Oh. No. Thanks."

She staggered out into the courtyard and leaned on the stable wall as the world tilted crazily around her. Stepper was gone. Logan was gone.

No. No, no, no. This could not be happening!

"My lady? Thea? Are ye well?"

She looked up to see Rian standing in front of her, a worried expression on the young maid's face. "I...um...I don't feel so good."

"Come," Rian said kindly. "I'll help ye back to yer room."

Thea nodded dumbly as Rian took her by the arm and guided her back through the corridors of the castle and to her room. Once inside Thea couldn't help glancing at the rumpled bed sheets, sheets that Logan had slept on only a few hours ago.

He couldn't be gone. He wouldn't do that to her. He wouldn't abandon her. Would he?

Rian began straightening the bed covers. "Is the room to yer satisfaction, my lady? If not, I can move ye to one of the other guest chambers, although this one does have a lovely view of the valley."

"What? Um, no. I mean, yes, the room's lovely, thanks. And please don't call me 'my lady.'"

Rian nodded. "Very well. Thea. Have ye come a long way to visit with the laird? I dinna recognize yer accent."

A long way? Thea thought. *You have no idea.*

"Yes," she replied. "A long way."

Rian came over and patted her hand. "It must be very daunting being so far away from home but I'm sure yer long trip will be worth it. The laird seems quite taken with ye. I'm sure things will work out well between ye."

Thea blinked at her. What did she mean? Her brain was too foggy to make sense of it. "Yes," she muttered. "I'm sure."

Rian knelt by the fireplace and began laying a fire. Thea gazed out of the window. On the horizon she spotted a lone horseman making his way up the road out of the valley. Was it Logan? Was he standing there looking back at her? She shook her head. *Don't be idiotic,* she told herself. *That's not Logan. He'll be long gone by now and if he's given you a second thought, it's probably only to think how relieved he is to be rid of you.*

Her heart twisted and a shot of anguish went through her. She leaned on the window sill, fighting back a sob that threatened to escape her. Sucking a deep breath through her nose, she steeled herself.

Information. She needed as much as she could get if she was to figure out exactly what the hell was happening to her.

She turned to Rian. "Do you know the laird well?"

The woman looked up from where she was laying sticks in the fireplace. "Aye. My family has served the laird's family for generations. I've been working in the castle since I was sixteen. My ma is a cook and my da the stable master."

"So you were here when the previous laird was around?" Thea asked. "What can you tell me about him?"

Rian's brow furrowed and her eyes took on a faraway look as though searching for a memory she couldn't quite grasp. "I...I dinna remember," she said at last. "There was...someone...before Laird Eoin, I'm sure, but I canna picture their face."

Only Eoin seemed to know who Logan really was. Why? There were so many questions here, questions she had to find the answers to.

"You know, I'm feeling a little restless," she said to Rian. "I'd like to stretch my legs and maybe get to know this place a bit."

And look for Logan, she thought. *He can't have just left me here. He can't.*

Rian grinned. "Then how about I show you around the castle? I know it like the back of my hand as my ma likes to say. We'll soon have ye feeling right at home!"

Thea smiled. "Thanks. I think that's exactly what I need."

Rian stood, wiping her hands on a cloth. "This way then, my lady, um, Thea I mean."

Thea followed Rian out of the room and down the corridor. She soon realized how fortunate she was in having Rian as her maid. She really did know the castle like the back of her hand and Thea would no doubt have been utterly lost within minutes without Rian to guide her.

First, they went to the Great Hall where Malcolm and Margaret greeted Thea warmly. She asked if either of them had seen Logan but they both shook their heads and said they hadn't seen 'her companion' since the day before. Despite serving Logan when he'd been laird, neither of them remembered who he was.

Next they visited the kitchen where Thea met Rian's mother, Magda, and the stables where her father Baldwin, ruled. Everywhere they went they had to step around piles of weapons and supplies and weave their way through groups of armed men. The castle was bursting with warriors with more arriving by the hour.

"Dinna worry, my lady," Rian said as they stood on the steps and watched a group of ten mounted men ride through the gates. "It isnae usually like this. They're here for the muster and when this business with the MacKinnons is over, they'll soon go back to their homes and the castle can get back to normal. There's going to be a battle. The word is that the day after tomorrow the laird will ride out against the Laird MacKinnon. He's been mustering at Drover's Pass for weeks. Men must have their wars, regardless of whether they make us women widows. Damned fools the lot of them if ye ask me."

Thea muttered in agreement, watching the newcomers as they swung down from their horses and led them towards the stable. The day after tomorrow. That didn't leave much time for Thea to figure all this out.

"Come, we'll go through the back entrance," Rian said. "And avoid all this rabble."

She led Thea along a narrow path through rose bushes that hugged the base of the castle and to a small door that was used by the serving staff. Inside the passages were narrower and the decor plainer but somebody had gone to the trouble of hanging bunches of dried flowers from the rafters so their delicious scent wafted through the corridors. They made their way up a winding staircase heading back to Thea's room. Halfway up they passed a small half-landing which housed a large door with a thick padlock.

"What's through there?" Thea asked.

A strange look crossed Rian's face. "The laird's private study," she replied. "We dinna go in there. It's out of bounds."

Rian began climbing again. Thea paused for a moment, looking at the door. Then, on impulse, she laid her palm flat against its surface. The wood was smooth and oddly warm. A tingle flared along Thea's palm and an image suddenly flared in her mind. A wind-lashed sea and tall stones rising into the night. Something moving through those stones, searching for her... Thea gasped and snatched her hand away. She hurried after Rian.

She was glad to reach the door of her room. She was just about to follow Rian inside when a voice called behind her.

"Ah! Lady Thea!"

She turned to see Laird Eoin approaching. His corn-yellow hair was tied at his neck by a leather band and he wore riding gear as though he was just about to go out. Thea clasped her hands and turned to face him, forcing a smile onto her face.

"Laird MacAuley."

He waved a hand. "Pah! Call me Eoin. I hope ye are feeling better."

Better? Thea thought. *What a stupid thing to say. How can I feel better knowing your cousin has left me?*

But all she said was, "Yes. Thank you. Rian has been most helpful."

"I should hope she has!" Eoin laughed. He stepped closer, closer than Thea would have liked but the wall was behind her and she couldn't back away. His eyes were a pale icy blue as they looked her over. "Ye will join me for dinner tonight. As my honored guest."

Thea stifled a groan. Dinner? That was the last thing she wanted! All she wanted to do was curl up on her bed and cry. But she remembered Kara Harris's warning. There was a war coming and Thea had to figure out how to stop it if she was to ever have a chance of going home. Dinner with Eoin might just provide the opportunity for some information gathering.

Forcing a smile, she inclined her head. "Dinner. Yes. Great."

He grinned then reached out and curled a strand of her hair around his finger. "Until tonight then."

Chapter 17

THEA FELT ABOUT AS uncomfortable as she could ever remember. The dress she was wearing—sent to her room as a gift from the laird—was so tight around the bodice she could barely breathe and the neckline so low she'd be afraid of leaning forward in case she spilled out the front. Never had she appreciated the simple dresses Ailsa had leant her, nor had she ever missed her friend as much. She wondered how she and Rhodry were faring and whether Anna had recovered yet.

She pushed away a sudden pang of longing and concentrated on putting one foot in front of the other. She was following Rian through the castle on her way to meet with the laird. She'd been a little surprised when, instead of leading Thea downstairs to the Great Hall, Rian had turned left up a set of winding steps to a level above, which was even more lavishly furnished than the guest quarters below. Rian stopped at a door and knocked.

"Come!" came the laird's voice from within.

Rian smiled at Thea. "Enjoy yer dinner, my lady. I'll come to help ye to bed a little later."

Thea swallowed thickly, set her hand to the door, and pushed it open. Eoin was seated at a rectangular table with a goblet in his hand, one leg thrown over the arm of his chair. He stood when he saw Thea, putting his goblet down on the table. His eyes swept over her, lingering on her cleavage longer than was necessary.

"Lady Thea," he breathed. "Ye look...beautiful."

Thea didn't reply. She realized there was nobody else in the room and the table was set with only two places. So, she was to dine with Eoin alone. Great.

Eoin gestured to a chair opposite his. "Sit, please."

Thea slid into the chair. Eoin poured her a goblet of wine before resuming his seat. He eyed her in silence for a moment.

"So, how do ye find Dun Ringill?" he asked at last.

"Big," she replied honestly. "And a little overwhelming."

He barked a laugh at that. "Aye, I imagine it is. Still, ye will soon feel right at home I'm sure."

"I'm sure." She cleared her throat. "What exactly did Logan say to you when he gave you that letter?"

Eoin put down his wine glass and sighed. "Thea, ye must waste no more thought on my cousin. He is gone, that's all there is to it. Ye know he's cursed. He's done ye a favor by leaving."

Really? Thea thought. *Then why does it feel like my heart's been torn out?*

"But why now?" she persisted. "You know what a stickler for honor Logan is. Why would he leave without saying goodbye? It makes no sense. It's almost as if something happened to make him leave so suddenly."

"Enough!" Eoin said sharply, annoyance flashing in his eyes. "Will ye ruin our meal with talk of my damned cousin?"

Thea was saved from answering by a polite knock on the door and then several servants entering bearing platters of food. Thea watched as they laid out the meal, feeling Eoin's eyes on her the whole time. To cover her discomfort, she took a long gulp of wine and found it surprisingly good.

"I dinna stand on ceremony," Eoin said when the servants had left. "Please, eat."

He followed his own advice and began tucking into the meal. Thea looked down at her plate. It was piled high with roast grouse in some sort of sauce and glazed vegetables. She found she had little appetite but she forced herself to place some in her mouth and chew mechanically.

While they ate, Eoin spoke. He regaled her with tales of his hunting prowess and how he had beaten Laird Campbell in a wrestling match that spring. Thea listened closely, hoping that she might learn something useful, but when she tried to steer conversation towards the coming clash with the MacKinnons, he gave only vague answers. Of Logan, he said not a word.

Thea said, "I was surprised when you recognized Logan, seeing as nobody else remembers that he used to be the laird."

Her words had the desired effect. Eoin paled, his grip tightening on his goblet and a wary, calculating look came into his eyes. "How much did he tell ye?"

Thea shrugged. "He told me about his bargain with the Fae and the curse that followed. He didn't tell me how it all came about though. Do you know?"

He stared at her for a long moment. "That is between myself and my cousin," he said at last. He rubbed his chin and the gaze he fixed on her was sharp. "I'm more interested in ye, Thea Thomas. Who are ye? Where do ye come from?"

"I'm just a traveler."

"Aye, but a traveler from where? And why did this Irene woman bring ye here?"

Thea felt heat rising in her cheeks. She was suddenly very, very sure that she didn't want Eoin to know about her being a time-traveler. There was something hungry, almost predatory in his gaze. She stood abruptly.

"I...I'm very tired," she said. "I think I'll retire for the night."

It was a lame excuse and she half expected Eoin to insist she stay and answer his questions. She was surprised then when he nodded.

"Aye. It has been a tiring day for ye no doubt. Would ye like to call Rian to escort ye back to yer room?"

"No," Thea said quickly. "I can find my own way. Thanks for dinner. Good night."

Eoin bowed. "Good night, my lady."

Thea turned and scurried from the room. Once outside she didn't return to her bed chamber. Instead she hurried along the corridor then ducked around the first corner, pressing herself against the cold stone wall. She waited, keeping very still and very silent. The minutes passed and just when she was about to give it up and return to her room she heard Eoin's door creak open and then the sound of receding footsteps. She peeked around the corner to see Eoin striding quickly away down the corridor. With a quick glance around to make sure nobody was watching, Thea followed.

If there was one thing Thea was good at, it was sneaking. As a wildlife photographer, she'd quickly learned how to move without being seen or heard. So Thea padded quickly along behind Eoin, staying far enough back that he wouldn't hear her soft footfalls but close enough that she didn't lose sight of him. To her surprise, he didn't enter the main part of the castle but instead moved into the quieter, less-used servants' corridors at the back.

Here the passages were dimly lit, with only the occasional torch fixed to the wall. This meant there were large patches of shadow that Thea had to creep through. Eoin reached a spiraling stairwell and started to climb. After a moment she heard the rattle of a lock and the creaking of a door. Thea recognized the stairwell as the one she and Rian had used earlier that day.

She paused at the bottom, biting her lip. There was not a soul in sight. It must be getting late and the serving staff were most likely already in their beds. Still Thea hesitated. It was all very well following the laird in the corridors where she could claim she got lost but how would she explain creeping up these stairs? But she had no choice. She was sure Eoin had something to do with Logan leaving so suddenly and this might be her only chance to discover what that was. Taking a deep, slow breath, she set her foot on the first step and moved cautiously upwards.

Before long she spotted the half-landing above her that housed the door to Eoin's private study. This time the padlock that had held the door was gone and the door itself stood slightly ajar as though Eoin had forgotten to close it properly in his haste. Heart thumping, Thea stepped closer. From somewhere within she heard the sound of voices. One was Eoin's but she didn't recognize the other and they were too quiet for her to make out the words. Who was he talking to in there?

The gap in the door was too narrow for her to squeeze through but she might be able to spy through the crack. Careful to make no sound, Thea pressed her eye to the gap and peered into the room beyond. The room's walls and floor were unworked stone and it was bare of furniture. The only decoration was a chalk circle scrawled on the flagstones with four rounded stones marking the cardinal points.

What the hell? Thea thought. *What is this?*

And yet this was not the strangest sight.

A small, square table sat in the center of the chalk circle and an old man was seated at it. He was small, shorter than Thea herself, and seemed old beyond measure. His skin was brown and wrinkled like boiled leather and there was not a single hair on the smooth scalp. The eyes that looked out of his weathered face were as black as onyx. Something about him put Thea in mind of Irene MacAskill but where Irene radiated a kind of grandmotherly warmth, all that shone from this man's eyes was malevolence. A shiver walked down Thea's spine. Who was this man?

Eoin, who was standing just outside the circle of stones, crossed the threshold and took a seat at the table opposite the old man. He had something in his hands which he was turning over and over. It looked like a branding iron with hair tied around it. The design of the brand was a series of interlocking coils that looked exactly like... Thea shivered.

It was the same design as Logan's tattoo.

"Ye summon me for this?" the old man growled at him. "To ask me to enchant some lass into yer bed? Ye overstep yerself, mortal!"

Eoin glared. "She is my cousin's woman. They are besotted with each other. What better revenge than to take the woman he loves? To have him watch as she falls in love with me instead?"

The old man smiled. "Ye have a cruel streak in ye worthy of any Fae, Eoin MacAuley. But the petty carnal desires of humans have no interest for me. If ye wish to bed some lass, ye will have to win her yerself."

"Have ye not been listening? This is not just 'some lass'. She's different. She knows things. She knows about Logan's curse and yet is unaffected by it. And I think she suspects my part in it."

At this the man's eyes flashed. "Does she now?" He scratched his chin. "Nay, it isnae possible. My enchantment holds. No highlander may remain near the MacAuley brothers and remain unaffected."

"She's no highlander," Eoin replied. "Irene MacAskill brought her here."

At that the man's head came up and a look of pure fury crossed his face. "Irene MacAskill? That meddling old harridan?" The anger faded and he looked suddenly thoughtful. "Then ye may be right. Perhaps there is more to this lass. Irene has the power of time and I'm willing to wager the lass does too."

Eoin's eyes widened. "Then I claim her. She will be mine. She will be my wife and give me this 'power of time'. I claim it as my right."

"Yer right?" the old man said, his eyes flashing. "Careful, mortal. We have nay bargain concerning the lass."

"Then I'll make a new bargain. Give her to me and I'll do yer bidding."

The old man laughed harshly. "What could ye possibly offer me that would be worth her?"

"Ye said yerself she may hold the power of time. Think of what we could achieve with her under our control."

The old man looked thoughtful. "Aye. Maybe ye are right. Very well. If ye win the battle with the MacKinnons, I will give the lass to ye. Give me what I want: war, chaos, glorious misery, and I will grant yer paltry desire."

"I want her now," Eoin growled. "I know how ye will twist and turn and try to get out of any bargain we make. Just like ye did with Logan, Camdan and Finlay. They were supposed to die! Instead they are still out there, living and breathing. I will not have ye reneging on this bargain!"

The old man's eyes blazed. "I am Fae!" he bellowed and a ripple of power rolled through the cavern, charging it with electricity. "And we fulfill our bargains how we see fit! I never promised to kill yer cousins for ye! I promised to take their lives—and take them I did. In return ye were to bring war and death to the Highlands—something ye are yet to fulfill—so dinna dare speak to me of reneging on a bargain!"

Eoin gritted his teeth and Thea saw a vein throbbing in his temple. He was clearly furious but also afraid of this man. After a moment he nodded. "I will fulfill my part of the bargain when I take the MacKinnon's head. Ye will have the strife ye so crave and I will have power over all the Highlands." He fixed the old man with a stare. "And I will have Thea Thomas as my wife."

Thea's blood ran cold and her heart began to thump in her chest. *No you won't, you lying, cheating bastard*, she thought. *Never. I'd die first.*

She turned on her heel and quietly crept away. Only when she'd gone far enough that Eoin wouldn't hear her footsteps did she give into her panic and run. She pelted through the darkened passages, her pulse pounding in her ears. She had to get out. She had to find Logan and warn him. Somehow they had to stop Eoin from waging his war.

She took the steps two at a time. She remembered that a door lay at the bottom. She'd go from there to the stables, beg or steal a horse, and then make a run for it.

She almost sobbed in relief when she reached the door. She lost precious seconds trying to throw back the heavy bolt and she kept glancing up, expecting at any minute to hear heavy footsteps descending. At last the bolt shot home and Thea pushed open the door, tumbling out into the blessedly cool air of the bailey.

Pausing for only a heartbeat to orient herself, she set off, hugging the base of the castle to make it harder for any guards on the battlements to spot her. Reaching the corner of the castle, she grabbed the hem of her dress so it wouldn't trip her then sprinted across the bailey.

She reached the stable block without incident and leaned against the rough wooden wall, grateful for the shadows that hid her from prying eyes. The door was secured with a wooden cross-beam but it was easy enough to lift out of its metal brackets. Thea pushed open the door and stole inside. The musty smell of horses assailed her and the soft sigh of their breathing and the occasional stamp of a hoof was the only sound.

Thea didn't have time to be picky so she crossed to the first stall where a brown gelding was drowsing with his head hanging down. He awoke at Thea's approach and stepped forward eagerly, ears swiveling in Thea's direction. He wasn't too big, not as tall as Stepper, for which Thea was grateful.

"How about we go for a little ride?" she whispered to the horse, rubbing the velvety skin of his nose.

"I would advise against it," said a voice behind her. "It's a cold night and there are brigands about."

Thea whirled. Eoin MacAuley was standing in the doorway, his arms crossed and a small smile on his face.

Thea backed away. "Stay away from me."

"Is that any way to treat someone who's offered ye sanctuary?"

"Sanctuary?" Thea spat. "You never intended to help me! You just wanted to get rid of Logan in case he upset your plans."

Eoin raised an eyebrow. "My, but ye are a fiery one. I can see why he likes ye. Now come inside and we will see if we canna sort out this little misunderstanding." He took a step towards her. Thea backed away.

"I'm not going anywhere with you. I'm leaving. Now stand aside and let me go." She was grateful that her voice came out steady.

"Nay possible I'm afraid. I know ye were listening at the door and heard my plans. It would be very stupid of me to let ye go wandering with such knowledge wouldnae it? And it would be even more stupid of me to allow someone with the power of time to escape me, dinna ye think? Imagine what we could do together! Imagine where we could go!"

Thea's heart was thumping so hard she feared it might crack her ribs. "Logan will never let you get away with this," she said. "He'll come for me."

Eoin barked a sharp, savage laugh. "Logan? It was Logan who brought ye to me in the first place! My cousin may have many fine qualities but the judgment of character isnae one of them. He's always been a trusting fool. He handed me the lairdship and now he brings me my wife! Oh, he'll not be coming for ye, lass."

"I'll never be your wife. "I'll never marry you."

Eoin sauntered closer. "Oh, ye will. Ye see, I've made a new bargain and ye are the prize. Once the battle is over ye will marry me willingly. Ye will be devoted to me and willnae even remember who Logan is. Until then, ye willnae be going anywhere."

Chapter 18

"THERE! YE LOOK BEAUTIFUL, my lady!" Rian said, standing behind Thea as she examined herself in the mirror.

Thea sighed and turned to look out of the window. Men were clustered in ranks in the bailey below, and in the lower part of the town too. The MacAuley army, ready to march out and meet the MacKinnon. And after that if Eoin had his way...

No! Don't think about it! she told herself savagely. *You'll find a way out of this. You will.*

Rian peered over her shoulder at the men below. "My, dinna they look grand?" she said, a note of pride in her voice. "My Ma always said the MacAuley clan were the pride of the Highlands. Now I see what she meant."

But most of those aren't MacAuley men, Thea thought. *Most are mercenaries bought by Eoin. And they don't look grand to me. They look like men ready for violence.*

Rian gave Thea an encouraging smile. "Dinna worry, my lady. Ye and Laird Eoin willnae be anywhere near the fighting. Ye'll be in no danger. Then afterwards we'll be having a double celebration—victory in war and the marriage of our laird!"

Thea bit her lip to keep from screaming. Rian's eyes were bright, her cheeks rosy. She looked the picture of exuberance—but there was something wrong with her, just as there was something wrong with everyone in this damned place.

Meeting the woman's gaze directly and pronouncing each word clearly Thea said, "Rian, for the hundredth time, I do not want to marry Laird Eoin. I never agreed to it. He is forcing me into this and keeping me here against my will. I'm a prisoner."

A glazed look came into Rian's eyes. For a moment she looked puzzled but then her smile returned. "We'll have games and dancing out on the green. It will be a grand day."

Thea threw up her hands in exasperation. It was the same no matter who she spoke to. After her altercation with Eoin last night she'd been escorted back to her chamber and woke with a raging headache and an urgent desire to get as far away from this place as possible. But everyone she'd met had quietly stopped her from leaving. The stableman had laughed gently when she asked him for a horse and told her that Laird Eoin had forbidden her from riding. The guards on the gate had escorted her back into the castle with friendly smiles, and when she'd told them she was a prisoner, they had merely nodded and wished her well for her big day. It was like they couldn't hear her. Whatever she told them about Eoin seemed to bounce off them, leaving no impact at all.

It was the same thing that happened whenever she'd asked Ailsa and Rhodry about the old Laird MacAuley. They'd get that same glazed look as though trying to piece together thoughts that wouldn't come. It was the work of

Logan's curse and she was now sure that everyone in Dun Ringill was under the same kind of enchantment, Fae magic making them believe whatever Eoin wanted them to believe.

Her stomach tightened with anger at the thought of that man. Oh how she'd love to slap his grinning face! How she'd love to knee him right where it hurt and see him crumple to the ground! But even that small satisfaction wouldn't be enough. The scale of the evil that Eoin had wrought was staggering. He'd betrayed his cousins, made pacts with an evil Fae, and led his clan to war. And for what? For power. He had to be stopped.

"Are ye ready, my lady?" Rian asked.

Thea drew a deep breath and nodded. She followed Rian down to the bailey. A wall of noise hit her as she stepped outside. Men shouting orders, dogs barking, horses snorting. Thea halted at the top of the steps. The sea of people in front of her seemed endless. Weapons glinted in the morning sunlight.

And they will all die unless I stop this, she thought.

"Ah! There ye are, my dear!" Eoin swept up to her.

He looked resplendent in his MacAuley plaid and long crimson cloak. His golden hair shone in the light, his handsome face lit with a smile. He was every bit the impressive Highland warrior and she could well understand why Rian stared up at him with longing in her eyes. But Thea knew the outward beauty hid an inner corruption. Eoin MacAuley was not the man everyone thought he was.

She smiled sweetly at him. "Touch me and I will kill you."

Eoin laughed. "Ah, my fire-tempered beauty." He gave her a courtly bow. "Shall we?"

Gritting her teeth, Thea allowed Eoin to lead her to the horse that had been set aside for her. It was a magnificent dapple mare, done out in gaudy finery. A stable hand helped her into the saddle and she settled into her seat, stiff-backed and tense. She watched Eoin. As he approached his own horse, he hesitated for a moment and checked his saddle bag. Inside Thea spotted the branding iron Eoin had been holding when he met with the Fae last night, the one with the same design as Logan's tattoo.

The mark of the Fae burned into his skin, a brand for all to see, tis the sign of his fateful bargain, and the way to set him free.

The words in Irene MacAskill's book suddenly came back to her. Thea's heart skipped. *The way to set him free.* Eoin glanced at her and she quickly looked away but her mind was suddenly whirling.

As the laird heeled his horse and led the way out of the gates, Thea gritted her teeth in determination. She *would* find a way to stop Eoin MacAuley if it was the last thing she ever did.

LOGAN SAT IN THE GLOOM and waited. Enough light fell through the small, barred window to illuminate the manacles that chained him to the wall but little else. Footsteps approached the cell door and he heard voices talking outside. The door opened and the sudden torchlight was bright enough to make Logan squint and throw his arm in front of his face.

Two guards stepped inside, one carrying a tray, the other a drawn sword. Both watched him warily as they set down the tray. Logan grinned at them and they paled, stepping back a pace. He had been far from a model prisoner. One of the guards sported a black eye, the other a bloody nose.

Logan said nothing as they backed out of the cell and closed the door behind them. After a moment he shuffled over to the tray, the chains just long enough to allow him to reach it. A bowl of broth and a hunk of bread sat on it but Logan wasn't interested in the food. Instead, he grabbed the spoon and held it up to the light. Made of pewter, it was cheaply crafted with a thin handle that was easily bent.

Logan smiled. Good. This was exactly what he needed.

Shuffling back to his spot by the wall, he carefully went to work on the spoon handle, bending it into the required shape. Eoin was a fool. Had he forgotten that Logan was a blacksmith now? That he made manacles and chains for a living? Did he really think these would hold him?

Eoin.

The thought of his cousin sent a hot surge of fury pounding through Logan's veins. He'd trusted him, brought him into his counsel, depended on him for advice. And what had he done with that trust? Used it to destroy him and his brothers and to bring his clan to the brink of war.

He suddenly thought of the day it all began, the day that changed his life forever.

"We should evacuate," Finlay said as Logan sat with Eoin and his brothers in the laird's study at the top of the tower.

"Empty the town. Send the people to shelter with the MacKinnons."

Camdan looked up, anger flashing in his steely gray eyes. "That's yer advice, little brother? That we should run like cowards? That we should give up everything we've fought for and allow the Irish to take our lands?"

Finlay met his brother's stare calmly. He was never ruffled by Camdan's temper. "Nay, brother. I say we save as many of our people as we can. Everyone not able to fight—the women, children, the old and sick, they should go. Everyone else stays. If we abandon the lower town and defend the castle, we should be able to hold them off."

"For how long?" Logan interjected. "If we give up the lower town, they'll use it as a base. They'll lay siege to the castle and starve us out."

"I'll not sit here like a rat in a trap!" growled Camdan. "I say we ride out head on and meet them. Drive the bastards back into the sea and burn their ships so they can never plague us again!"

Logan sighed. The same old arguments. They'd been going around in circles for hours. It came down to one thing: they didn't have enough warriors. The MacAuley clan was large and powerful but the raiders coming across the sea numbered larger still. Rumor was that there had been strife in Ireland and that many young warriors had been displaced, swelling the ranks of the raider captains. Now, having plundered their homeland for all they could get, their eyes were firmly set on MacAuley lands.

He sighed. "Aye, we'll make a good fight of it and take many of them with us. Perhaps we'll even cull them enough to give the MacKinnon time to send to the king for reinforcements. It's the best we can hope for."

Eoin looked up from the book he was reading. His eyes were red-rimmed and Logan guessed he'd been up all night again, poring over his books and old documents. "What if it isnae? What if there's another way? Something that will wipe the raiders out before the battle is even joined?"

Camdan laughed. "Have ye found something in yer books that will give us power over the weather, cousin? If ye could drum up a storm to drown the bastards before they even set foot on our shores that would be mighty welcome."

Eoin smiled thinly. "Nay, I dinna have that power." He tapped his book. "But I know of something that might."

And so he'd told them of what his research had led him to: a way to ally with the Fae. Camdan had been horrified but Finlay had been more open to the idea and after much arguing and debating Logan and Camdan had agreed to try. After all, what did they have to lose? If it didn't work, they'd be in the same position as before and they'd all likely be dead by sundown tomorrow, their people with them.

But if it *did* work, they had a chance to save their clan. Their lives were a small price to pay for such deliverance.

Logan snapped back to the present. A cold hand seemed to grip his heart and squeeze it. Eoin. He had been the one to broker the pact with the Fae. He had been the one who had taken over the lairdship from Logan. The man was a snake who would do anything, use anybody, to get what he wanted.

And I brought Thea to him, Logan thought with a sickening lurch of his stomach. *I have to get her away from him.*

He shifted position so that the light shone directly on the manacles and began picking at the lock with the bent piece of metal. He worked diligently, brow creased in concentration, and was rewarded when the manacles suddenly sprang open. He tugged them off his wrists and threw them and their chains onto the floor.

Tucking the lock-pick up his shirt-sleeve, he padded across to the closed door and put his ear to it. He could hear nothing from the other side but he knew it would not be long before the guards returned to collect his crockery. He grabbed the tray and stood behind the door, settling in to wait.

From the movement of the little patch of sunlight on the floor of his cell, Logan guessed that just over an hour had passed when he finally heard footsteps outside his cell. A key rattled in the lock. Logan tensed then, as the door swung open, he leapt forward, smashed the tray into the startled face of the first guard and followed it with a swift elbow to the temple that laid him out cold. The second guard staggered back with a startled cry and tried to draw his sword. Logan didn't let him. He grabbed the man's arm, yanked him forward, landed a knee into the man's stomach that doubled him over, then sent him crashing to the ground with an upper-cut into his jaw.

Logan quickly took one of the swords then dragged the unconscious men into his cell and locked it. Hefting the sword in one hand, he padded carefully along the length of the dungeon. He might have escaped his cell but before he could get out of the dungeon, he would have to get through the guard room where at least five guards were stationed at all times.

On cat's paws he rounded a corner and came in sight of the guard room door. It stood ajar and he could hear raucous laughter coming from within. Logan was grateful for their carelessness.

He crept up to the door. The guards were gathered around an empty beer barrel playing a game of cards and they didn't notice as Logan stepped noiselessly into the guardroom. Then suddenly one of them looked up, shouted a curse, and the guards sprang into motion, scattering and reaching for weapons.

Logan leapt forward, cracked one on the head with the hilt of his sword and grabbed another by his shirt and hurled him into the beer barrel, sending it and the card game flying. That left three men standing and they'd recovered from their initial shock now. They spread out in a line, swords drawn, blocking Logan's escape.

"Dinna do anything stupid," one of them, an older man, said. Logan knew him. His name was Jamie and he'd been a member of the garrison since Logan was a boy. "There's nay way out of here, lad. Dinna force us to kill ye."

"Stand aside," Logan growled. "I dinna want to hurt any of ye."

Jamie shook his head. "This willnae end well for ye. There are three of us and only one of ye. Do ye really fancy those odds?"

The man was right. Logan would be hard pressed to take down three of them in such a confined space but he would try anyway. He tensed, preparing to spring, when a voice suddenly rang out.

"Leave him be, damn you!"

Surprised, the guards glanced behind and Logan took his chance. He sprang at Jamie, bringing his sword down in a sweeping arc and sending the older man's weapon clattering to the floor.

"Sorry, friend," he murmured before punching him in the stomach and sweeping his legs out from under him. Jamie thudded to the floor, groaning.

The other two guards were fighting the newcomer. Logan couldn't get a good look at his benefactor but he waded in, grabbed one of the guards by the shirt, yanked him around to face him, and cracked him on the skull with his sword hilt. The guard collapsed without a sound and his benefactor dispatched the last remaining guard with a swinging haymaker to the chin.

Only then did Logan get a good look at the newcomer. With a start he realized it was Rhodry. His friend doubled over with his hands on his knees, breathing heavily.

"Oh Lord," he wheezed. "I'm very out of practice."

"Rhodry!" Logan cried. "What in God's name are ye doing here, man?" He strode over and pulled him into an embrace.

"Looking for ye," Rhodry replied. "Although I have to say I didnae expect to find ye escaping from the laird's dungeon." He looked around at the fallen guards. "Lord above, what have we done? We are going to be in serious trouble for this!"

Logan placed a hand on his friend's shoulder, forcing him to look at him. "Why did ye come looking for me? What's happened? Why aren't ye with Anna?"

To Logan's surprise Rhodry broke into a grin. "That's why I came to find ye. Anna has awoken! She seems a little tired but Ailsa reckons she'll make a full recovery. "

For a moment Logan just stared at him. Anna was awake? Recovered? But how? She'd been cursed. Hadn't she?

"What's wrong, man?" Rhodry asked. "Ye've gone as pale as milk."

Logan shook his head. "I'm fine. Just a little taken aback—and pleased of course. That's mighty fine news."

Rhodry nodded. "I rode to yer croft to tell ye but was surprised to find it empty. Then I bumped into old Gregor and he told me he saw ye riding to Dun Ringill in a hurry and that Irene MacAskill had been spotted here. That's why I came: to let Thea know that Anna is well before she left us to go home." His face folded into a scowl. "But when I came up to the castle, they told me that Thea was riding with Laird Eoin and that ye'd been thrown into the dungeon. Well, I didnae like the sound of that so I came here meaning to talk to the guards and find some answers. I thought it must all be some misunderstanding but here ye are breaking out of the cells. Logan, what is going on?"

Logan waved his question away. "What do ye mean Thea is riding with Eoin?"

A troubled expression crossed Rhodry's face. "That's what they told me at the castle gates and the whole town is full of the gossip."

"What gossip?"

Rhodry shifted uncomfortably. "That Laird Eoin means to wed Thea."

Logan staggered, steadying himself on the wall. "That bastard," he breathed. "I'll kill him. I'll cut his black heart from his chest."

Rhodry's eyebrows rose in alarm. "Logan, are ye going to tell me what is going on? Why would Laird Eoin want to marry Thea? And why would he throw ye in jail?"

Logan straightened and looked at his friend. It was time he told him the truth. "Rhodry, do ye trust me?"

"Of course. Ye are my closest friend."

Logan drew a deep breath. "Laird Eoin is my cousin. I was laird before him but I stepped aside in his favor. This was my castle, my dungeon, my land—once."

Rhodry barked a laugh. "Dinna be ridiculous! Ye are a blacksmith!"

"Think, Rhodry. Can ye remember the laird before Eoin?"

"Of course! He was...he was..." Rhodry's brow furrowed. "Actually, no. I canna seem to recall anyone before Eoin."

"That's because there is a Fae enchantment laid on me—one instigated by my cousin." He held his friend's gaze, willing him to believe him.

Rhodry stared at him. Then he said slowly, "Ailsa's mother is always going on about the Fae. She still leaves milk and a slice of pie out for them sometimes. I always thought her old stories were a load of horse dung. Ye mean to tell me they are true? That the Fae are real?"

"Aye," Logan said quietly. "They are real."

Rhodry ran a shaky hand through his hair. "God's teeth! What have I gotten myself into? Ailsa is always telling me I've got a nose for trouble."

"And I'm mighty glad ye have," Logan replied. "I thank ye for yer help but ye must go home now, back to Ailsa and the bairns."

"What do ye mean to do?"

Logan sheathed his sword. "I have to go after them. I have to get Thea away from Eoin and I need to put an end to this madness with the MacKinnons. Somehow."

Rhodry straightened. "Then I'm coming with ye."

"Nay," Logan said, shaking his head. "Ailsa needs ye at home. This is my battle, my friend."

"Do ye think Ailsa would ever forgive me if I let ye ride off alone? God above, man, she would tear strips off me. I'm coming with ye whether ye like it or not."

Logan watched his friend for a moment and then nodded. "Well then, how do ye feel about a spot of horse rustling?"

Chapter 19

"WOULD YE LIKE ME TO heat some water so ye can bathe, my lady?" Rian asked.

In truth Thea would like nothing better than to sink into a hot bath and soak for a while. They'd ridden hard all day and her muscles were aching something fierce. But she shook her head.

"No, thank you," she said to the maid. "I'm a little tired. I think I'll retire for the night."

Rian smiled. "Aye, it will be a big day tomorrow. Well, good night."

"Good night, Rian."

Thea held her smile in place for the time it took for Rian to leave then the smile slid from her face like a knob of butter from a knife. She looked around at her tent. It was more like a pavilion, large enough to stand up in and house a low bed and two folding chairs. It was a luxury that most of the fighting men weren't afforded. If they had a tent at all, it was a small, threadbare piece of cloth that would barely keep out the incessant wind that blew down from the pass and moaned around the camp like a banshee.

She waited a few moments to be sure Rian had gone and then lifted her chin, plastered a haughty look on her face, and marched to the entrance. The two guards that Eoin had placed there for her 'protection' glanced up as she opened the tent flap.

"If anyone comes to see me, tell them I don't wish to be disturbed," she instructed.

The guards shared a glance but then nodded. "Aye, my lady."

She glanced over at Eoin's tent. It was erected next to hers but was much larger with the colors of the MacAuley plaid sown along the seams. Candlelight burned within. Thea returned to her own tent and seated herself on one of the chairs, waiting.

Gradually, after what felt like hours, the sounds of the camp began to quieten. She rose from her seat and padded over to the back of the tent. The canvas had been staked down but none too securely. There was just enough give in the fabric to allow her to wriggle underneath. Trying to keep as quiet as possible, Thea burrowed her way beneath the wall and into the cool night air on the other side.

Around her the MacAuley camp stretched out, a sea of campfires. In the darkness they looked liked hundreds of tiny fireflies hovering in the night. Thea drew a deep breath, tiptoed to the side of her tent and peered around it. Her two guards were crouched playing a game with dice. Whilst their attention was fixed elsewhere Thea took her opportunity to quickly dash across the gap between her tent and Eoin's and to hunker down in the shadows of the larger pavilion.

She pressed her ear against the canvas and heard the sound of soft, even breathing from within. Good. The bastard was asleep. Creeping around to the entrance, Thea quickly ducked inside. Her heart was hammering in her chest and her palms were sweaty but she pushed away her fear and forced herself to concentrate.

Her plan was a simple one—steal the branding iron he seemed so fond of and run for it. She hadn't been able to come up with anything better.

She paused for a moment to allow her eyes to adjust to the darkness. Shapes gradually materialized out of the gloom. She made out chairs in a circle in the center of the space with a table between them. A curtain sectioned off Eoin's sleeping area.

Biting her lip she looked around, searching. Her eyes alighted on a traveling chest by the far wall. She quickly crossed to it and knelt on the canvas floor. Laying her fingers on the polished wood, she lifted the lid. It creaked and Thea froze, waiting for the hitch in Eoin's breathing that would tell her he'd awoken. It didn't come.

Letting out a slow breath and trying desperately to calm the frenzied beating of her heart, Thea reached into the trunk. At first her questing fingers found nothing but folded clothing then they brushed against something hard hidden beneath. She lifted out the object and saw that it was indeed the branding iron. The feel of it was strange. It felt warm and sent a tingling up her arm. Bringing it close to her face, she examined it more closely. The hairs wrapped around it gleamed a dull bronze and she had no doubt that they belonged to Logan. Curse Eoin! What did he want with this thing?

She heard the footstep behind her a moment too late. She snapped the lid shut and whirled around just as Eoin grabbed her by the throat, lifting her until she stood on her tiptoes.

"Give it to me," he hissed.

Thea choked, desperately trying to snatch a breath and held out the brand. Eoin snatched it and released her. Thea staggered back, gasping for breath, and massaging her throat where Eoin's fingers had been. He carefully placed the brand back in the trunk and closed the lid.

"Do ye know the punishment for stealing from the laird?" he asked softly. "Hanging. Should I hang ye, Thea Thomas?"

"I...I...wasn't trying to steal it," Thea gasped out. "I was curious that's all. I just wanted to see what it was."

"And what did ye see?"

"Nothing. Just a brand. Something you use on cattle, I guess."

He stared at her for a long moment. Thea forced herself to meet his gaze. He suddenly smiled.

"Damn it all, but I like a woman with spirit! Ye will make me a fine wife. Ah, the things we will accomplish together!" Eoin moved so close she could smell the sour wine on his breath. "I will forgive ye this transgression, my love. After all, ye havenae learned to obey me yet, have ye? But ye want to. Ye want to do anything I say."

He stared at her, unblinking. His gaze caught hers and for a moment Thea felt her will slipping away. Why was she trying to defy him? Hadn't he done well by the MacAuley clan? Hadn't he been a good laird? A better laird than Logan had ever been? Why would she disobey him? He was strong and powerful and the most handsome man she had ever seen. She felt herself take a step towards him.

"No!" she yelled. She scrambled backwards and the glamor suddenly vanished. "What the hell are you trying to do to me?"

Fury crossed Eoin's features. "Curse ye!" he yelled at the ceiling. "I want her now! Give her to me!" He cocked his head as if listening to a voice Thea couldn't hear. A slow smile spread across his face. "Aye, mayhap ye are right. The wait will make her all the sweeter." He turned to Thea and the hungry look in his eyes made her blood run cold. "Ye will return to yer tent now, my love. If ye try to leave it again without my permission, I will have ye tied up. Oh, dinna look at me like that, like ye want to stick daggers in my eyes. That will all change after the battle is won. Then ye willnae entertain any notions of disobedience. Ye will live to please me."

He yelled for the guards and they entered the tent and roughly escorted Thea back to her own. As she sank down onto the bed her tightly held control cracked. She leaned forward, hugging herself, as tears leaked from her eyes and sobs racked her body.

Feeling her free will slipping away had been utterly terrifying. It was a Fae glamor, just like the one that kept people from recognizing Logan. If Eoin won the battle, the Fae had promised to use it on her. She would be in thrall to Eoin. God help her, she would *love* him and most likely forget that Logan ever existed.

His face suddenly flashed into her mind and memories of the night they'd shared together. It had been the most special night of her life, laden with hope and promise. Now that had all turned to ashes.

Logan, she thought as the sobs shook her. *Where are you? I need you.*

IT WAS WHAT HIS FATHER would have called a 'fine Highland evening' which meant it was lashing down with rain and howling a gale. As the sun had set clouds had gathered, turning the sky into a purple bruise.

Logan glanced at the storm clouds and a chill ran down his spine. The weather had been like this the night he'd enacted his bargain with the Fae, and again when he'd rescued Thea from the sea. Now, as he rode a stolen horse along the trail, the wind drove rain right into his face and made the path ahead all but invisible. It was beyond reckless to be riding in this weather and any sane travelers would have found shelter for the night. Not Logan and Rhodry. They couldn't rest. Too much depended on their mission. So they rode as quickly as they dared through the wild night, their clothes soaked through, urgency driving them on.

They rode all night, stopping for only short intervals to rest the horses, and the sun was well above the horizon when they finally topped a rise and found themselves looking down into the valley of Drover's Pass. The pass itself was a narrow cut through sheer cliffs. Beyond it lay the MacKinnon stronghold of Dun Varan. Surrounded on all sides by towering hills, Dun Varan was well defended, but what proved its strength was also its weakness. It meant that if an enemy took Drover's Pass they could effectively cut it off from the rest of the Highlands, gradually starving out its people. This had obviously not been lost on Laird MacKinnon which is why he'd marched his army to the head of Drover's Pass rather than letting an army lay siege to his castle.

As they pulled their horses to a halt, Logan saw that two armies were marching into position in the valley. To the east lay the MacAuley forces, to the west, and closer to Logan and Rhodry, lay the MacKinnons. His father's training kicked in and Logan scanned the forces, quickly assessing their numbers. His stomach tightened. The MacAuley forces outnumbered the MacKinnons three to one. This would not be a battle. It would be a massacre.

"Holy mother of God," Rhodry breathed. "Look at them all. We're too late."

Even as he said it, drums began to beat, pounding out the rhythm of the marching men.

"Nay," Logan replied. "There is still a chance but we have to hurry."

He set his heel to his horse's flanks and they went cantering into the valley—heading straight for the MacKinnon lines. It wasn't long before they ran into the MacKinnon scouts. A group of mounted men materialized out of the trees and blocked their path.

"Ye'll nay be going any further, friends," one of them said. "I suggest ye turn yer horses around if ye dinna wish to feel cold steel in yer guts."

Logan studied them calmly. They were seasoned fighters by the look of them, scarred men wearing the MacKinnon plaid. "I wish to speak with Laird MacKinnon," he said. "I come with an offer of terms from Laird MacAuley."

The two men shared a glance. "Really? Sneaking through the woods like this? If Laird MacAuley wished to offer terms he would wait until the parley."

"Aye, he might. Or he might send riders in secret in order to avoid bloodshed and allow both sides to ride out of this with their honor unscathed. Which is it?"

The men looked less certain now. Then they put up their spears. "Ye will give up yer weapons and follow us on foot."

Logan and Rhodry did as they were bid, handing over their swords and leaving the horses behind. They followed the men through the camp and were soon ushered to a spot high on a hill where Laird MacKinnon had gathered with his commanders.

Laird MacKinnon looked up from a map as Logan and Rhodry were brought forward. Logan's heart lifted at the sight of him. He was a big man past his middle years with wide shoulders and ruddy cheeks. Quick to anger, quick to laugh, Laird Angus MacKinnon had been Logan's friend for years uncounted. How many times had they played dice together? How many times had he sought this man's advice when he'd first come into the lairdship? Now their people were about to face each other across the field of battle.

The MacKinnon glanced at him, showing no trace of recognition. "My scouts tell me ye claim to have come from Laird MacAuley with an offer of terms. Forgive me for being a little skeptical where that snake's offers are concerned." He crossed his arms over his broad chest and fixed Logan with a glare. "Well, let's hear what yer lord has to say."

Logan glanced at the forces gathering below. The early morning light reflected off thousands of weapons. He gestured to the gathered armies. "I canna believe ye want this, my lord."

The MacKinnon's eyes narrowed. "Dinna presume to know my mind, boy," he growled. Then he sighed. "Aye, tis this laird of yers that wants strife and all the bloodshed that comes with it. War is an ugly thing, boy, which I think yer laird will discover before the end."

"Aye, it is. But what if there was a way to end this without a blow being struck?" Logan asked.

The MacKinnon laughed. "Then I would say that whoever manages such a thing is a better man than I!" Behind him his two warriors laughed.

Logan did not join in. Looking the MacKinnon square in the eyes he said, "I can deliver such a thing. But I need something from ye first. I need yer word that if I prevail ye will retreat from the battlefield and allow the MacAuley forces to withdraw."

Laird MacKinnon's eyebrows pulled down into a frown. "Have ye gone mad, boy? Ye think I'd fall for such a trick?"

"It isnae a trick. I will do all I can to get the MacAuley forces to withdraw without engaging. Will ye do the same?"

"Who are ye? How, by Heaven, could ye claim such a thing?"

Logan shook his head. "Who am I doesnae matter. What matters is that I'm offering ye the chance to avoid bloodshed and save yer people. I have some influence with Laird MacAuley and believe I know a way to end this without anyone getting hurt. I need yer word, Laird MacKinnon." He met the old man's gaze, willing him to take him at his word and not ask him to explain. Once, he would have done so without question.

The old man stared at him for a long moment, his eyes narrowed. "Ye know, boy, ye remind me of someone I used to know, long ago. Who are ye?"

Logan shrugged. "Just a clansman who wants to save his people. Will ye agree?"

"Aye, lad. If ye get Laird MacAuley to withdraw, I will do the same. I think ye may be a little unhinged but what have I to lose? If ye are successful we all go home. If ye aren't, we'll ride to battle as planned."

Logan held out his hand and Laird MacKinnon clasped it, wrist to wrist. "My thanks."

He and Rhodry strode to the door but Laird MacKinnon called for him to wait. Logan turned and saw the old man had a puzzled expression on his face.

"Are ye sure we havenae met before?"

Logan smiled wryly. "Many times, my old friend. Many times."

Then, without further explanation, he turned and left.

"What was that?" Rhodry asked as they walked through the MacKinnon camp, escorted by his scouts. "How could ye hope to achieve such a thing? Logan, what are ye planning?"

Logan halted and looked at his friend. Around them the MacKinnon lines were forming up. In a few hours time most of these men would be dead, their wives widows, their children fatherless. Unless Logan did something about it.

"I'm going to do what I should have done from the start," Logan growled. "I'm going to kill Eoin MacAuley."

Chapter 20

THEA FELT SICK TO HER stomach. She stood rigidly on the hillside, watching as the battle lines were drawn up below. Last night's rain had blown through, leaving a crystal clear morning. For many of the men down there, it would be their last.

She closed her eyes, trying to block out the sight, but her other senses assailed her instead: the smell of sweat and leather, the creak of harness, the thump of booted feet against the ground. She couldn't escape it. This was really happening. She really was in the middle of a battle with a madman at her side.

Eoin MacAuley stood next to her, eyes alight with an avid fervor as he surveyed the valley. "Station archers along the marshy ground to the east," he instructed one of his commanders. "They might be desperate enough to try the crossing once we get into them and make sure the mercenary captains know to keep their formation. I'll not have them turning into an undisciplined rabble." The commander nodded and walked away.

Eoin was clearly enjoying himself. He looked resplendent in his battle gear and ermine-trimmed cloak as he stood surveying his troops.

Oh, how Thea hated him.

"Not long now," he said, turning to look at her with a grin. He had a pouch containing Logan's branding iron attached to his belt. He didn't go anywhere without it, not since Thea had tried to steal it. "We're almost in position and soon it will all begin."

"You expect me to be happy about that?" she hissed. "You expect me to be pleased I'm about to stand here and watch men die?"

Eoin's smile widened. "I expect ye to stand here and watch as I fulfill my destiny, then afterwards, when the battle is won, ye will give yerself to me and I will enjoy the fruits of my hard-earned victory."

"I'll kill you first." She took a step towards him but her two guards grabbed her arms and stopped her going any nearer.

"That's it, ye stoke that fiery temper of yers," Eoin said. "It will make taming ye all the more pleasurable."

Thea opened her mouth for a scathing reply but a sudden murmur went through the ranks. Turning to look at what had caused the commotion, she saw a single rider riding out from the MacKinnon lines and crossing the no-man's land between the two opposing armies. He carried a spear with a red flag attached to it, which snapped in the wind.

"A challenge!" the cry went up. "The MacKinnon's send a challenger!"

The rider reined in just out of bowshot of the MacAuley front line and reared his horse. "Eoin MacAuley!" he bellowed, his voice ringing out clear and sharp. "I call ye out for the bastard ye are! I challenge ye to single combat! Do ye dare to face me?"

Thea's heart skipped. She'd know that voice anywhere! She stood on tiptoe, trying to get a good look at the man over the heads of the gathered warriors and as she recognized him a flood of joy and hope surged through her.

"Logan!" she screamed.

Eoin's face turned white. Thea couldn't tell whether it was fury or fear or both. A vein throbbed in his temple and his mouth pressed into a hard, flat line.

"Eoin MacAuley! Will ye hide behind yer men? Are ye too much of a coward to face me?" Logan shouted.

"How, by hell, did he get here?" Eoin hissed. "Arrogant bastard! He willnae be so arrogant when I shove three feet of steel up his arse!"

He took a step forward but one of his officers held up a hand. "Ye canna accept the challenge, my lord. This is a trick of the MacKinnons."

"Ye dare tell me what I can and canna do?" Eoin growled. "Step aside."

The man stood his ground. "My lord, I would advise against this. If ye were to die—"

"Ye think I canna deal with one preening peacock? Ye think yer laird to be weak?"

"Nay, lord," the man stammered. "It's just that—"

"Out of my way!"

Eoin grabbed Thea roughly by the arm and yanked her forward. The men parted to let them through and as they stepped out onto open ground, Thea's eyes flew to Logan.

He seemed unharmed although his clothes were grimy and she didn't recognize the horse he rode. Seeing them, he dismounted and approached. Eoin dragged her across the no-man's land and they met Logan in the middle, halting a few paces away.

His eyes were fixed on her face. "Thea," he breathed. "Are ye all right? Has this bastard hurt ye?"

"No, I'm fine," she stammered. "Oh god, Logan! He's in league with the Fae! It's been him all along!"

"I know," Logan replied, his gaze transferring to his cousin. "I know it all."

"Well isn't this reunion touching," Eoin rasped. "Pity it won't last very long. It will only take me a moment to kill you."

"Send Thea to safety," Logan replied. "This is naught to do with her. It's between us."

"I disagree. It has everything to do with her. After all, she is to be my wife. She will stay. She will watch as her husband kills her lover."

Without warning Eoin drew his sword and launched himself at Logan. Logan threw his sword up just in time to parry the blow and the two blades met with a ring of steel on steel. A cheer went up from the watching armies.

"Thea, get away from here!" Logan bellowed. "Run!"

Thea staggered back, away from the fighting men, but she didn't run. She couldn't. She had to help Logan!

The two men circled each other warily. They looked so different, one light in coloring, one dark, one tall and broad-shouldered, the other whip-thin and wiry. But they were equally matched in skill. As they came together, blades slashing and parrying, Thea saw that Eoin's sword-craft matched Logan's. Of course it would. They had been trained together after all.

Eoin darted in, kicked dirt into Logan's face and slashed his blade at Logan's throat. Logan staggered back, clumsily parrying the blade as he dashed the dirt from his eyes, and the tip of Eoin's sword nicked his shoulder, causing a line of red to bloom on his shirt.

A cheer went up from the MacAuley forces.

"First blood to me, cousin!" Eoin called. "Now I'll take yer head."

"Ye always talked too much," Logan replied. "Mayhap I'll cut yer tongue out before I kill ye."

With a growl Eoin attacked. He came at Logan with a series of lightning blows, his sword glinting as it swung. Logan blocked and sent a savage riposte that opened a wound on Eoin's bicep. This time a roar went up from the MacKinnon forces. Eoin grunted in pain and took a step back. Logan seized his chance. He pushed forward, his blade catching the early morning light as he slashed and cut. Eoin parried each stroke but the wound in his bicep was hampering him and his movements were a fraction slower than they were.

Logan pressed his advantage, driving his cousin back several paces. Then Eoin let out a roar and flung himself forward. Their blades met. Eoin sent a punch into Logan's unprotected face, making him stagger back a step. Eoin followed instantly, his blade slashing at Logan's throat. At the last second Logan dropped to his knees and rolled under the slashing blade before hooking his ankle around Eoin's and tripping him into the dirt.

He grabbed Eoin's wrist and twisted savagely. With a cry Eoin let go of his sword. Logan swept it up and pressed the blade against Eoin's throat.

"Do ye yield?"

Everything had gone deathly quiet. All Thea could hear was the roaring of blood in her ears.

"Do ye yield?" Logan bellowed.

Eoin glared up at him. Then, to Thea's astonishment, he began to laugh. It was a cruel, brittle sound that set Thea's hair on end. There was no mirth in it, only savage glee.

"Fool!" he laughed. "I will enjoy watching ye die."

"Yield," Logan growled. "This was a trial by combat and ye have lost."

"Enough of this," said a voice suddenly.

A sudden wave of force rolled through the battlefield as though a door had been opened and closed. "I tire of yer petty squabbles."

The air rippled and the old man who Eoin had met in Dun Ringill suddenly appeared. He flicked his hand and Logan's blade suddenly burned white-hot. With a gasp of pain, he dropped it to the ground where it smoldered, setting the surrounding grass aflame. The old man walked forward, smiling malevolently.

"Thea," Logan instructed, backing away and watching the man as though he was a viper. "Get behind me."

Thea scrambled to Logan's side. His shoulder was leaking blood and sweat smeared his forehead. The old man looked around at the gathered armies and then lifted his nose and sniffed like a dog.

"Ah! The air is rank with fear. Do ye smell it? Isnae it glorious?"

"What do ye want?" Logan demanded.

The old man's black eyes snapped to Logan. "Only what was agreed. Naught more, naught less. A bargain was made, Logan MacAuley, and ye willnae be allowed to interfere with it."

"Damn yer bargains! I've had my fill of them! I willnae let ye cause any more strife."

"Oh?" the man asked, lifting an eyebrow. "And how, exactly, do ye plan to stop me? Ye are a dead man, Logan MacAuley, a ghost, yer life merely a shadow of what it once was."

"Aye, maybe it is," Logan replied. "But I'll spend what's left of it trying to stop ye. I may no longer be laird but I'm still a MacAuley. I willnae let ye hurt my people."

"*Yer* people?" he said. "Those same people who are baying for yer blood? Listen! Can ye not hear how much they hate ye?"

It was true. The MacAuley forces were jeering and hollering, calling for Eoin to slay the challenger. Thea looked up and saw violence and hatred written on their faces.

"It doesnae matter," Logan said. "They have been tricked, as I was tricked. I call our bargain null and void, Fae. It is over!"

The old man's eyes blazed. "It is over when I say it is over! Ye are mine and I will do with yer life as I see fit! We made a bargain and it canna be broken!"

Thea was suddenly grabbed from behind, her arms pinned to her sides. "What did I tell ye, wife?" Eoin said by her ear. "I told ye ye would watch my victory. Well here it is. Are ye enjoying it?"

"Let her go!" Logan bellowed. He launched himself at Eoin but a force suddenly grabbed him and froze him in place.

"Ye have proven quite irritating, Logan MacAuley," the old man said, a flicker of annoyance passing over his wrinkled face. "I think maybe ye are right. It is over. For ye, anyway."

He held out his hand and squeezed. Logan suddenly began to choke, thrashing against unseen bonds.

"No!" Thea screamed. She struggled, trying to break free but Eoin held her fast. "Leave him alone!"

"Give me the anchor charm," the old man said. Eoin swung the knapsack from his shoulder and held it out to the old man who snatched it and pulled out the brand. He spoke a word and the metal flared to life, burning so hot it reminded Thea of the coals in Logan's forge. The Fae stepped towards Logan and tore away his shirt, revealing the tattoo crawling across his chest.

The Fae smiled. "I'm afraid this is going to hurt."

Logan, unable to move, glared at the man. There was no fear in his eyes, only raw fury. Not so for Thea. Cold horror drenched her, turning her legs to water as the Fae advanced on Logan. Her legs buckled and she would have collapsed but Eoin held her up. She turned her head away but Eoin grabbed her chin and forced her head around.

"Nay, ye will watch."

The brand was only inches from Logan's skin now. The white-hot metal would brand him like cattle, leaving a scar for all to see. Thea's eyes widened suddenly. A scar for all to see. Like storm clouds parting before the sun, everything suddenly became clear.

The mark of the Fae burned into his skin, a brand for all to see, tis the sign of his fateful bargain, and the way to set him free

The way to set him free.

And suddenly, finally, Thea knew what she had to do.

Feigning weakness, she went limp in Eoin's grasp. He relaxed his hold slightly and in that moment she rammed her elbow into his stomach with all her strength. The blow caught Eoin off guard. He doubled over and staggered back a pace, releasing Thea. She threw herself at the Fae. He turned to her, shock flaring on his face, as she snatched the branding iron from his hand. She backed away, holding the iron in front of her like a poker.

"Bitch!" Eoin growled. "Ye will pay for that."

He advanced on her from one side, the Fae from the other and Thea slowly backed away.

"Stay back!"

"Or what?" the Fae asked. "Surely ye dinna think that can hurt me?"

Thea glanced at Logan. The Fae's power still held him trapped but his eyes had swiveled and were following her, wide with anguish.

"You know, you are way too self-centered," Thea said to the Fae. "You think everything is about you. It really isn't."

Then, before either could react, she sprang at Eoin, pressing the brand against his cheek. Eoin screamed and the stench of burning flesh wafted through the air. Horrified, Thea dropped the iron as though it was a snake. Eoin collapsed to his knees clawing at his face where a design had been burned, a design of swirling, inter-locking coils.

It matched the one on Logan's chest—the mark of a Fae curse.

The old man stared at Eoin and then at Thea. His face had gone very pale. "What have ye done?"

Logan suddenly gasped and Thea turned to see that the tattoo on his chest was glowing red and angry, like a brand that had just been burned into his flesh. Then, as she watched, it flared brightly and then faded, leaving behind no trace of the brand or the tattoo, only bare, unmarked skin. Instead, the mark on Eoin's face began to darken until a black tattoo swirled across his cheek, sealing his bargain with the Fae,

A silent concussion suddenly rocked the ground and Thea was thrown from her feet. When she looked up, she saw Logan collapsed on the ground a few feet away from her. She crawled over to him, laying a trembling hand on his cheek.

"Logan? Logan?"

His eyes fluttered open and fixed on her. "Thea? What happened? I feel...strange. Like a weight has been lifted from around my neck."

"No!" hissed a voice. "I willnae be thwarted! Ye will die for this!"

Thea looked up to see the old man standing over her. His face was contorted into a mask of fury. He raised his hand and power crackled across his fingers. Thea ducked her head, throwing up her arm to shield her and Logan from the coming blow.

But then a calm voice spoke. "Stop. Ye willnae hurt them."

Thea looked around and her eyes widened in shock to see Irene MacAskill standing a few feet away, gray hair tied back in a bun, hands clasped in front of her, regarding the old man calmly.

"Ye! Ye meddling fool! Ye think ye can stop me?" sneered the old man. He brought his hand crashing down towards Thea and Logan but the power crackling around his fingers suddenly fizzled and died. He spun on the old woman. "What have ye done to me?"

"I?" Irene replied. "I have done naught. Ye are merely subject to the bargain ye made. Ye canna harm Logan MacAuley or Thea Thomas as ye have no bargain and therefore no power over them."

"What are ye talking about?" the old man spat. "I bargained for the life of the MacAuley laird and it was given willingly, sealed with the mark of the Fae!"

"Aye," Irene agreed. "And ye *have* the MacAuley laird, marked and claimed by yer bargain. He's right there." She pointed at Eoin who stared up at her in terror.

"Ye have tricked me!" the old man raged. "The bargain doesnae stand!"

The wind picked up suddenly, swirling around them. "I think ye will find that it does," Irene said. "Even our kind canna escape the laws of the balance. The balance which has now been restored. Go now. Ye have no further business here."

The old man glared at Irene but the wind suddenly howled around him so fiercely that dirt was whipped into the air, blocking Thea's view. When it subsided, both the old man and Eoin were gone.

Irene MacAskill turned to look at Thea and Logan. "That," she said. "Was what people in yer time would probably term a 'close shave.'"

Thea scrambled to her feet and faced the diminutive woman. "Where are they?" she demanded. "What happened to them?"

Irene smiled. "Far away where they canna bother any of us again. They are now bound together. I dinna think either of them will like the experience."

Logan heaved himself to his feet. He tottered a little and Thea held out a hand to steady him. He moved to Thea's side and looked down at Irene MacAskill. He towered over her but she seemed not in the least bit daunted.

"Now?" he growled. "Ye choose to appear now? After we've been searching for ye all this time? After Eoin nearly caused a war?"

"I couldnae interfere," Irene replied. "What ye did, ye had to do of yer own free will. If I had done so, the balance would have been tipped and all would have been lost. My granddaughter risked much by talking to ye."

"Kara?" Thea asked.

"Aye, she still has much to learn. I will be having words with her. Still, all is well that ends well, eh? Listen! They are calling for their laird."

Thea and Logan turned to look at the MacAuley lines. The men were stamping their feet and chanting. "MacAuley! MacAuley!"

"They are calling for Eoin," Logan said.

"Nay," Irene said, shaking her head. "They are calling for ye. Ye are, after all, Laird MacAuley."

Logan went very still. "I dinna understand."

Irene smiled. "Ye will, lad."

Just then they heard hoof beats and turned to see two men riding towards them from the direction of the MacKinnon lines. Thea recognized Rhodry on one of the horses but riding the other was an older man. They reined in the horses and dismounted. The older man approached Logan. He had a puzzled look on his face.

"Logan? Is that ye?"

Logan frowned. "Ye recognize me?"

"Of course I recognize ye!" the older man cried. "I may be getting old but I'm not yet blind! I've known ye since ye were a bairn! Young Rhodry here has been telling me a mighty strange story—something about our clans going to war! I would have told him he was cracked but for the evidence of my own eyes. I feel a little strange, I must admit. Kind of foggy. What are we doing here, Logan? Why are our forces arrayed for battle?"

"Ye have awoken from a long sleep, Laird MacKinnon," Irene said. "But all will be well."

Logan stepped forward and gripped Laird MacKinnon's hand. "My friend, will ye withdraw yer forces from the field?"

"Of course I will! I havnae a cursed idea why we are here in the first place!"

"Then the MacAuley forces will do the same. Ye must trust me, my friend. There is much I must tell ye but that must wait until later. So what now?" Logan said, turning to Irene.

"That depends on the two of ye," she replied. "And the choices ye will make." She turned to look at Thea. "Ye have done all I asked of ye and ye have my thanks, lass. What do ye now wish? Do ye want to go home?"

Home? Thea thought. *The twenty—first century?* It seemed so strange now she thought about it, like an alien land rather than where she had spent most of her life. It was the Highlands that felt like home now—because of one man.

She looked at Logan and found him staring at her with an expression she'd never expected to see. Fear. He held out his hand.

"Dinna go," he whispered.

"This isnae yer choice," Irene interjected. "It is Thea's to make. What will it be, my dear?"

"You cannot send me home, Irene," she said. "Because I'm already here." She took a step closer to Logan and stood looking up at him. "You're my home, Logan, and I'd like to stay here, if you'll have me."

"Have ye?" he said hoarsely. "God in Heaven, Thea, of course I'll have ye. I've never been so scared in all my life. For a moment there I thought ye were going to leave me." He drew in a deep, steadying breath and then laid his hands on her shoulders. "Aye, lass. I'll have ye. I'll have ye for the rest of our lives—if ye'll have me. I love ye, lass. I love ye more than life. I want ye by my side for all time. Will ye marry me?"

Thea's heart skipped a beat. Her heart swelled and she suddenly felt as light as a feather. "Yes," she breathed. "Of course I'll marry you."

Logan bent his head to kiss her and Thea's eyes slid closed as their lips met, euphoria sweeping through her like rain on a desert. A huge swell of noise erupted around them and she realized the MacAuley forces were hollering and cheering— cheering a name.

"Laird MacAuley! Laird MacAuley!"

Chapter 21

THEA WAS SO NERVOUS she was sure she was going to throw up. The air in her chamber felt stifling even though a cool breeze was blowing through the open window. From the courtyard below came the sound of Highland pipes playing and raucous laughing as the guests started enjoying themselves.

"Are ye ready?" Ailsa asked.

Thea turned away from the window, focussing instead on her friend who was kneeling by the fireplace making last minute adjustments to Anna and Maisie's bridesmaids' dresses. Thea sucked in a breath.

"Ready as I'll ever be."

Ailsa laughed and climbed to her feet. "Dinna worry, every bride gets nervous on her wedding day. Lord, when I wed Rhodry I almost bolted back down the aisle. It was only my father's grip that stopped me!"

"I know," Thea breathed. "But all those people!"

It wasn't the thought of marrying Logan that was making her nervous—hell, just the thought of that sent delicious tremors right through her body. No, it was the thought of the MacAuley clan—her new clan—and so many others watching that had nerves fluttering in her belly like butterflies. Logan had invited half the Highlands, it seemed. Now that he was laird again he was eager to re-cement old bonds and what better excuse than a wedding?

Not that those bonds needed re-cementing, mind you. It seemed that whatever magic had sealed his bargain with the Fae had transferred from him to Eoin. Now nobody remembered Eoin MacAuley at all and everyone thought Logan had always been the laird. It was most strange.

Only Ailsa and Rhodry knew the truth. One of the first things Logan had done was bring them up to the castle and make them the new housekeeper and steward. Margaret and Malcolm were more than happy to retire and Logan had given them a comfortable suite of rooms in the castle as well as a generous pension. Ailsa and Rhodry had taken to their roles with ease and it was good to see the children racing around the place with their new friends. Even Mary approved of the change—mostly because she got to order servants around.

Thea did a little twirl. "Well, how do I look?"

"Like a princess!" Anna cried.

Maisie waved a chubby hand. "Princess Thea!"

She laughed. "Hardly a princess but thank you for the compliment." She looked around at them all. "Well, shall we get this show on the road?"

They filed out of the room. Ailsa, as Thea's maid of honor, walked by her side, holding Maisie's hand. Anna walked behind holding a bouquet, taking her duties as bridesmaid very seriously indeed. The corridors of the castle had been decked out with flowers and ribbons. They stood in vases and hung in bunches from the walls—testament to Mary and Ailsa's wedding planning.

As they walked, Thea felt a flicker of sadness. She'd always hoped her grandad would give her away and that her grandma would be there to hold her hand. But they weren't and they'd be mighty shocked to see the life she'd chosen.

But they'd be happy for me, she thought. *They always wanted what was best for me and they'd love Logan. I don't doubt they're here in spirit.*

By the time they reached the doors to the Great Hall the nerves in Thea's stomach were wriggling like snakes. The doors had been thrown wide open and from the hallway outside Thea could see rows and rows of people craning their necks to watch her.

Ailsa gave her hand a reassuring squeeze and Thea forced a smile. Oh god! They were all staring at her!

But all her nerves fell away as she stepped into the room and her eyes found Logan. He stood with Rhodry and the priest at the far end, his eyes fixed on her. The guests, the Great Hall, the entire world seemed to fall away until all she saw was him. Dressed in the MacAuley plaid, with his copper hair falling onto his shoulders and his eyes shining, he was quite possibly the most beautiful thing she had ever seen.

And he was hers.

Thea kept her gaze locked on Logan's all the way down the aisle. Only when she reached him did she glance at the crowd and spot the two figures standing at the back. Irene MacAskill and Kara Harris both had broad smiles on their faces and Thea was sure she could see the twinkle of tears in Irene's eyes. For a moment their eyes met and Irene inclined her head. Thea nodded and then gave them both a smile before turning to her intended.

Logan stood for a moment looking down at her, saying not a word. He didn't need to. His emotions were written clearly on his face: in the way his eyes shone and his lips turned up in a joyous smile.

"Thea," he said softly. "Ye look...perfect."

He took her hands in his and they faced each other as the priest began the ceremony. It seemed to pass in only a heartbeat and she barely heard any of the words. All her attention was fixed on the man before her, this wonderful, amazing man.

Then it was done and the priest was announcing that they were husband and wife and Logan was picking her up and twirling her around, to the delight of the guests who cheered and applauded loud enough to lift the roof. Finally Logan set her on her feet. Cupping her face in his hands, he leaned down and kissed her deeply enough to set the crowd cheering even louder.

"My wife," he breathed. "I will spend the rest of my life making ye happy."

"You already did," she replied, tears filling her eyes. "You already did."

THEA COULDN'T REMEMBER the last time she'd had so much fun. These Highlanders sure knew how to throw a party. She had no idea how the kitchen staff had managed to produce so much food and drink but it had flowed all afternoon and long into the evening until everyone—the kitchen staff included—were what her grandma would have called a little bit 'merry'.

There had been games in the bailey, singing in the Great Hall, and so much dancing that Thea feared she'd be unable to walk come the morning. Her current dancing partner was Laird MacKinnon and although he was old enough to be Thea's grandfather, he was still sprightly on his feet, twirling Thea and leading her through the steps like a much younger man. By the time the music came to an end, Thea was laughing and breathless.

Laird MacKinnon leaned over, his hands on his knees. "Ah! Mayhap my wife was right when she said I'm a silly old fool who thinks I can still keep up with the youngsters."

"Nonsense!" Thea replied. "You could teach the youngsters a thing or two I reckon!"

"Ha! That's kind of ye to say, lass, but I think I'll take a breather all the same."

Thea helped the old man to his chair then looked around for Logan. There was no sign of him. He wasn't dancing and his chair up at the main table was empty. Thea thought for a moment then wove her way across the floor—excusing herself from requests to dance—and out into the bailey. Hiking up her dress, she made her way around it and ducked into the stable.

It was blessedly calm and quiet after the bustle of the wedding. The only sound was the horses munching on their hay—and the 'swish, swish' of a horse being groomed. Thea made her way down the central aisle towards the sound. At the end she found Logan grooming Stepper. The white mare had been discovered amongst the mounts of Eoin's garrison, much to Logan's relief. Still dressed in his wedding plaid, he held a comb in one hand and was meticulously brushing out Stepper's mane.

"You know, some brides might be offended by their husband making a quick get away from their own wedding."

Logan spun towards her. He grinned. Dropping the brush, he grabbed her around the waist and kissed her.

"Then it's good ye are not most brides isnae it?"

"Aye," she replied, mimicking his accent. "I suppose it is." She ran a hand through his hair and looked up at him. "What are you doing here, Logan? And don't say you're grooming Stepper. I can see that. *Why* are you grooming Stepper?"

He released her and stepped back. "Ah, I'm sorry, lass. It all got a little...overwhelming." He gestured at the space around them. "All this. It's taking some getting used to. Everyone acts as though I've never been away, but I have, and I'm not the same person they remember."

"No," Thea agreed. "You're a better one."

"Do ye think?"

"I do. Blacksmith MacAuley is the best man I know but I've a feeling Laird MacAuley will be even better."

He smiled and brushed his thumb across her cheek. "Ah, lass, ye a balm on my soul. I only wish Camdan and Finlay were here to see this. It feels wrong being this happy when I know their curse still holds them."

Logan had questioned Irene long and hard about his brothers' fates but the old woman would not be drawn, saying only that they had their own paths to tread. It was a source of great sorrow for Logan that he could not help them.

"We have to hope," she told him. "You found a way to break your curse, who's to say they won't as well? Maybe one day they'll both come home."

Logan smiled. "Aye, lass. I'll pray for that."

"Come on," she said, taking his hand. "We'd best get back, we've got guests waiting."

He held her hand. "Just one moment. I find I'm enjoying being alone with my wife."

He pulled her hard against him and kissed her. His lips were warm and insistent, his arms strong as they circled her. Thea felt herself melting into him. She kissed him back fiercely, wrapping her arms around his neck as arousal flared along her nerves.

"You know what?" she said breathlessly. "Stuff the guests. I find I'm enjoying being alone with my husband—and I'd like more of it, please."

"As ye command, so I obey, my lady," he replied.

He bent, grabbed her around the waist and behind the knees and lifted her into his arms, cradling her against his chest. Thea laughed and wrapped her arms around him as he carried her from the stables and round to the back of the castle where it was quieter and up the servants' stairs to the laird's chambers. *Their* chambers, she reminded herself.

He kicked the door open and nudged it shut behind them before carrying Thea over to the bed and laying her down. Somebody—Ailsa probably—had been in to draw the curtains and light the candles and the room was filled with a lovely golden glow.

Logan looked her over, his eyes drinking her in and she saw they had gone dark with desire. An answering tingle lit inside Thea. She grabbed his plaid and yanked him down on top of her, finding his mouth with hers and kissing him, her tongue tangling with his, her teeth nipping his lips.

Logan's hand went behind her neck, expertly untying the ribbons on her wedding dress and then pulling it down to expose her breasts. He took one in his mouth, his tongue flicking the nipple until it went hard, eliciting a gasp of pleasure from Thea. She curled her fingers through his hair as he trailed his tongue across her chest, making her skin tingle with desire.

Giving her an impish smile, he reached down and slipped his hand under the hem of her dress. Thea gasped as his fingers traced a line up her inner thigh and she arched her back as he slipped beneath her panties and found her sweet spot, massaging expertly with the pad of his thumb.

Something like electricity tingled along her nerves and every cell in her body seemed to come alive with craving for him. She tugged at Logan's plaid, wanting it gone, wanting to see every inch of his body, and he obliged by yanking it over his head and dropping it to the floor. She wriggled out of her wedding dress and undergarments and Logan gently caressed her hips as he lay down next to her, both of them naked now.

Thea placed her hand on his pectoral, over his heart where the tattoo used to be. Now there was only unblemished bronze skin. She looked up at him.

"I love you."

Logan took her hand and kissed it. "And I ye, lass. More than ye will ever know."

He leaned down and pressed his lips against hers and hunger raged to life inside her. She moved her knees apart and Logan swung atop her, curling his fingers through hers and pinning her hands to the bed.

"Ye are mine," he whispered. "For all time."

Then he thrust his hips and drove himself deep inside her. Thea cried out, a sense of completeness engulfing her as their bodies joined and his hot skin glided over hers. With a shudder Logan withdrew and thrust again, the movement sending a hot spear through Thea's body. They began to move in time, their bodies finding a deep, pulsing rhythm that lit Thea's senses. Logan drove into her again and again and Thea rose to meet him, each coming together pushing her further and further towards a peak of indescribable ecstasy. Logan's movement intensified, his tempo increasing as their passion built, eliciting gasps of pleasure from Thea that began to build as the inferno spread through her body, along her nerves to the very extremity of her limbs.

She came apart. With a shuddering cry she arched her back beneath him, wrapping her legs around his hips as her climax swept her away. Logan groaned by her ear and his whole body shook as he reached his own peak, driving himself deep with one final piercing thrust and holding himself there for a long, eternal moment.

Slowly Thea regained her senses. She was breathing heavily and their bodies were covered with a thin sheen of sweat. Feeling the ecstasy ebb, to be replaced by a deep, all-encompassing joy, Thea wrapped her arms around Logan's neck, holding him close. He pressed his forehead against hers and his hair fell forward to brush her cheek.

Finally, when his breathing eased, Logan lifted himself off her and lay on his side beside her, his head propped on his hand. Thea rolled to face him. He was watching her, a smile on his face. He reached out and gently brushed her nose.

"Thank ye, Thea."

"For what?"

"For giving me a second chance at life. I feel like I've been reborn."

She kissed him. "We both have. Our second lives start right here, right now."

He threw his arm around her and pulled her into an embrace. Thea snuggled against her husband, the warmth from his skin seeping into her body. For the first time in her life she felt utterly complete.

"Although you do realize in your haste to escape you forgot to dance with Mary?" she said.

Logan groaned. "Oh Lord, she willnae let me forget it either."

Thea laughed. "Oh, the hardships of being a laird."

"Well, if I'm in trouble anyway, I may as well make the most of it," Logan said. He rolled over and kissed her.

After that, Thea forgot all about their guests.

THE END

Want some more Highland adventure? Then why not try the other books in the series? www.katybakerbooks.com[1]

Would you like to know more of Irene MacAskill's story? *Guardian of a Highlander*, a free short story is available as a free gift to all my newsletter subscribers. Sign up below

---

1. http://www.katybakerbooks.com

to grab your copy and receive a fortnightly email containing news, chat and more. www.katybakerbooks.com[2]

WHAT DO YOU DO WHEN destiny comes knocking?

Irene Buchanan is running from hers. Gifted with Fae blood, she is fated to become the Guardian of the Highlands.

But Irene wants none of it. Soon to be married to her childhood sweetheart, she has everything she ever dreamed of. Why would she risk that for a bargain with the fae?

But Irene can't run forever. When a terrifying act of violence rips all she loves from her, she realizes she must confront her destiny. If she doesn't, she risks the destruction of all she holds dear.

The fate of the Highlands lies in her hands.

---

2. http://www.katybakerbooks.com

Printed in Great Britain
by Amazon